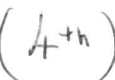

Every Daughter's Fear

Joanna Warrington

Autumn 2023

Text Copyright 2023 by Joanna Warrington

All Rights Reserved

ISBN

DISCLAIMER AND BACKGROUND

Every Daughter's Fear is part of a series, *Every Parent's Fear*. I hope that you will enjoy *Every Mother's Fear*, *Every Father's Fear* and *Every Son's Fear* before reading this 4th book in the series.

All characters in this publication, other than those who are known public figures, are fictitious, and any resemblance to real people, living or dead, is purely coincidental. All opinions are those of the characters and not my personal opinions or the opinions of real people.

The story reflects the situations and experiences that families and thalidomide survivors might have faced, draws on real events and real experiences, and has been thoroughly researched. I have spoken with many thalidomide survivors at various events.

Georgia Southwestern State University in Americus is a real institution, but the events described in this story related to this institution are fictional and purely reflect the way that disabled people were treated in the 1970s.

This is a fictional story based on the thalidomide disaster, one of the blackest episodes in medical history, which had devastating consequences for thousands of families across the world. Thalidomide was used to treat a range of medical conditions. It was thought to be safe for pregnant women, who took it to alleviate morning sickness. Thalidomide caused thousands of children worldwide to be born with malformed limbs, and the drug was taken off the market late in 1961.

There is also mention in this book of other medical scandals which weave into this story and are used in a fictional way.

The story is set in the autumn of 1976. The events are loosely based on events of that year, in particular the US presidential election. Thalidomide was not approved in the United States in the 1960s, but as many as 20,000 Americans were given the drug in the 1950s and 1960s as part of two clinical trials operated by the American drug makers Richardson-Merrell and Smith, Kline & French. On August 1st 1962, President John F. Kennedy issued a warning to every woman across the country to check their medicine cabinets and not to take this drug. As part of an investigation, the FDA instructed its inspectors to interview every doctor who had received thalidomide and to investigate if any babies were harmed. This investigation proved to be extremely difficult and the true story of thalidomide distribution in the United States lay buried for half a century.

St Bede's, the school that Toby attends and where Bill works as caretaker, is loosely based on Chailey Heritage School in East Sussex, the first purpose-built school for disabled children in the UK. It was founded in 1903 and is where many of the British thalidomide survivors were cared for and educated. There are various schools around the UK called St. Bede's. The name is coincidental and bears no relation to any of these schools.

I have used the word 'handicapped' and 'handicap' in this book because this was the terminology used at the time, rather than the more modern term, 'disabled' and 'disability.'

ACKNOWLEDGEMENT

A book like this would be impossible without the help of the thalidomide community, the many conversations with survivors about the challenges they've faced over the years, as well as hearing about their many achievements. I hope this book helps to keep them in the public's mind.

Thanks to Stuart Higgins who is a volunteer with the RDA (Riding for the Disabled Association). We connected when Stuart kindly offered to make new riding straps for the thalidomide survivor I support, so that she can continue to enjoy carriage driving. Stuart played a very special part in the book's creation. I will fondly remember the hours of scribbling and discussions we had in the Hart Café in Haywards Heath over French toast and coffee!

Thank you to my cover designer, Jane Dixon-Smith, and to my proofreader, Julia Gibbs.

THE STORY SO FAR

The story begins with book 1, Every Mother's Fear. To purchase this book please click this link which will take you to Amazon.
https://amzn.to/43Nrugf

Toby was born in 1961 as a result of a night of passion in Brighton between Sandy and Jasper. The couple parted when Jasper headed north for a new job and before she was aware of her pregnancy. Being unmarried, Sandy was forced by her mother to make plans to have the baby adopted. Sandy took thalidomide during pregnancy for morning sickness, and as a result, Toby was born without upper limbs. Not expecting the baby to survive, the doctor ordered Rona the midwife to put him in a cold room to let nature take its course.

Heartbroken because she and husband Bill had not been able to conceive, Rona kidnapped Toby and the couple brought him up as their own child. Sandy meanwhile was told her baby had died.

Jasper never forgot his first love. He wrote to Sandy, but she didn't receive his letters because her mother destroyed them.

Jasper and Sandy reconnected when by a chance encounter they were both in New York on business. They married.

After Rona's death from cancer, Jasper met Bill and Toby through his newspaper interviews of thalidomide families, and when he found out that Toby was his, he kept it a secret from Sandy for three years to protect Bill.

The secret was revealed when Sandy's mother, Irene, opened a letter that was only supposed to be opened in the event of Jasper's death.

The revelation has fractured two families and this book explores the fallout.

CHAPTER 1: 1976

Toby's bedroom was his sanctuary, but it had also become his self-imposed prison. He felt safe, but also trapped. Ever since his chat with Sandy in the Wimpy bar, all he wanted to do was hide away from the world and not talk to anybody.

As he sat up, the book resting on his chest thudded to the floor. *The Life of Stalin.* It was a turgid read, not the usual material for a boy of his age.

He felt totally rejected. Three weeks on and the memory of the events of that day, the horrifying truth about his life still left him angry and hurt.

He refused to come out of his room. In all this time he'd not spoken to anyone and couldn't face even going to school.

Toby's senses were primed for the sound of Bill's slippers shuffling on the bare floorboards. Then the bang on the door. He could set his watch by Bill's arrival every mealtime like a synchronous clock. His constant nagging to open the door pushed him to breaking point, but he had no intention of letting him in. Bill had done enough damage for a lifetime.

Why can't he understand I have nothing to say to him?

'Dinner's ready.' Bill's voice sounded weary.

'I've told you before, just leave it on the tray, I'll eat it when I'm ready.'

Toby waited for Bill to go downstairs before it was safe for him to open the door. The knock came again, more insistent, more agitated this time, reminding Toby of a demented dog. He just didn't want to speak to him.

'Leave me alone. I don't want to talk. You've destroyed my life and Sandy's. I can understand how she must feel. All this time I've had a proper mum and dad and I never knew. All these years you've let me believe you and Rona were my mum and dad. How could you be so cruel?'

Toby turned his face to look out of the window as a distraction.

He hated being nasty but didn't care right now what he said because he couldn't get his head around any of it. Bill and Jasper couldn't hurt him any more than they already had.

'Toby, we need to talk, you can't go on locking yourself away, life has to go on.'

'Yes, life goes on. I'm about to take my O levels. Now you've ruined my chances by playing with my mind.'

He knew Bill's heart was cracking but he wasn't going to let him in.

'Please, Toby.'

'And you're an expert on life are you, Dad? Only thing you're an expert on is how to drown your sorrows in a bottle.'

'I'm sorry.'

If he heard that word sorry again, he'd scream. It was an empty word.

He wondered what Bill had told the school. More lies, he imagined. He had no intention of slipping behind. He loved learning, it was his escape. He was determined now more than ever to pass his exams, go to university, get away, start again, make a new life for himself. He didn't need a family. The characters in the books he read were his family. The fact they weren't real made it easier. Reading filled his days. Since being cooped up, he'd read *Moby Dick*, *Pride and Prejudice*, and *Crime and Punishment* and he'd dipped into a few biographies. He delighted in these parallel worlds and the escapades of others.

Another tap at the door took him by surprise.

'We want to talk to you, Toby, please.' Bill's voice was pleading, laced with despair. 'You know we've got to keep this to ourselves.'

He understood the reasoning, but why should he be expected to keep this secret for the rest of his life? It was impossible.

'That's all you care about, keeping it a secret.' In a loud voice, he said, 'And what if I don't?'

'Stop this. Just open the door, Toby.' He didn't answer but went to plonk himself on the bed and stared at the closed door.

'Jasper's coming over to take you for a drive.'

'Tell him not to bother. I'm not playing happy families with anybody.' He couldn't contain the sarcasm as it bitterly twisted through him.

When he thought of Jasper and Sandy, there was nothing about them that made him think of them as his parents.

Toby heard a big sigh and wondered when Bill would crack.

'Okay, do what you like, stay there and wallow in your own self-pity. I'll let you know when Jasper comes.'

'Sod Jasper, sod you. Can't believe he kept it a secret too, all the time pretending to be my mate. He's just a user. I'm the freak, another subject for him to write about. And you'd know about wallowing in self-pity, wouldn't you? Who are you to preach to me? At least I don't drown myself in alcohol.'

A twinge of shame pinched at him. It didn't feel right to lash out, but it was the only thing he felt able to do and there was something rather cathartic in these angry outbursts.

'I know, I'm not perfect.'

'You're far from perfect. You're a complete idiot, why the hell did you agree to go along with a kidnap?'

Bill, an accessory to kidnap. The very word shook him to the core.

He knew it was wrong, he should have returned me to hospital.

And yet, if he had, what would have been my fate?

It was Rona's mission to have a child, not Bill's, that was why she'd taken him from the hospital. Her role as midwife had made it possible. Even though he'd been a good dad, Toby sensed that fatherhood had been a chore he could have done without.

'If she hadn't kidnapped you, you wouldn't be here now and would have been left to die on the cold hospital windowsill.'

'I wish you bloody hadn't. You could have adopted any baby, with all its bits in the right place, but she chose me, an imperfect baby.'

At some point he knew he'd have to emerge from this pit. There were clothes strewn over the floor, dirty dishes piled in one corner, the odour of socks and dried food, crumbs in his bed, crumpled sheets that needed changing. His socks were all standing up in the corner like soldiers on sentry. His room had come to resemble the state of the rest of the house he loathed so much.

His mind flashed back to his mum. Rona was terrific at looking after the house. She was good at laundry, she knew how he liked his bed. It had to be just right, if not she used to take it all off and start again. God, how he missed her, everything about her.

Getting out meant opening the door, the door to that crap world that he was trying to suppress from his every thought. There seemed no escape from the torment in his mind.

CHAPTER 2: TOBY

Toby was mesmerised by the steady beat of the rain against the windowpane, watching as the water made a crazy pattern across the glass. It was hypnotic, made him calmer, dream-like. He'd been cooped up for fifteen days.

His mind drifted; he wondered what it would be like to be a lighthouse keeper, alone for days, weeks at a time, staring out at the horizon for ships, the turbulent waves, the salty wash battering the domed glass, that solitude, time to think. Looking through that glass would be like looking out on his own life, seeing out so clearly, but nobody could see him. That comforted him, his feelings were safe.

Despite the safety of his four walls, a yearning stirred inside him. He had to get out. He was going stir crazy being cooped up like a wounded lion. What if he lost his confidence, became like Howard Hughes? What then?

After the early rain, the sun came out. Hearing the front door slam, he jumped up from bed and watched Bill start his truck and head along the lane to work. It was Saturday and there was always something to fix at the school: a blocked lavatory, a broken desk, or lightbulbs to replace.

Jasper hadn't come round. He had to get out. He needed to clear his head.

There was no coming back from the ordeal that Bill and Jasper had put him through. He'd never be the same person again.

He headed downstairs, and in the living room took a sharp intake of breath. The place was a complete tip. The kitchen counter was piled with dirty dishes, food crusted on plates, half-drunk mugs of tea, saucepans soaking in soapy water, empty beer cans. His hackles rose.

Bloody slob.

Was this what Bill had become in Toby's absence, a grown man who couldn't cope? It was pathetic. He was a hopeless wreck.

Toby reached the front door and hooked his foot around the handle to open it, desperate to escape the splattered mess of his father's miserable life. He wouldn't go far, just take a stroll through the grounds of the school. He skirted the bracken along the rutted lane and through the cluster of silver birches en route to the garden. A light breeze snaked through the tops of the trees, which whispered to each other as if sharing secrets.

The trees knew.

Toby stopped and stared through the leaves; the sun illuminated the pattern of veins, each vein representing an avenue of his life, all the paths that could have been, might have been. Left to die on the cold windowsill, it would have been a short journey--cot to grave. He would never have existed, no youth, no history, no friends, no nothing.

The thought gave him a sense of desolation. Adopted via the correct channels and he would have had a completely different set of parents, a different name, different life entirely.

A thought snagged in his mind, and he peered down at the ground in self-pity and collapsed against a tree. What if nobody had wanted to adopt him, what then, what might his life have been like? The fact was nobody would have wanted him. Rona had always told him that there was nothing more beautiful than perfect imperfection. She'd taken him despite his imperfections.

He was tired, tired of the same thoughts circling. It was as if a murmuration of starlings had come to inhabit his head. He took the path which led through a brick archway into the western side of the garden. He heard gentle sobbing and stopped, stepped behind one of the bushes, unsure whether he should go back. He crouched and peered through the greenery. He recognised the back of her head. Sue's hair was the exact colour of his old hamster, Elvis, a blend of peanut and warm gingerbread. He'd barely said two words to her in the three years he'd been at St Bede's. There was something about talking to girls of his own age. He felt self-conscious, awkward, and always felt the heat rise to his cheeks because he didn't want to make a fool of himself. It was different with Lucy. She was easy to talk to, maybe because she was older than him, although he had been very nervous at first.

Sue was friends with a gaggle of girls who sat at the opposite end of the classroom to him and his friend Si. They always put boys at one end and girls at the other as if they had some contagious disease. He'd noticed them in a huddle at break time poring over a silly magazine called *Jackie* or a transistor radio listening to the latest hits or drooling over pictures of Donny Osmond. He was more comfortable talking about girls than to them, sharing thoughts of who he'd kiss given the chance.

As he watched her, something shifted in his mind like a bolt being released. He wasn't alone and never would be. Others at the school had problems too, issues they were dealing with. They were all suffering, not just physically. The mental scars were just as damaging and destructive, and ran deep through the seams of their family lives and were harder to fix than any impairment.

The damage that drug had caused was immeasurable.

He couldn't ignore her and creep away, but he wasn't used to talking about people's problems and what if she didn't want company? Propelled by a sudden memory thudding into him of those dark times back in Blackpool, he decided he'd risk it and if she told him to go away, well at least he would have tried. He took a step, crunching on a twig. Her head flicked around.

'Toby.' She sniffed, quickly looking away as if ashamed she'd been discovered.

'I didn't mean to intrude.' There was a bench next to where she was sitting in her wheelchair, and without asking if he could join her, he dropped onto the wooden slats and gave a sigh.

'Someone said you'd left.' He hated the rumour machine, and he still didn't know what story Bill had spun.

'I've been ill. Coming back Monday.' He hadn't planned to, but now that he'd said it, he was committing himself. 'Have you missed me then?' he asked with a cheeky laugh, hoping it might break the ice.

She looked at him. Her eyes were red and sore from all the crying. 'Chickenpox? Most of us had it a few years ago.'

'No, nothing like that.'

'What then?'

The question was blunt, and his brain froze. What was he going to tell his school mates? 'I'd prefer not to say, it's personal.'

It was a ridiculous answer, what the hell would she think? Never mind all the fresh rumours that would circulate. He couldn't come up with some mystery illness, but he hated lying. 'I wasn't actually ill,' he blurted.

She frowned at him.

'Just family stuff, I don't want to talk about it.'

'Family stuff?' She slumped forward, dipped her head. 'I know all about family stuff.'

'What's up?'

She didn't answer, kept her head dipped. 'Family stuff.'

'You were proper crying. Don't worry, I won't tell anyone.'

'Living in this place, it gets to you. It's alright for you, you've got a home, I mean a proper home and your dad works at the school. He's always around for you. Must be nice.'

If only she knew the truth.

'Bet you don't appreciate how lucky you are. Wish I had a dad like yours.' There was jealousy in her voice.

Images of the disgusting state of their kitchen shimmied into view, his dad's drinking, the lies, the deception. He wanted to blurt, "my life is a lie".

'I'm being serious, Toby, you don't realise how lucky you are. The others say the same. You're the envy of the school, we'd all like your charmed life.'

Toby clenched his toes. He couldn't stand to hear any more. He had to get away before he told her the truth, but he still hadn't heard what was bothering her. He abruptly jumped up and said, 'I'm okay, but I don't like to see you sad.'

'What about your family? Don't they come at the weekends?' he asked.

'When they're not busy, when Mum hasn't got a church event and Dad isn't playing stupid cricket or away on business.'

'I'm sorry. That must be hard. Where do they live?'

'Miles away. Near Chelmsford. Other side of London. Takes a couple of hours to get there. I think about them a lot and imagine what it would have been like to grow up with them. I have dreams about it. Having a room of my own, like my younger brother and sister. The house has four bedrooms. One of them is Dad's study with bookshelves on each wall and a big desk. I think that would have been my room. I'd have had a line of teddies on my pillowcase, and nobody would touch or hide them because they'd know it was my room.'

'You're too old for teddies.'

'Never too old for teddies.' She chuckled. 'I often imagine messing around with the other kids in the close, playing on bikes, walking to school together, maybe learning the times tables on the way. And going for tea at their houses and eating a whole stack of Marmite sandwiches.'

'Yuk.'

'Love Marmite.'

'Your family, they couldn't come this weekend then? That's why you're upset?'

'I told them not to.'

'Why the hell did you tell them not to come?'

'I wasn't being serious. I thought they'd turn up, but why, why do I always assume? I shouldn't assume anything where my parents are concerned. Aren't parents supposed to love you, but heck, what do I know? This life of ours, it's fucked up, we're fucked up. Don't suppose you've got a ciggie?'

'Don't smoke.'

'I shouldn't be at St Bede's. They're not poor, they could have hired a nanny. And just because I don't have legs, my arms are strong. They do everything my legs would do. I just do things differently. But Mum used to say the staff here knew what they were doing, they're professionals and could look after me better than she could. Looking back, I think it was just an excuse.'

Toby smiled. That was exactly the way he thought about his own handicap. His legs doubled as arms too.

'You came here as a baby?' he asked.

'Yep. Doctor told Mum to forget me, put me in an institution, go home and have another baby. A year later my twin brother and sister were born.'

Toby had heard similar stories. It struck him then how confusing it must have been, growing up in the care of nurses, only occasionally seeing your parents.

'Yesterday I got the nurses to dress me in my best outfit and I waited downstairs with the others, but no one came for me. The nurses tried to get me to have dinner, I refused. I couldn't believe they weren't coming. I felt like a right nana, and I'm sure that Nurse

Morgan smirked at me. She doesn't like me. She's a stickler for getting us to bed on time. My brother and sister can go to bed when they like. They get to watch *Morecombe and Wise* and *The Avengers*.'

She was rabbiting on, but Toby didn't mind, he liked the company. But he had the feeling that he was missing something. He didn't quite understand why she'd told them not to come. But maybe there was a lot about these families that he didn't understand and never would; come to think about it, he had never really asked, had he? He'd been so wrapped up in his own world, he'd never stopped to think about the others at the school.

I have a home. A bedroom of my own. The trappings of family life. Three people who care about me even if they do lie. So much I should be grateful for.

'Why did you tell them not to come? Doesn't make sense, Sue.'

She gulped, pulled a hanky from her pocket, and blew her nose. He envied her then, that simple act, how easy it was when you had arms. He dreaded colds, did everything to avoid catching one.

'So much happened the last time I stayed, three weeks ago.' She sighed, glancing up as if reliving the events of the weekend. 'I overheard Mum and Dad talking in the garage. He was having a go at her, telling her not to bother with her prayers and her Holy Communion, and all her God-fearing claptrap, it wouldn't change a thing. "That girl's deformed, that's why we sent her away, so that we can get on with our lives". Then Mum said something like, "God's still punishing me, it's hard work when she comes, it's disruptive on my routine, and I hate doing that awful journey. You know I get car sick". And Dad had replied, "It's not easy for me either. Do you think I like driving all that way, especially after going on one of my business trips? And you're forgetting I struggle to drive at night down those country lanes. Would have helped if you could drive but you didn't want lessons".'

Toby stared at the ground; the cruelty of those words was shocking. Sadness washed over him. He couldn't imagine how awful overhearing the conversation must have been.

My reality was so different.

Rona, she would always be his mum, his true mum. Her heart had ached for a baby, she wanted him despite his handicap, despite the enormous challenges he would bring, and despite Bill's resistance. He'd had the love of a mother.

But now I have Sandy too and that feels freaky. She can't replace Mum, but she is my biological mum.

He suddenly laughed to himself; the word biological reminded him of the box of Fairy Snow in the kitchen cupboard. He wondered if there was a link.

CHAPTER 3: SANDY

As Sandy rocked Angela to sleep after her early morning feed, the dawn was breaking, the black sky softening, tinged with a faint streak of orange.

She glanced round the poky room, feeling like an exile in her own home, forced to sleep in a single bed in the spare room, Angela's cot wedged beside her, because she couldn't bear to be anywhere near Jasper. When he'd confessed to her that Toby their long-lost son had not perished soon after birth as she'd always believed, she was shocked to the core. To think that Bill and Jasper had meticulously kept the truth from her for a staggering three years was mind-boggling and bewildering, and worse, if her mother hadn't opened the letter, she might never have found out.

It was all she could think about, her husband's big fat ugly lie. Maybe not a lie exactly, but a withheld truth, hard to separate the difference. The revelation left her questioning the very foundation of their marriage and made her wonder whether she could ever trust him again. This had gone on for three weeks, dancing in the shadows around each other, not wanting to give any indication of hurt or submission and sleeping apart. Late evening, they said goodnight, but it was more a grunt than actual words. The longer this went on, a pattern was formed, a pattern that she knew would be hard to break. At first Angela had been the perfect excuse––she didn't want to disturb his sleep, he needed a clear head for work, but now that she'd left the marital bed, she didn't want to return to it anytime soon.

The baby I thought had died is alive. How the hell could I have ever prepared myself for this?

Toby was born fifteen years ago, so long ago yet no time at all and now he was practically a grown man. Her heart ached––she'd missed his whole childhood, knew so little about him. His whole life was before him and the challenges that would bring. The tears flowed down her cheeks, he was hers, but she did not know him. The pain was unbearable. Her son, her boy, her past coming back to haunt her like the chains around Jacob Marley's neck. And she'd now be a part of that, and she didn't know how she felt about it, didn't even know if she wanted it because it had all been foisted on her, this new responsibility, this person she thought was dead. Toby…it was hard to even say his name. Was it the name she would have chosen?

When she'd found out, she outwardly accepted him, took him out a couple of times, had wanted him to understand her, get to know her, because what choice had there been? Only a heartless cold-blooded and callous woman would have turned her back on her own son. Yet there was a disconnection. When she looked at Toby, it was like looking at any other teenage boy. She wouldn't have picked him out in a crowd or a line-up and declared, yes, he is my son.

What was she supposed to feel, and after all this time? The process of developing that maternal bond had been severed. Her heart had hardened to the growing child inside her womb. She would have done anything to rid her body of him, as if he were waste. Her pregnancy hadn't been a time to fill her heart with love, hope, and joy. Nineteen and unmarried, practically disowned by her parents, viewing her pregnancy as a grave sin that tarnished their reputation and brought shame on the family's name. The weight of this judgment compounded an already difficult situation. They made it clear the baby would be adopted. And in that chink of time when the doctor had hit her with the news that her baby had died, her mother had coldly whisked her away and in fifteen years they'd never spoke about it.

But now––there was this heavy expectation that she could somehow conjure love from a bag of tricks like a magician. How was she going to do that? Toby was her son, her flesh and blood, yet she didn't know how to love him.

How could she suddenly drop her life to accommodate a sadly deformed child? She didn't have the tools, the experience, as Rona had. And she had her own baby to look after now. Her life had moved on. Toby was her past, a brief part. He'd survived fifteen years; he could survive without her now.

Her head was screaming for her to unlock the key to her heart, to let the love flood out, but there was no love, the chamber was empty. All the love she had was blinded for Angela, all-consuming as a mother's love should be. It was planned love, had taken nine months to nurture.

She slid her little finger into the baby's palm, smiling when Angela's tiny fingers closed around it. Her heart swelled, and in that moment, she felt it.

Like no other love she'd ever known before.

A mother's love.

The sweetest, purest, tenderest, most indulgent love on earth. So intense, so all-consuming. No one could take that away. Angela broke away the darkness, the hidden crevices of her heart, reaching parts of her she didn't know existed until now. She had created something magical, perfect in every way. How was this possible? As she traced a finger around her face, Sandy's eyes trailed over every crease and every fold in her skin, the patch of cradle cap, pale eyelashes, rosy lips. All that was beautiful was here in her arms, every small last detail. When was the last time she'd stopped to examine the beauty of a living creature? Maybe as a child playing on the beach, collecting seashells, marvelling at the wonder, the shape, the creation of such an incredible object that you could put to your ear and hear the waves.

Sometimes when she looked at Angela, it was hard to believe that she had grown inside her, a collection of cells the size of a lentil, to a kidney bean and after just nine months fully formed and perfect in every way. The agony she'd endured, exhausted, bloated, bruised, that dreadful pain that took over her whole body, forgotten so quickly in the euphoria of new life. The baby was blood-splattered, slimy, wormlike and screaming, but she was perfect. She couldn't believe it, felt overjoyed but also dumbfounded, kept looking at her vernix-smeared limbs. She was raw, unedited, but all that was beautiful was there: two arms, two legs, two ears.

She gently lowered Angela into her cot, trying not to wake her before slipping into the single bed sandwiched between the wall and the cot. She pulled the covers around her, a wave of shame crashing over her now. The horror of those thoughts when she'd first seen Angela, they hit her suddenly. The sheer relief, the overwhelming feeling of gratitude for her perfection, that she wasn't deformed with tangled limbs and God knows what else. And telling herself that she could now put the past behind her, that she was over her first-born, could forget him, relegate him to a box somewhere in the dark corners of her mind and shut the lid tightly as if his life hadn't mattered. Like tossing a broken biscuit in the bin, like shooting a wounded deer on the road.

Why didn't she feel this same love for Toby? She was his mother, her own flesh and blood, she'd created him, and despite those lost wilderness years, surely that unadulterated love was there, hidden inside her waiting to reveal itself? That broken baby whom she'd thought all those years ago to be dead was alive--how the hell was that even possible?

If only I had a sibling to turn to.

A familiar ache cut across her chest. She'd always grieved for the brother or the sister she'd never had. When she was a small child, an imaginary sister frequently entered her dreams at night and in the daytime. She must have stopped doing this at some point but couldn't remember when this was.

Didn't Toby deserve that same love?

Am I prepared to walk away from him? Reject him because he is not perfect? I want something bigger, a closer relationship. But how?

She tried to sink into the pillow. Angela would wake again soon, but her mind was fired, thoughts crowding in and preventing sleep. The mattress was lumpy, not comfy like the bed she shared with Jasper. How she'd always hated it when he went away on business leaving her alone in the house, the click and tick of its rhythm, unsettled at night in the king-size bed all alone, and now she didn't want to sleep in the same room as him. How could they possibly go back to the way they were? Their relationship was changed forever.

She drifted back to sleep, and a while later, sunlight slanted through a gap in the curtain waking Sandy with a start. She twizzled round, in a daze. She knew she'd overslept, but Angela should have woken by now. Something was wrong. She sat up, threw the covers off and reached over to the cot. She couldn't see the rise and fall of her chest. She settled her on her tummy, as she seemed to like that position best. She reached over, panic setting in as she touched the baby's head with a trembling hand. Angela snuffled and Sandy gasped with relief, plonking herself back on the bed. Was this normal, to be so panicked, so fearful of something happening to her? She was so delicate, so fragile and utterly dependent. As these thoughts trailed through her mind, a sickening shiver swept over her, a surge of horror slamming into her.

Baby Toby was put on a cold windowsill to die.

If Rona hadn't snatched him, he wouldn't be alive today. His life would have ended, snuffed out, days old, but she rescued him. Was she supposed to feel gratitude or anger? That martyr of a woman who'd risked everything and loved her son with all her heart even though he wasn't hers. And the worst of it––had loved him more than his own mother and by volumes, a love with no bounds. This thought Sandy found so hard to fathom, and guilt suddenly wrapped itself tightly around her. She owed everything to Rona.

As Sandy watched her baby sleep, she contemplated getting dressed. She hadn't heard Jasper get up and was glad it was Saturday because he usually left the house at around eight for a round of golf with a neighbour, returning at lunchtime, then retreating to his study to continue an article he was working on. For the whole morning at least, she could relax, she had the house to herself.

Opening the door, still in her nightdress, she nearly smacked right into Jasper and the cup of tea he was holding. She stepped back to let him in, ruffled because she'd told him several times not to bring her up a cuppa.

'Put it there.' She waved her hand at the chest of drawers without so much as glancing at him. She didn't care that she sounded like a stuck-up lady of the manor giving orders to her maid.

He put it down and went over to the cot, his hands in his pockets, jangling coins. Another habit of his that now drove her mad.

'How was last night? Did she keep you awake?' His tone was cheerful.

She wasn't going to respond to his pathetic attempts to pacify her. Pretend this nightmare hadn't happened, forgive him. He'd betrayed her and that left a fork in the road for their marriage. Right now, she didn't know which road she wanted to take.

'She woke once.'

'Once? If she's sleeping through, why can't you bring the cot into our room, that way we can be a family? We've never slept apart.'

Sandy looked up at him, incredulous.

Snarling, she said, 'That's all you care about, that we haven't done it in weeks. Family isn't about rearranging the furniture and papering over the cracks.'

'I know you're struggling with all this. I know I screwed up. It wasn't easy for me; I don't think you get that even after all the explaining I've done.'

'Oh I get it alright, you lied to me for three years. You kept a secret, not just any old secret. I think if you'd had an affair, gone off with some tart in the village––that, Jasper, would have been nothing compared to this. This is huge and it's you that doesn't get it.'

'But you're my wife, we love each other, we're so close, we tell each other everything, we can get through anything. This isn't going to break us. You trust me, don't you?' His face was pleading.

'Huh.' She threw her head back in disbelief. 'You're kidding me. The one thing, the most important thing of all that we should have talked about, and you kept it hidden. If it hadn't have been for my mother, I'd have never found out. So don't you dare tell me we're close. We're about as far apart as the moon is from Earth.'

'Us bickering, biting slices out of each other isn't going to help. We should be coming together, supporting each other, we can get through this. We both caused this in our own stupid way.'

He took her wrist and pulled her towards him, and she was

forced to look at him. She recalled the expression on his face when he asked her to marry him, staring into those eyes and making her feel special as he always did. She saw that same expression now and fleetingly felt conflicted, angry that he had this way with her. He'd always had that power over her with his relaxed manner, never stiff or unsure, charming, and always acting with such confidence and self-assurance.

She shook his hand away, as if it had burnt her. 'I don't want to come anywhere near you, it's bad enough being in the same house as you. I certainly don't want to sleep in the same bed.'

'I miss you, holding you at night.'

'You should have thought about the consequences of your actions then, shouldn't you?'

She left the room and Jasper followed as she headed downstairs to the lounge, where she plumped cushions and gathered items of Angela's. The place needed a tidy-up.

'It tormented me for three bloody years. I wanted to tell you, more than anything. Bill pleaded for me not to.'

'You're pathetic,' she said, clutching a cushion to her chest. 'You put that bloody man, an ignorant school caretaker before your own wife. The pair of you connived behind my back.' She jabbed her finger at him. 'I can't forgive you for that.'

'I could hardly watch while the poor bloke was carted off to prison. He did a pretty good job of bringing up our son.'

'Who says he would have gone to prison?'

'You might have gone to the police––you might still do.'

'You don't trust me. You make judgements, assumptions. You don't know me at all.' She slumped onto the settee, crestfallen. 'You have the audacity to talk about trust. You've ploughed a bulldozer right through our marriage, I'm not sure there's any going back from this.'

He leant towards her, tears filled his eyes, pointing a finger at her, his face angry, and in a sharp tone he said, 'Don't you lecture me on trust. You had a baby and didn't think to tell me.

You were planning to have our child adopted, for Christ's sake. If I hadn't bumped into you in New York, I'd never have known. Do you ever stop to consider how I felt?'

His words fanned a flame, the crossing of a line. Something inside her cracked and she struggled through tears to get the words out. 'I did everything to find you, you know that. My mother destroyed your letters.'

He knelt beside her. 'I'm sorry for everything. But it's not going to help, us sleeping apart.' He looked lost now, sorrow and regret eddying through his words. 'Please don't cry, we can work through this.'

She wiped her eyes, looked up at him. 'I don't know that we can, Jasper.'

'I'll do anything for you, Sandy, anything. You're my world.'

'I'm not sure, we're broken, that's how it feels.'

He stood up, went to gaze out of the window, hands stuffed in his pockets. He was shaking, trembling like a scolded child, and was silent for a few moments. Then abruptly he raised both his hands, slapping them onto his thighs.

'I don't know what you want from me.'

He didn't get it; he didn't get her. She was now the one in the wrong for being stubborn, for wanting time alone, for punishing him. But did she understand herself? She felt strangely detached from her own feelings. She felt devoid of all emotions apart from those she felt towards Angela.

'Just go to your golf. Get out of my hair, I can't stand the sight of you.'

His face hardened. 'Fine, I will do, if you're going to be like that. I might play a full round and stay on for drinks in the clubhouse. Don't stay up for me.'

'You do what you bloody like, it's what you're used to.'

He swept from the room and a moment later she heard the front door slam and the car engine cough to life.

CHAPTER 4: JASPER

Jasper's friends left the golf club after a couple of beers. He didn't want to go home, what was the point, Sandy would still be in a mood. There was nothing he could say or do to reason with her. She refused to understand why he'd kept Toby a secret.

He ordered a bottle of wine and went to sit in a corner to contemplate what to do next. He glugged the first glass in seconds, savouring the taste and enjoying how relaxed he now felt. A simple pleasure he'd almost forgotten; the evening stretched ahead, he could unwind, put himself first for a change and best of all, he didn't have to get home for a specific time. If anything, Sandy would welcome him staying out for as long as possible. These days she barely spoke over meals. He hated the strained atmosphere, the tension that sat between them. He'd heat his dinner up later--how much easier that would be.

Heck, she'd throw him out given half a chance, have the house to herself. The thought jarred him. Was she plotting to end their marriage? There was a difference between the positive silence of a couple comfortable in each other's company and the silence that reflected tension, conflict, and disconnection. The type they were now trapped in. But to break that silence had become unsafe. Every conversation turned into an argument, a re-run of the same fight, turning the screw deeper and deeper. She accused him of lying but he'd never actually lied, just honoured a secret for everyone's sake. His lack of transparency now cast a long shadow over the marriage and all she did was pour more fuel on the fire. Each time she attacked him, dredging up his mistakes, it pained him, amplified his regret and resentment, a regret he now carried, but she kept throwing more ammunition. It was like ripping the scab off a wound over and over. There had to be an end to this, a moving on. Hadn't she punished him enough?

Jasper raised his glass as if giving a toast.

To Bill and Rona, you made Toby the fine man he is today. Without you, he'd be buried in a box.

The second and third glass slid down his throat like a serpent, slithering around his system and singing in his head. He wasn't used to drinking this much wine, it was rare for him, he was usually more restrained and didn't use alcohol like a blanket to smother painful emotions in the same way that Bill did. But tonight, he needed that crutch. He was surprised just how fast he could down a bottle, but it was smooth, fruity and mellow, one of his favourites.

Swaying over to the bar, light-headed, he ordered another.

'Think you've had enough, Jasper,' the barman said as he polished a glass. 'And we'll be closing soon.'

'Bit early.' Jasper glanced at the clock next to the picture of the Queen. 'It's only seven.'

'The guv wants to close early. It's been quiet this evening and he's got a builder coming round shortly to give an estimate.'

He was probably right, he should go. He couldn't stay here all night.

Jasper staggered to the door, his head spinning. Out in the fresh air, he felt suddenly woozy, and collapsed against the car as he fumbled for his keys. He slumped to the ground feeling bile rise in his throat. He hadn't eaten for hours, there was nothing to line his stomach. No wonder he felt rough. He leaned over and was violently sick. He pulled a handkerchief from his pocket and mopped his mouth. He hated to be in this state, an overwhelming sense of self-loathing washing over him, but how low he felt.

In the dimly lit car park, he squinted, trying to make out the figure rushing towards him. It was Mike, the manager of the club. He hadn't seen him all day, he must have been shut away in his office catching up on paperwork and accounts.

Mike reached for the keys Jasper was clutching. 'Mate, you're in no fit state to drive. Let me call you a cab.' He helped Jasper to his feet, his legs nearly giving way. He felt like a newborn foal. 'Come and wait inside.' He took him by the arm and helped him back to the clubhouse where the barman had begun to switch the lights off.

'You okay, Jasper, this isn't you, what the hell's going on?'

'My wife doesn't love me anymore,' he slurred.

'I'm sure that's not true.'

'Huh, you've not seen her lately.'

'Come on,' Mike said, nudging the swing door with his knee and guiding Jasper over to a chair. 'This is the drink talking. Perhaps it's her hormones. My wife was all over the place when our nipper was born.'

'If only it was just hormones. She won't let me near her or the baby. I feel like an outsider.'

Mike stared at him with a frown on his face. 'The baby's yours, right?'

'Huh, apparently not.' Jasper didn't know what he was saying. His head was fuzzy. Angela might as well not be his, it didn't feel as if they were a family. Sandy wouldn't let him hold her, she was being so damn possessive, like a kid with a new toy. How could he bond with his child? These early weeks were so precious, but Sandy had built an invisible iron curtain around their baby.

As the taxi pulled up on the driveway, Jasper felt as if the house was watching his arrival with a lack of enthusiasm. Darkness wrapped itself around the bricks like a glove. The floodlights came on, lighting his way. Crunching and staggering from side to side over the gravel, nearly at the porch, he glanced up, stepping back to look up at the nursery window now bathed in an amber glow.

She's awake.

Instead of feeling dread, his heart soared. He imagined her dressed in a cream silk negligee, the short one with a lace trim around the bust that hugged her curves so beautifully.

The singing head, the post alcohol thump in the gut would soon disappear once he was in her arms. He needed her. It was just a wall but could be broken.

Inside, he went through to the kitchen, pouring himself a large glass of water and glugging it in one and refilling another to take upstairs. On his way up to the landing, he banged into the walls. At the last step, he plunged forward, the glass falling from his hand and crashing down the stairs, shattering against the wall.

Something sharp hit his head.

What the hell was that?

He put his hand to the source of the pain. A drop of blood. He'd gashed himself on something metal. What the hell had he left on the stairs earlier? He was always so careful, he knew the danger of stairs. The thought of Sandy having an accident, Angela in her arms. It filled him with horror. Their safety was paramount. He remembered a work colleague tumbling to her death after tripping on a hairbrush.

His yelp and the clatter of the object as it hurtled down the stairs disturbed Sandy. Now the landing was bathed in a blinding light, and she was standing there. She had that just woken appearance, eyes bleary, hair ruffled, but she was a picture of beauty in her thin cotton nightie. Peering up at her, he cast his eyes over her long, slender legs, and was reminded why he'd been attracted to her that evening they'd first met.

'You've cut yourself,' she said in alarm, rushing over and kneeling beside him. As she crouched, her nightie rose and he caught a glimpse of her thighs, the private parts of her body she now kept hidden.

How he longed for her, ached for her. The recent chill in her voice and facial expressions was replaced by concern for him.

'Something was left on the stairs, it cut into me.'

'Oh my goodness.' She gasped and clapped her hand to her mouth. 'It's my fault,' she said, glancing down the stairs and pointing to the cheese grater that had landed on the bottom winder. 'I was holding it when I answered the phone earlier. I must have forgotten to put it back in the kitchen.'

'It's okay, it doesn't matter.'

'It does matter, you've gashed yourself.'

He didn't care about the cut, just the shame of her seeing him in this pitiful state, how low he'd sunk, but she didn't seem aware that he'd been drinking.

'Come and sit on the bed.' She guided him into the bedroom, and he sat on the edge. His head pounded, the alcohol sloshing around his system, and now this sharp pain. She went into the bathroom, her nightie again rising as she reached up to the cupboard pulling cotton wool and plasters from the shelf. He watched her turn on the tap, dampen the cotton wool with her perfectly manicured fingers. It was a simple task and yet it was so loving. Pure lust and love overwhelmed him, melted him. In that moment all he wanted was her, to be close again, make love to her. As she turned and came over to him, gently dabbing his forehead, he knew she still loved him. She was concerned for him, the first time in a while she'd shown any interest in his welfare--it felt good. Their eyes briefly met and all he saw was pure love staring back, the love he'd seen many times in her eyes when she looked at Angela.

And then it was gone as she spoke her next words. Her tone icy, every hope of a reconciliation dissipated in the chilly air swirling between them. 'You've been drinking.'

'Only a couple.'

'Don't lie to me, Jasper. You've had far more than a couple.' Her voice was full of hurt as she jabbed at his head with the cotton wool, her previous gentle touch gone.

He'd done it again. He looked at her, completely lost, like a floating paddle on an ocean. She was his raft, always had been. He was nothing without her, he had to find a way back, he couldn't bear a life without her.

The sense of despair, lust, longing, all crashed into him at once. He reached over, pulled her towards him, his arm on her back, pinning her to him as his lips smacked clumsily into hers. His tongue forced its way into her stiff mouth, skidding across her teeth. He'd turn her on, get her to relax, they'd collapse on the bed. For a moment he believed this but then she pushed him away with a violent thrust of her hand.

'What are you doing, Jasper? You're disgusting.'

'But I love you, I want you. Don't you love me anymore?'

She stood up, her frame stiffening. 'Not like this. What's wrong with you?'

From nowhere an invisible mist descended before his eyes. He leapt up, preventing her from leaving the room. She couldn't go. He wouldn't let her. He couldn't bear it, couldn't watch her disappear to the nursery, another night alone in their bed. Tonight, he'd seen her begin to thaw, couldn't let this horrible chasm continue.

He grabbed her arm, yanked her back towards him like a rag

doll, pushing her onto the bed. She'd soon experience how he truly felt.

'Get off me, Jasper,' she screamed. He was covering her body now. She couldn't move. She kicked out, thrashed her arms.

'Get off me,' she screamed again.

Just then, the door flew open.

CHAPTER 5: BILL

*B*ill pulled up under an oak tree in the golf club carpark. It was getting dark, soon the clocks would be going back, and the days would grow shorter. As he got out of his truck a cold breeze ruffled the treetops, sending a flurry of golden leaves to the ground.

'Not getting out? You can sit in the lounge,' he said to Toby.

A minor victory had been achieved. Bill had coaxed Toby from his bedroom with the promise of a Chinese takeaway if he came with him to the golf club and waited while he fixed a leaking radiator. Bill smiled to himself. Although the lad had complex needs, he was a teenager and everyone knew what simple creatures they were, easily pacified--temporarily at least--with the lure of a treat. But succeeding in luring him away from his room was one thing, getting him to talk was another. Their journey over to the golf club had been in silence.

He'd wanted to talk and for Toby to be able to talk to him, but it wasn't going to happen. They'd muddle through until Toby left for college, but it wouldn't feel natural or relaxed. Ashamedly Bill realised he now longed for the day that Toby left home. He despised himself for this and felt huge guilt, but wouldn't life be easier if he didn't have to look at Toby every day and be reminded of the horror of what he'd done.

He felt stunted, as if parts of his brain had been surgically removed. He was good with his hands, could sort out any problem to do with the house or a car, but trying to fix a relationship, he didn't have the right tools or the skills. He was the adult, yet he felt about as useless as a chocolate teapot. He hadn't a clue how to break the ice. He felt panicked, out of his depth. How was he supposed to reach Toby? He loved that boy with all his heart but didn't know how to show it and couldn't find the right words.

Life––it wasn't supposed to be like this. He couldn't have children of his own, that was just the way that God had designed him. He wasn't supposed to have these challenges. He wasn't cut out to be a father––never had been. That's why he'd struggled for the past fifteen years and why he was struggling now.

He was an imposter, play-acting at being a father. A fraudster, he didn't deserve Toby. He'd played the role, gone through the motions, displayed a façade of fatherhood, fooled everyone, bluffed his way through but had always been haunted by the fear of being found out. And now that the truth was in the open, every lie and falsehood exposed, he couldn't live with himself, or with Toby. He wished he could curl up into a ball, go to sleep and never wake up.

'I'm staying here,' Toby said coldly. 'I only came because you promised me a Chinese. I'm starving.' Toby didn't turn his head to look at him and kept his gaze fixed on the tree in front of the truck, his eyes expressionless.

Bill's shoulders drooped and his chin trembled. He felt truly broken. Broken into a million tiny pieces. Toby loathed him. He could see it in that simple act, his body rigid in the seat, not turning to acknowledge his presence, it spoke volumes.

'Okay, I'll try not to be long.'

Toby didn't reply and he shut the door and headed over to the clubhouse, his chest tight with the enormity of what he faced with Toby.

Inside the clubhouse, Mike took him through to the men's toilet block and showed him a large puddle under the radiator. He turned off the radiator at the two control valves.

'I'm going to have to come back tomorrow. I'll need to buy some new seals and drain the system. It's getting late and it's not a quick job, I'm afraid. Put a bowl under the drip and I'll see you around midday.'

Occasionally Bill did odd jobs for cash. The extra money came in handy, but he didn't like to make a habit of it, couldn't risk the taxman finding out.

Mike was leaning against the wall watching him tighten the valves. 'That journalist friend of yours was here earlier.'

'Did he win his round of golf?'

'Not sure, but I was a bit worried about him. He was very drunk. I put him in a taxi, he was about to get in his car.'

Bill put his tool down, turned his head and stared at him. 'We are talking about the same fella, Jasper?'

'Quite sure. He had a couple of pints with the guys he played a round with. I was in for most of the afternoon. I came out later to find him staggering across the carpark pissed. His friends had long gone.'

'That's totally out of character. Jasper hardly drinks. I've only ever seen him drink one, two at the most.'

'Yes that's what I thought too.' Mike frowned.

Bill dug his hands into his pockets, thoughtful. 'You've got me worried now. Maybe I'll call in, see how he is.'

'I'd tread carefully if I was you. I got the impression he's got marriage problems.'

'They can't have, they've just had a baby.'

Mike lowered his voice. 'He mumbled something about the baby not being his.'

Jasper must have been very drunk to come out with such a clanger. What an idiot, this wasn't like him at all. And then it struck him. What if he went on another bender and blurted everything out? The man was a liability, a danger to him.

Shit, I could still go to prison.

Back in the truck, Bill told Toby about Jasper getting drunk. 'I'm worried about him. I think we should drop by on our way home.'

'But what about the Chinese? I'm starving and you promised.'

'Later,' Bill said as he reversed the truck and swept out of the carpark.

'I knew you'd go back on your word.'

'I always keep my word.'

'Course you do.'

His sarcasm was starting to niggle. 'Toby, if you've got something to say, then say it. Shout, scream, tell me what a shit I am because I'm fed up with this cold treatment. I've only ever done the best for you. I know I'm not your flesh and blood, but I was thrown into this, I never walked away from you.' He raised his voice and gripped the steering wheel to stop his hands from trembling. It took every effort to stay focussed on the road.

Toby sat, blankly staring out of the window.

Bill thumped the steering wheel. He hadn't a clue what to say. He couldn't bear to glance at him and kept his eyes firmly on the road.

'You stole my life,' Toby shrieked. 'You stole me from them, my real parents. I would have had a completely different life.'

Bill glanced in the mirror, indicated to pull over, then slammed his foot on the brake. He couldn't concentrate on the road and the conversation.

He applied the brake and switched off the engine. 'A better life, that's what you want to say. Go on, just spit it out, say it. He earns far more than I do, they've got a big posh house, a nice car.'

'I didn't mean that,' Toby pleaded.

'Yes, you did, you little shit, that's exactly what you meant.' Bill had gone a step too far, he didn't intend to be insulting, but he'd reached boiling point. In that moment he longed for Rona to be there to take control.

'I didn't have a say when your mum brought you home. I didn't know what she had done, it was like a nightmare for me. She was desperate to have someone to love; a baby to fulfil her dreams. We wanted children but the magic didn't happen. We tried so many times and every time it ended in heartbreak. Then she found you, broken, rejected and helpless. The joy on her face that she could make a difference, she was a new woman, unshackled from her own nightmare. How could I deprive her, Toby, after all she had been through? I am not proud of what we did, but I will always be proud that your mum saw beyond the challenges. You might not be proud to call me your dad, but I will always be proud to call you my son.'

Bill felt emotionally drained. He flicked the indicator, put his foot down and drove off towards Jasper's house in silence with tears burning his cheeks.

CHAPTER 6: TOBY

Toby stared ahead as Bill drove in silence through the village towards Jasper and Sandy's house.

He recalled the first time he met them. After being told that Jasper and Sandy were his real parents, time had stilled. He was still in shock. There was a buzzing noise in his ears, as if someone had stuck a whisking spoon into each ear and turned the speed to high. The past, the present, the future blended together into a murky abyss.

He wished he'd questioned the tiny warning signs that might have led him to the truth, because looking back now, there had been plenty. But that was plain daft. Kids didn't question what their parents told them--everyone knew that. They believed the daftest of stories including the one about the fat bloke dressed in a red suit who flew on a sleigh pulled by reindeer. He chastised himself nonetheless for being gullible, for eating the bullshit. If Bill or Rona had told him the earth was flat, he would have believed them.

He remembered going through a phase of asking lots of questions. It drove Rona mad. He must have been around eight or nine years old. "Be quiet for two minutes, I can't hear myself think," she'd say. He wanted to know about dinosaurs and planets and rainbows and ice and so much more. He must have been piecing together information to make sense of the world, or he was just naturally curious.

Closely his eyes, scrunching his face in the darkness, he tried to focus. The memories were so close, crouching in the shadows of his mind.

And then--a flashback.

Sitting on a bench, with Rona, swinging his legs back and forth while they waited for the bus into town. He must have been around eight years old. The bus arrived and a heavily pregnant woman laden with bags descended the steps right in front of Toby. His mother pulled him out of her pathway with a tut and an apology. The woman's bump was enormous, as if a football had been stuffed up her dress and he imagined popping it with a pin and watching it deflate, like a party balloon. He watched as she waddled off down the road struggling with her bags and looking like a duck. Later that day, Toby quizzed Rona. "What was it like to be pregnant? Was I a big baby? Did it hurt you when I came out?"

"You loved it when I had a bath. I'd lie back and watch my belly contort into weird shapes as you kicked, swirled and fluttered. I thought you were a girl practising ballet. I kept a jug by the bath, poured water on my belly, and you'd kick and roll even more. You were such an entertainment, and your dad would sit by the bath and laugh his head off."

So elaborate a description--all a cocktail of lies.

I feel so let down.

Bill picked up speed on the main road, maybe because he felt uncomfortable driving in silence and wanted the journey to end. Toby glanced down at the footwell, spotting a discarded half-eaten sandwich, perhaps Marmite, knowing Bill.

And there it was, another flashback.

Rona told him he was born in the kitchen. She'd been making Marmite sandwiches when her waters broke and there was no time to get to the hospital, so he was born on the kitchen table.

What codswallop. Anger mixed with sadness welled inside him. He needed to see his birth certificate. Did they even have one and if not, how on earth was he supposed to get through life without an official identity?

He wanted to ask about his birth certificate but dreaded more deceit and that horrible feeling yet again of being let down.

'There's an old sandwich by my foot.' He sighed. It wasn't important in the grand scheme of things, not compared to all the lies, but in this mood, Toby felt like lashing out.

Bill's nonchalant glance towards the footwell stoked a flash of annoyance, and Toby, unable to contain himself a moment longer, blurted, 'I don't know how the hell you can live like this.'

He knew he was overstepping the line, but the fine threads of respect were fast unravelling and there was nothing that Bill could say or do to repair it. 'You're a complete slob. If Mum could see you now, the pigsty we live in, she'd be horrified. She kept everything pristine and in its place, but now I realise she was just constantly running around after both of us, clearing up in your wake.' He knew he was pushing every button, but the venom was flowing, and he couldn't stop.

'I'm busy trying to support you, put food on the table.'

'I'm a burden then, that it?'

'I didn't say that.'

'You've got time to drink and put your feet up in front of the TV. The only reason you like *Steptoe and Son* is because their back yard reminds you of our living room.'

'I work bloody hard.'

'You don't understand what it's like for me. I can't just take a plate or a dish from a dirty stack. Maybe you should pile them all in the bath and I'll wash them with my toes.'

'You're being ridiculous now.'

'Am I? Type of thing Steptoe would do.'

Bill shook his head and stifled a smile.

'I don't know why you don't get a housemaid. No wait, no self-respecting woman would set foot in our gaff. It's a wonder Mum was even attracted to you.'

Bill turned into Jasper and Sandy's close and pulled up on the kerb outside their house. 'That's enough, I've had enough.'

'And I've bloody well had enough too. I want to live with my real parents. At least they keep a clean and tidy house.'

In that moment, as he glanced up at the large detached modern house with its neat front lawn and its big windows and garage to the side, the vision of a rosy life appeared before his eyes. The house decorated at Christmas time with a real spruce and coloured lights, presents and laughter. For the past few years, Bill hadn't wanted a Christmas tree and Toby had called him Mr Scrooge.

Jasper and Sandy were his real parents.

This is where I belong.

Had he ever loved Bill? He questioned it now. He felt shame for being so nasty, and confused, so damn confused.

The longing to be a million miles away or just here, living in this nice house with his real family. It was hard to hide his thoughts.

I have a sister too.

He'd always longed for a sibling and although Angela was much younger, a yearning rose inside him to be part of her life.

It was then that Toby noticed it. The front door, wide open.

Hastily, Toby got out of the truck and as he rushed towards the house, the floodlights pinged on illuminating the driveway.

He stepped inside, paused in the hallway, glanced round, confused. Why would they forget to shut the door? Behind him, Bill slammed the truck door and his feet crunched over the gravel. The mere sight of him, his shirt hanging out, an unsightly globule of egg on his chin, shoelaces undone––all of it sent tiny waves of irritation skittering through him.

And then he heard it.

A scream.

A surge of adrenaline shot through him. Sheer panic and animal instinct drove him up the stairs, two steps at a time and reaching the landing with pounding heart and legs that wanted to give way, he glanced round. What the hell was happening? Which room? Then he heard it again, louder this time.

'Get off me, you're hurting me.' She was crying. She was in pain. He didn't stop to consider who was in there, who was hurting her. His gut made the decision without a second's hesitation.

This was his mum. His defenceless mum, and she needed help.

Bill called from the bottom of the stairs, 'Toby what are you doing? Come down,' but it was too late, Toby had flung open the door to the main bedroom and stepped inside.

His head played a game of catch-up. Was this normal? Something wasn't right, he turned on his heels, glimpsing back.

Tangled limbs, Jasper's naked body. His bare bottom rising on top of her. Was he crushing Sandy to death? That's how it looked, an animal pouncing, ready for the kill. He was clenching her wrists, she was struggling, couldn't move, legs thrashing, her face red, sweaty. Distressed. Was he suffocating her, strangling her, what the hell was happening?

'Mum.' He screamed, then whimpered. 'Everything okay?'

Everything wasn't okay, he knew that.

All the admiration he had for Jasper, his incredible journalist father who he looked up to with pride--it was gone, evaporated in an instant.

She needed help, no she didn't. This was private, intimate.

Shit. He shouldn't be here.

Relationships--he didn't get them.

Blind panic took over. If only he could cover his face with his hands. Time froze, he backed out, and flew down the stairs, pushing Bill to one side who was standing there looking gormless.

He ran--ran like the clappers with no plan of where to go, what to do, who to see. He turned into an alley between the houses where darkness merged with the creepy shadows of trees. If only a streetlight could show him the way, but that was how his life was, there was no guide, no saviour. He was trapped in darkness and now even the darkness was staring back, swallowing him whole.

Who can I trust?

Where do I go from here?

Out of breath and sweaty he stopped, crouching against the fence. Over the road he had full view of the village hall all lit up. He could see a disco ball spinning and glittering from the ceiling, reflecting light in every direction. A cluster of skimpily dressed girls in their late teens were huddled together outside laughing and lighting ciggies, plumes of smoke eddying into the cold night air. He wondered what they were laughing about, but it didn't matter, they were having fun, they could forget their worries for one evening. The swing doors flew open and a gaggle of lads spilled out, the singer's voice escaping with them.

Lucy.

It was her voice above the clash of a cymbal and the strum of a guitar. She'd recently formed a band with two guys and had started playing in local pubs and venues. He wanted to see her now, performing in that hall, and more than anything just to melt into a crowd of people and soak up the party atmosphere, escape in some of his favourite songs. To forget about Sandy, Jasper and Bill for an hour would feel so good, the weight of them lifted from his shoulders. Right then, music was his tonic, his refuge, and when it hit his soul, he could crawl between the notes, free his mind, feel no pain, and the louder the music, the better.

He made a dash across the street and round the building, slipping in through the fire door wedged open with a brick. He wouldn't be spotted here by the staff checking tickets. The hall was full. Some were dancing, others straining to chat above the music, a few were going wild on the dance floor, free-spirited and without a care for who was watching, the type who'd dance anywhere––in rain, in mud, in war. There were a few couples snogging and Toby quickly averted his gaze and stood in the crowd, his eyes fixed now towards the stage. Between a gap in the crowd, he could silently admire Lucy undisturbed as she strutted the stage singing one of Abba's greatest, 'Waterloo', dressed in a flowing white cheesecloth dress and brown cowboy boots, twisting, and bending and with such passion in her voice and face, giving her all.

Towards the end of the song, she looked straight at him, their eyes meeting, her face breaking into a smile. She announced a twenty-minute break, put the microphone down, hugged her guitarist, then descended the steps, spoke to a couple of well-wishers as she wove through the crowd towards him. He loved how sociable she was, the way confidence oozed from her, just comfortable in her own skin and admired by all. How he'd love to be like that. What was her secret?

'Toby, I didn't know you'd be here.' She reached out, pecked him on the cheek.

'Neither did I.' He laughed. 'You were amazing.'

'Who you with?'

He shrugged. 'On my own. It's a long story.'

'Want to come outside? It's a bit fresh but I need a ciggie.'

He followed her out of the fire exit and away from the building onto the playing field beside the hall.

'It's going well then, your band?' he asked while she flicked a lighter and took a cigarette to her lips.

'Really well. We're busy most weekends now. We've got a couple of weddings coming up and an eighteen-year-old's birthday bash. Word gets around.'

Toby thought how beautiful she looked in the moonlight, but it wasn't just the way she looked, it was what was inside her, the way she was and everything that continued to make his heart flutter in her company. He'd long accepted that he stood zero chance with her romantically. She was three years older for starters and had never thought of him that way. They were just friends and he hoped it would stay that way and for the long haul.

'Something's troubling you.' She tilted her head, exhaled smoke into the damp air.

'Why do you say that?' He could feel his cheeks burn and briefly glanced away.

'I can just tell, I know you well, Toby Murphy.' She winked.

He winced at the sound of his full name, that link to Bill and Rona.

'I haven't heard from you in weeks.' She looked at him directly now and there was no escaping that power of hers, that ability to unlock his soul, make him melt. Everything laid bare.

Could he trust her? His heart was breaking, desperate to confide in somebody, but not anybody. He didn't imagine she could keep a secret and her dad was on the town council. If she blurted his secret, the whole town would get to hear. But damn it, right in that very moment, maybe that was what he needed.

Trust was so fragile, easy to break, easy to lose, but hard to rebuild. Broken trust was like a shattered mirror, like the million tiny pieces of glass in a disco ball. He was willing to take that risk, how much worse could things get? He was consumed with hatred towards Bill and if someone was to slip into a police station and blab, he didn't care, it would be a small triumph, a victory of sorts.

'I found out that I'm adopted.'

His words hung in the silence that unfolded between them. She took a puff of her ciggie, stared up at the sky as if drawing inspiration from the stars above.

'I don't know why,' she said after several moments, 'but I always knew that.' Her eyes were bright, almost animated as she turned her head and looked at him, but all he felt was bleak despair, his insides hollowed out.

Everyone else knows. I am the last to find out.

'How, why, what makes you say that?'

'I don't know why, just an inkling, a feeling I had, it wasn't something I gave much thought to so it can't have been a strong feeling. You don't look like Bill. You look like Jasper though.'

Toby stared at the ground, his shoulders slumping. That likeness––maybe everyone had seen it, commented on it. There was no proof though. No proof with any of it. All he had was their word.

'Do you think so?'

'I know so, Toby, my parents have long commented on it.'

Toby sighed. 'Well… there we are then.'

'Jasper made some comment once.'

'What comment?'

'I can't remember.' Her voice sounded weak, pathetic.

He turned to stare at her, desperation in his voice. 'Why can't you remember?'

'I'm sorry, I just don't, but the comment made Dad wonder about you and Jasper, that's all. Look if he's your real dad, you should be very proud. He's a very successful guy and he clearly thinks the world of you.'

That was the last thing Toby wanted to hear. Everybody admired good old Jasper, but they didn't know what a brute he really was, they hadn't seen what he'd seen earlier on. It might change their minds.

'I've got to go, they'll be out looking for me. I'll come and watch you again if that's okay?'

The only place he could go to was back home to the cottage. Whether he liked it or not, that was where he lived, where his belongings were.

CHAPTER 7: SANDY

Sandy woke in the half-light of dawn. She couldn't remember feeding Angela during the night, her head was groggy and still playing catch-up. She glanced into the cot; the baby was sleeping soundly.

She slipped out of bed, and on wobbly legs staggered through to the bathroom. There was a stinging sensation as she peed, and it felt like spilling vinegar on a cut. Shooting pains rose and she pressed her hand against her pubic area, trying to alleviate the pain. She hadn't recovered from the tear following Angela's birth although the stitches were out.

Back in the room, she went to stand at the window and peered across the lawn, the morning dew like tiny pinheads dotting the blades of grass. A bloody-fingered dawn fringed the horizon, the sky ablaze. All the pain of her body was reflected in that sky. Her heart breaking, bleeding all over the world.

Last night was horrible.
I feel dirty, disrespected.
It was the worst experience I've ever had.

It was his strength she remembered. So drunk, he couldn't have penetrated her. He was like a dead weight bearing down on her. She'd struggled to push him off, it felt as if he was crushing her, clamping her. The way he'd pulled her around as if she were a rag doll. All she'd wanted was to get back to the spare room, curl up and fall asleep.

It was the drink––because what sort of caring, loving husband in their right mind would do that? She'd never seen him drunk. He rarely had more than one, two drinks at most. How much had he consumed? The drink had changed him. But as much as she wanted to justify what had happened, she knew deep down that alcohol was no excuse for such awful behaviour.

She turned from the window and as she went to sit on the bed, the most shocking memory of the previous night hit her.

Toby.

Why on earth was he in the house, how did he get in? And then the penny dropped. Jasper must have given him a key and without even bothering to ask her if it was okay. But how would it be possible for Toby to open the door? She'd never seen him use a key, she didn't know how he'd go about it.

She grabbed the milk-stained muslin which was draped across the side of the cot and in frustration wound it around her wrist as her mind flitted back to Jasper. What would it be next? He'd invite Toby to live with them. Their spare room wrecked by a teenage boy, the daily challenge of moodiness, loud music, and rows of dirty cups to clear up. The very thought of it––two males in the house.

Angela was stirring and she lifted the child and prepared to feed her. Afterwards, Sandy lowered her into the cot and tucked a blanket around her. She went through to the bathroom and splashed warm water on her face, stopping to stare at herself in the mirror. She no longer recognised the person staring back. Who was this woman––this woman whose feelings could be bulldozed? There were echoes to her past, the decisions her mother had made supposedly in her best interests. Not only did she feel as if her life and marriage were violently shifting but she didn't know how to stop the momentum.

Even though it was impossible to forget what had happened the night before, she showered away the scent of him and put on clean clothes before heading downstairs. In the kitchen, she made coffee, relieved that Jasper was still in bed. She was dreading the sight of him.

Last night he'd treated her like an old sack of potatoes, she felt violated, trampled on.

She busied herself feeding cutlery into the drawer, putting crockery away and folding Angela's laundered sleepsuits. She had no idea what she would say to Jasper and how it would be received. It would be easier to give him the silent treatment, slope off to the spare room and shut herself away, but what if he came for her again?

Wrapped up in these thoughts, she didn't hear his soft steps on the stairs, but sensing sudden movement behind her, she turned, startled. He was standing in the doorway and looked dreadful. His hair was sticking up in all directions, a light dusting of stubble peppered his face and there were dark circles around his eyes. He rubbed his forehead and let out a groan.

'Any aspirin?' He glanced round looking helpless as if the packet might jump from a drawer and then he slumped on a chair, looking completely winded as if his feet couldn't hold him up any longer.

She couldn't smile and couldn't help lashing out even though she reminded herself of the way her mother often spoke to her father. 'If you've got a headache, it's your own fault.'

As if reading her thoughts, he said, 'You sound just like your mother.'

She did, but maybe her mother had been right about him all along. The thought jangled at her nerves and sickened her.

'I feel like death warmed up,' he grumbled. 'How long did I

stay out? I don't remember getting back.' He glanced out of the window. 'Where's the car?'

She studied him for a few seconds before answering. He looked pathetic, not at all the man she'd married and admired.

'I've no idea, Jasper, maybe you'd like to enlighten me, where is the car, because I'll be needing it later?'

He went to the front door, opened it, and stared out onto the empty driveway, squinting against the bright light. Surely, he remembered what he'd done. Was he playing games with her?

He leaned against the doorframe, covered his eyes, and let out a groan.

'Maybe you had the good sense to leave the car at the golf club and take a cab.'

He frowned, his hands on his cheeks as he stared blankly at her. 'Everything's foggy, I think Mike or that barman put me in a cab, but I don't remember much.'

Her heart was banging in her chest. 'So you don't remember trying to fuck me then?'

He stepped towards her, his face a picture of horror. She had his full attention now. 'Sandy, I would never fuck you, as you so crudely put it. I love you and I've always made love to you. But you won't let me do that, you won't let me be the loving husband I want to be.'

She folded her arms and straightened her back. 'Ask your son if you don't believe me.'

'What's he got to do with it?'

'While you were helping yourself to the pleasures, Toby suddenly appeared at the foot of the bed before backing away in horror and dashing from the room.'

'What the bloody hell would he be doing here?'

'I haven't got a clue, Jasper.'

'He doesn't have a key and how would he open the door? The lock's too high for him and too tricky. Did you speak to him?'

'Of course not. I couldn't move. I had your dead weight stuck on top of me, you were snorting, and reeking of alcohol and sweat.'

He slumped onto one of the chairs, resting his head on the table, his hand on his forehead and let out a big moan.

'You and your bloody head is nothing compared to the pain I'm feeling right now, and you can't even remember last night.'

He glanced up. 'I'm sorry I don't remember any of it. Explain to me. You're talking in riddles. What do you mean Toby was here?'

She pulled out a chair and took a deep breath. 'You were trying to force yourself on me. It's only a few weeks since I had the baby. I don't know if I can trust you anymore, Jasper. You're no longer the person I fell in love with.' They were the saddest words she'd ever spoken and sounded so final. Hearing them made her well up.

He reached over, a pleading look in his eyes as he covered her hand with his. 'I'm very sorry, I've not been able to love you for so long.'

'You could have waited longer.'

'I needed you.'

'You couldn't wait a few weeks, when I've had to wait fifteen years to find out the truth? My fifteen years have brought fifteen years of pain. He was still alive, I had no knowledge, no input.'

They were silent for a few moments then Sandy spoke.

'I've never seen you drunk. You only ever have a couple of drinks.'

He straightened his back and stared at her. 'Don't forget I'm hurting too. You're blaming me, I've not lied to you, I didn't know. For three years I tried to protect you. I did what I thought was for the best. You have to believe me otherwise what do we have, there is no us?'

'I don't know, Jasper, what I believe anymore. I need space.'

'Space?'

She sighed. 'Maybe we need time apart.' The idea shocked her. Where would she go? 'Because right now, we aren't making each other happy, we both need time to think.'

'I don't. I know what I want and it's you, Sandy, it's always been you. It's only ever been you. I'm just finding it hard to cope, I'm mixed up, I'm hurting inside and all I get is a frosty reception when I come home in the evening. I just want to come in and throw my arms around you, but you won't let me. I just want to make everything go away and it to be as it was.'

'Right now, I can't be the loving wife you want me to be. Last night you drove a wedge between us.'

Jasper looked shot to pieces. She wished her heart would turn, reach out to him, but she felt like dead wood inside. The desire was gone.

He ran his finger along a seam of the table. 'I don't think time apart is the answer, it's one step on the slippery slope. Where would you go? Or if I went, I've no idea where I'd go. Stay with a friend? Is that really what you want, for our friends to know our business, to think we've got marriage problems and so soon after the baby?'

They sat in silence, staring at the grooves in the table, as if they'd reached a stalemate, spent and uncertain where this was leading.

He rubbed his forehead, slammed his chair back and headed for the kettle. 'There's no way you're going to your parents. They caused this mess in the first place.'

She wheeled round and stared at him, remembering when her mother was here last and found the letter written by Jasper to Sandy to be opened in the event of his death. The letter had explained that Toby was their son. He hadn't wanted her to know.

'If Mum hadn't been a nosey cow and opened your letter and told me, how long would it have been before you did?' She wasn't defending her mother but, in that moment, felt strangely defensive of her. Not that her mother deserved this because Sandy knew that her sole motive for telling her about Toby was one-upmanship–– finally being able to prove to her daughter what a poor choice of husband she'd made. She'd never liked Jasper, and this gave her reason to gloat. Seeing the glee in her eyes had nearly destroyed Sandy. There was so much she needed to say to her mother, so many questions she wanted to ask, and she wondered when that opportunity would come. She had to be strong emotionally, that much she knew. Having Angela had made her think about her own childhood, about motherhood and about family.

THE NEXT FEW days were strained, they didn't speak much, and she did her best to avoid him. She found it hard to sleep, with everything weighing down on her mind and the worry that he might force himself on her. And if he was going to start drinking, she didn't feel safe. Jasper tried yet again to coerce her back to the main bedroom.

One evening after dinner when Sandy was about to prepare Angela's feeds for the night, her mother phoned out of the blue.

'It's your bloody mother,' Jasper called from the hall, as he held the phone out for her, his hand covering the mouthpiece. He was a picture of pent-up anger and if looks could kill, his scowl could have slain her mother. 'I don't want to talk to her, I've got nothing to say.'

'I'm busy, what does she want?' She dried her hands on a tea towel and tossed it over to Jasper. She stared at the phone as if it was about to bite her, feeling instantly tense and still reeling from what had happened the last time her mother was here. Snatching the phone from him, she covered the mouthpiece and braced herself. Whatever she was calling about, this wasn't going to be easy.

'How the hell should I know? To apologise?' He smirked. 'Doubt it, after all this time.' Jasper stood back, his arms folded while Sandy took the call.

'Mum. Is everything alright?' She didn't feel like being pleasant, but it was hard not to be.

'Your father's broken his leg.'

She sensed what was coming. There was usually an ulterior motive where her mother was concerned. 'And?' She almost wanted to chuckle into the phone at the absurdity of him breaking a leg. This was her father, the most unadventurous man she knew.

Her teeth were gritted as she glanced at him.

'I need you, Sandra, I can't cope on my own,' she pleaded.

'I can't just drop everything. I've got Angela to look after.'

'I'm really struggling, you know I've got a bad back.'

She sighed and asked, 'How did he do it?'

'He missed the ladder and fell out of the loft.'

It sounded amusing but could have been worse. Lucky, he didn't plummet down the stairs.

'That will be his dodgy eyes. I told him a while back to get them tested. He needs new glasses.'

Jasper was standing next to her, a frown on his face, hands planted on his hips, mouthing, "no" over and over.

'Hang on, Jasper's trying to say something.'

'Selfish man––doesn't want you to help me. Thinking of himself as usual. You pander to him, Sandra, have done since day one. About time he learned to cook his own dinner and wash his own dirty socks.'

She covered the mouthpiece. Caught in the crossfire, it was like balancing on a high wire trying to please everyone. 'She wants me to help her, just for a few days.'

'Have you lost your mind, Sandy? This is your mother, my toxic monster-in-law.' He pointed a finger at her, angry and despairing. 'Have you forgotten all the trouble she's caused us? We wouldn't be in this mess if it wasn't for that cow.'

'Dad's had a fall and she needs my help.'

'Huh,' he said dismissively. 'She knows the right tricks, pushes all the right buttons, and you rise to the bait. You don't see it, do you?'

'See what?'

'You go up there, she'll drive an even bigger wedge between us once she gets her claws into our marriage problems. Meddling woman. She's toxic.'

'Be reasonable, Jasper. They are my parents. I feel I have a duty to them.'

'When have they ever been reasonable to you?'

She didn't disagree with him, but he was trying to make decisions for her. He had no right, not after what he'd done.

There were advantages to a short stay with her parents. Peace, quiet, the chance to get away from Jasper, Bill, and Toby for a while and get her head around things, return to a semblance of familiarity--her childhood home--however uncomfortable that experience would inevitably be.

Her mother was the only person who knew the truth about Toby and even though she wouldn't have anything pleasant to say, there were questions she desperately wanted to ask. She particularly wanted to finish that awkward conversation they'd had the last time she was here.

Sandy returned to the phone call, still wavering, and feeling pulled in two directions.

'I can't just drop everything here, Mum. I've just had a baby.'

'I knew it would be useless asking for your help. You're all we've got. If we had another child, I'm sure they would have been much more helpful and accommodating.'

Such a ridiculous thing to say--how could she possibly know that?

'Mum, I haven't heard from you in weeks. Not since you left in a taxi, leaving a storm in your wake, no apology, no kindness, no nothing.'

'It's you that needs to apologise, Sandra. After everything we do for you. Do you bother to ring, to find out how I am after all that digging and prying into my past, picking at old wounds, collecting fodder for your husband's next newspaper article?'

'I was curious, you were upset, I wanted to help. I was mortified when you told me your mother abandoned you when you were a little girl.'

'All you did was stir up a hornet's nest. I've not been the same since.' She sounded bitter, twisted, yet needy and vulnerable, making it hard for Sandy to turn her back. The softer side to Sandy was winning the day and she was on the brink of relenting.

'I'll come for a few days, but that's all,' she said firmly, instantly regretting her decision and watching Jasper's mortified face. 'The baby's got a routine, I need sleep, I'm still recovering.'

'You've had a baby, Sandra, not a triple bypass. Back in my day we didn't sit around basking in the glory of babyhood. There was work to be done.'

After the call had ended, she faced Jasper who looked as if he was quietly seething.

'Even after all these years, you're behaving like the scolded child. She snaps her fingers, you go running.'

'That's not fair.' No matter what her parents had done, she felt obliged to step up to the plate, try to be that perfect daughter they'd always wanted her to be, but knowing deep down that no matter what she did, she could never live up to their high expectations. They always raised the benchmark. 'We need a break, Jasper. If we don't have some space soon, we'll end up killing each other. This atmosphere is not good for Angela.'

'And you think there will be a better atmosphere at your mother's. Well, you can think again.'
'Well, it won't be any worse than here.'

CHAPTER 8: JASPER

On Monday morning, Jasper stood on the pavement watching Sandy drive away, his child in the back and the boot jam-packed with bags and baby paraphernalia. And Tibs the dog on the passenger seat. He wondered how Irene and Arthur would cope with the dog. He hadn't remembered Sandy mentioning to her mother about the dog going too. Maybe that was a good thing. Any luck, she'd turn them away.

When the car disappeared around the corner, it was a while before he finally turned and wandered back towards the house. Everything inside him hurt and he desperately wanted to weep. There was something about their flat goodbye that had felt so final, leaving him with a sad ache, a longing for her return even though she'd barely gone.

About to enter the house, he glanced back at the empty driveway, his insides hollow, half expecting her to change her mind and the car to pull up on the gravel. He clenched his fists. That wasn't going to happen, not now that dreadful woman, his bloody mother-in-law had Sandy firmly in her clutches, like a hawk with a mouse in its sharp talons. Everything that woman had ever done was to scupper their happiness and cause strife.

As he'd married Sandy without her mother's blessing, she was always going to make things difficult given the chance, and finding out about Toby had given her a perfect opportunity to cause maximum damage. He wondered why she was like this, so self-absorbed, uncaring, and bitter, why she hated to see Sandy happy. While it infuriated him that Sandy had given in to Irene's demand to drop everything and go and help them, it was sad because he could see why. Sandy so desperately needed her mother's approval. Maybe it had always been this way. If only she could escape from her clutches and be her own person.

He went into the house and leant against the newel post. The house felt eerily quiet. The sounds of their life together were silenced. The irony of this new situation. Since Angela's birth, he'd thought that silence would be a welcome reprieve, but he shuddered now––it was less comforting than he'd imagined. And it seemed empty. The pram gone, no handbag or clutter spread across the hall table. The green phone pushed to one side, crouching there like a big toad––alone and bereft.

He caught sight of his grey, puffy face reflected in the mirror above the table and took a brutal look at himself.

He stared into the mirror into his own eyes, and it was like staring into his soul, an unsettling feeling washing over him.

I've been a complete idiot. How can she ever forgive me? How can I forgive myself?

He vowed not to touch another drop of alcohol. Drinking was never the answer, he knew that. He'd seen what it did to Bill. What the hell had happened that night and why couldn't he remember forcing himself on her? She'd sworn that was what had happened. The shame, the horror of it. This wasn't who he was. He prided himself on being the perfect gentlemen. To be anything less, he couldn't bear it, couldn't live with himself. And hurting her, that was the worst of it. He never wanted to hurt her, physically or mentally but he'd succeeded in doing both.

Poor Sandy. How will I ever make it up to you?

He must have been so out of it, but that was hardly an excuse. If he had been out of it, how could he have forced himself on her? An erection in a state of inebriation--that was impossible. And yet he did remember lying on top of her, trying to cuddle her. Beyond that, his memory was patchy.

With mounting shame, he turned from his reflection and headed into the kitchen. She'd left it spotless. It was never this clean and he wondered if it was deliberate, to make a point that she wasn't coming back. He tried not to think of that possibility, it was too awful, too overwhelming.

He made a coffee and went to sit at his desk. It was Sunday but with nothing else to do, he'd crack on with the article he was writing. Seconds after draining the last of the coffee, he looked down at the mug in his hand and saw what was printed on it.

The world's best husband.

A Valentine's present given to him a few years back.

I hate myself.

He stood up and with an almighty sweep of his arm threw the mug at the wall. It crashed, smashing into pieces, and landed on the carpet, coffee staining the cream paintwork. In that instant something snapped inside him--something had to change. He'd lost Toby. He couldn't lose her too, or his daughter. Their baby--he'd barely spent any time with her, the weeks would gallop by, she'd grow, change, develop, all without him. Her first smile, first laugh, was he going to be around to see any of these important markers? It wasn't fair, she was his too, she needed a dad. He hadn't been there for Toby, history couldn't be repeated, that would be agony.

So many occasions, he'd dearly wanted to tell Sandy about Toby, only keeping it a secret to protect Bill. How foolhardy that had been. And now he stood to lose his whole family. He couldn't let that happen.

He strode into the hall, grabbed the phone, and dialled Bill's number.

'We need to talk.' His tone was blunt, but he didn't care. Let Bill know that he wasn't happy with him.

'Fancy a walk on the heath? I can meet you up there this afternoon, two?'

'I don't have a car, you'll have to pick me up.'

'Oh.' There was a short pause. Jasper could sense his surprise. 'See you at two.'

He slumped to the floor, still holding the phone, the disconnect tone ringing out. Something inside him cracked and tears flooded down his cheeks. It was easier to blame Bill, blame Irene, the NHS, blame anyone else, but he knew deep down that much of this could have been fixed by himself. There were so many "if onlys" and "what ifs" whirling through his head robbing him of a clear way forward. He wished he could declutter his mind like he could his garden shed.

A vision of his grandma entered his head. If only she was still alive. Passing away in his late teens, she hadn't been around to witness his adult journey. He needed her now--the one person he would have turned to for support, wise words, and a warm hug. What was it she used to say to him?

You reap what you sow.

Up on the top of the heath where the views were spectacular, Bill parked the truck by the ice cream van. The car park was heaving, people walking their dogs, joggers in Lycra, young families getting fresh air and exercise. As he glanced round and watched children put on wellies, eat ice creams, a dad lift a small child into a baby backpack, Jasper's heart quietly ached for his own family.

'I'm glad you called,' Bill said after they'd chosen the path that skirted a clump of pines and down towards the base of the valley. A woman on a horse nodded as she passed, the horse's hooves sending a spray of dry mud into the air. Bill dug his hands into his pockets. 'We need to talk about the other night.'

Colour rose to Jasper's cheeks as he prepared himself for embarrassment.

Toby.

In their bedroom.

'Please don't tell me it's true, that Toby was in our bedroom.'

'Afraid it is.'

Jasper didn't immediately reply, and they carried on walking.

'How did he get in the house, why was he even there?' He stopped walking and stared at Bill. He shouldn't have left it until today to call Bill, but he'd been so engrossed in the fallout from that night. 'Jesus, mate, this is all I need right now.'

'I was really worried about you, I popped over to the golf club to fix a toilet and Mike mentioned you'd been there for hours. You were very drunk.'

Jasper cringed. He wanted to forget that evening. 'We both agreed, it wasn't like you. I know things are difficult, but you really don't want to go down that road.'

They carried on walking. 'It wasn't my finest hour, and the prize of the evening was Sandy accusing me of forcing myself on her. And now she's gone to stay with her mum.'

'Toby was pretty shaken up after what he witnessed.'

'Shit.'

'I did it once--walked into my parents' bedroom in the middle of their love making. I was only bringing them a cup of tea.'

'How did he get in?'

'The door was wide open.'

'Bloody hell. I must have forgotten to close it. To be honest, Bill, I can't remember any of the evening, I couldn't even tell you how much I'd drunk but it was a lot. I'm struggling to cope, mate; I'm finding it so difficult. My world's changed in a matter of days.'

'That's the danger of drink. I've been trying to cut down for years, but booze always comes back fighting and I end up back to where I started. The bottle of whisky on the kitchen shelf, it's a persistent stalker, my trusty old pal. Sometimes when I look at it, it seems to have a face, eyes, a mouth, and it looks at me and says, give me one more chance, I can make things better, you're miserable without me.'

He sounded so casual, flippant, making light of his drink problem. His son had grown up with an alcoholic and worse than that, an unremorseful one.

He grabbed Bill by the collar and shouted, 'This isn't a bloody joke. I don't want my life to be sucked into a whisky bottle. I don't want Toby and Angela to grow up thinking I need buckets of alcohol to cope like you do. For me, the other day was a one-off. I don't intend to make that mistake again, but you––you do it over and over, you never bloody learn, and my son's had to witness it. All the time you continue to drink, you're not fit to be a father.' Still gripping his collar, Jasper pushed him back, watching the startled look on Bill's face. He'd never been like this with Bill before and his heart pounded in his chest. It felt as if everything was coming to a head, his patience with the situation was stretched, he wanted something to change. None of this was good for any of them.

Jasper turned and headed back up the hill towards the truck, calling over his shoulder, 'You're useless, did you know that? My life has collapsed because of you. If I'd come clean three years ago, my marriage wouldn't be in this mess, and protecting you has lost me three precious years of my son's life and may have cost me my wife as well.'

'I'm sorry,' he pleaded. 'We did what we both felt to be right at the time.'

'What was right for you, you mean?' Jasper hissed.

'I'm in the same mess as you,' Bill shouted.

'So how do we fix it?'

'For a start there's no point in dwelling on the might-have-beens. We've got to think of Toby and his future, what's best for him, and right now I'm worried sick. That's why I wanted to meet up with you. He barely comes out of his room, he's rude, surly. He's changed, Jasper. My boy has changed.' He looked at Bill and saw the rawness of his pain in those dark eyes. 'And I think it's too late, I don't think I'm going to get him back.'

Jasper stopped walking and gazed across the gorse and to the horizon. The vast landscape stretching for miles seemed to represent his own internal wilderness. He'd never felt so lost. But they were both lost, and they had to find a way forward, for Toby's sake.

'I think we need to talk to him, properly, the pair of us together.' Jasper's voice was calm, conciliatory.

'That's a good idea but how the hell do we do that when he's blanking everyone? If only that boy would wake up and realise how lucky he is. He's got two dads who care and are worried sick.'

'Bloody kids, who'd have 'em? I'm sure we'll come up with a plan. At the end of the day, he needs us, both of us, he's upset right now but give it time, he'll come round. It will take him a while, it's a lot to get his head around.'

CHAPTER 9: SANDY

Sandy parked the car and glanced up at her parents' house. Even though it had been years since she'd visited, nothing had changed. Her mother was still meticulously scrubbing at the steps, keeping up appearances. Kneeling, brush in hand, hair in rollers under a green net with a pinny tied round her waist, she looked just like Hilda Ogden. Polished steps, finished with a donkey-stoned white line were so important to her, and yet the tired paintwork peeling off the windowsill and the rusty downpipe didn't seem to bother her.

As Sandy got out of the car, Irene turned and rose to her feet, making a great play of rubbing her back and lumbering along the path, each step an exaggerated effort for her daughter's benefit.

'Why have you driven?' Sandy was jarred by her harsh, unwelcoming tone. 'He should have driven you. All that traffic across London.'

It hadn't occurred to Sandy, but her mother was right, Jasper could have dropped them off, the journey had given her a headache, she didn't particularly like driving and he knew that and could have suggested it. Now she was here, she didn't need the car.

'I suppose he didn't want to see us.' She folded her arms and gave Sandy her beady-eyed look. 'When was the last time he came over, when was the last time either of you bothered to come over? Just as well,' she said, opening the car back door, 'I haven't got much to say to him. I suppose he's too busy with his investigative whatever it is.'

She leant down and peered into the carrycot. 'How's my little granddaughter?'

The dog flew out of the car, wagging his tail.

Irene stepped back onto the pavement, startled. 'I didn't say you could bring the dog too,' she shrieked. 'You know how your dad hates dogs. Where's it going to sleep? It's not going upstairs. I hope it's house-trained. I don't want piddly puddles all over the floor. I've just spent hours cleaning it before you came. And does it bark? I don't want the neighbours complaining.' Tibs was sniffing a clump of grass and Irene eyed him suspiciously.

'Mum, he has got a name, he's my Tibs.'

'Stupid, it's a cat's name.'

'I couldn't leave him with Jasper. He might get called away.'

'Called away?' She stared at Sandy. 'But you've got a baby. He can't swan off on business and leave you. I wouldn't have tolerated that if your father had gone away, business or otherwise. He did what I told him to. You're too weak, that's your problem.'

Sandy lifted the carrycot from the back seat and scoffed. 'What are you talking about, Mum? I was born in the middle of the war, men had to leave their families, otherwise Hitler would have stormed in and taken over this country.' She put the carrycot on the pavement while she opened the boot and handed Irene a couple of bags, while quietly seething under her breath.

With the dog tethered and the carrycot in Sandy's arms, as

she stepped towards the gate, Irene grabbed her wrist, dropping one of the bags.

Before she'd even spoken, Sandy could read the scorn mapped out on her face and was chilled by the disdain in her dark eyes. 'Before you go in,' she said, her voice dropping to a whisper and her grip tightening, 'there are a few house rules, my girl, that you need to obey.' She kept her wrist tight, and it started to hurt. 'I can't have you running roughshod over my regime. You are not to mention Toby's name in this house, or at any time to one of my friends or anyone in the neighbourhood. Your father doesn't even know he's alive.'

Sandy looked away, too shocked to meet her mother's eyes. Her hand was tingling as her grip tightened.

Releasing her wrist, she grabbed Sandy's face instead, forcing her to look at her like a scolded child who'd committed a wicked deed. 'No noise after 8pm, no loud noises, take your shoes off before you come in. Side door for the mutt and he's not to leave the kitchen. You understand.'

'Yes, Mum.'

She released her hand and stepped away, but her forbidding eyes were still fixed on Sandy's. 'This is not a guesthouse so don't treat it like one,' she added stiffly, pausing before turning to head up the path. 'Don't go thinking we're hard up, because we're not, but we aren't flush either, so don't use reams of loo paper and a fresh teabag each brew. I know what you're like with your la-di-da ways. This is not Surrey. Things are different here.'

The windows were steamed up in the tiny kitchen as Sandy headed in, breathing the aroma of suet and bacon pudding––a favourite dish of her dad's. Instantly she was transported back to a time when she did whatever she could to avoid eating these heavy meals. Tripe and faggots, semolina, toad in the hole. Being a model, keeping a slim, trim figure was paramount. Her boss wouldn't have kept renewing her contract if she'd piled on the pounds.

The kitchen was exactly as she'd remembered, and it felt like stepping into a museum. She couldn't understand why they'd never updated it. The old, chipped Belfast sink, the two-toned walls--half green, half magnolia—the Formica table still under the side window, three chairs tucked underneath, the red tiled floor, the high shelf running along one wall where the pots and pans were kept. Her eyes were drawn to the white linen tablecloth embroidered with pastel flowers.

'I don't remember this tablecloth, Mum. It's beautiful.' She picked up the teapot to examine a lacy doily. 'You didn't make these, did you?'

'Don't sound so surprised. Of course I made them.' Irene went to the sink and filled the kettle up before lighting the stove.

'I didn't know you could embroider?'

'You're not very observant, Sandra, you never have been.'

This was going to be hard work, much harder than she'd imagined. It seemed that every subject was off limits for different reasons with tetchy remarks and snide digs. How was she going to cope?

'I hope you haven't cooked dinner especially for me?' She tried to sound bright and polite. All she wanted was a small sandwich. She hadn't eaten big dinners at midday since childhood.

'I've still got your father to feed.'

'Where's Dad?'

'In the front room with his leg propped up. Get yourself sorted out first then you can pop your head round the door.' She glanced down. 'And get that dog from under my feet.'

'I'll put him in the garden for a bit.' She went to unlock the back door, coaxing Tibs into the garden. The dog shivered, looking up at her through doleful eyes, clearly feeling as sorry for himself as Sandy did for herself.

Upstairs, Sandy hurled her suitcase onto the bed and burst into tears.

What the hell am I doing here?
I should be at home.

She slumped onto the bed, a rag doll emptied of stuffing, tears flowing. On reflection, what did she expect? Her parents were never going to welcome her with open arms. Her mother wasn't going to change. They were never going to be close, never going to understand each other.

She hoped that seeing her dad wasn't going to be as painful. Her dad had always been her mum's staunchest defender. When she was growing up he'd always seemed passive, but then she came to realise there was nothing passive about standing by, retreating to the safety of his garden shed or hiding behind a newspaper. There had been times when he'd left her confused about loyalty and trust. Her mother was always critical and sniped at her unfairly and constantly. It seemed she never let an opportunity go by to put her down or ignore her and if she messed up, she'd go on and on about what a failure she was. With successes, such as passing exams or job offers, she'd pretend they hadn't happened or tell her they weren't important. If she pushed back, her dad would step in and appear to acknowledge that she was hurt but then tell her to placate her mum or apologise. He'd say, 'it's just the way she is,' or 'she just wants the best for you,' or something that made her feel as though she'd been sold down the river. That was as damaging in the end as her mother's sniping.

She opened her case and took out a neatly folded pile of clothes. About to put them into the set of drawers that had once stored her clothes for all those years, she paused and sniffed the air. Traces of her perfume and talcum powder lingered after all these years, or was her mind playing tricks? She glanced round.

The room looked smaller than she remembered. The walls were still a shade of pink and the floral curtains a semi opaque texture that sent shards of light softly onto the candlewick bedspread at the start of a spring day. It had turned into a nondescript guest room, but she knew it was her room because the integral reminders of her childhood remained. The hallowed poster of Audrey Hepburn whom she'd fiercely admired, not just for her beauty and talent but for how fearless, admirable, and selfless she was. Despite hardship and heartache, Audrey never stopped loving life and people and remained a huge inspiration. Sandy remembered the battle with her parents because she hadn't asked permission for the poster to be put up and it would wreck the wall. She stood back and smiled. The edges of the poster were curled, the colours had long faded, but it still adorned the wall, triumph to a rare battle she'd won. Odd though, she mused. They could have long binned it but hadn't.

A row of her once favourite Steiff teddies and a doll sat on the dresser beside a yellowed photo in a frame of herself and two friends, Deirdre and Silvy, whom she'd not seen in many years. Was she supposed to feel cocooned and connected to her youth amid this sea of nostalgia? Had her mother kept this as a sanctuary, a mausoleum in case her marriage to Jasper hit the rocks?

Sandy sat on the bed still holding the clothes and wiped her eyes. She could vividly recall afternoons reading *Girls' Fun and Fashion Magazine*, *Woman*, and *The Lady* sitting on the carpet or Deirdre and Silvy's visits and showing them her new poodle skirt and conical bra. She opened the wardrobe, half-expecting the clothes she'd worn back then to still be hanging, but the cupboard was bare apart from a 1960 copy of *Woman*. It was almost as if it had been planted there to torment her by stoking memories of that year, the year she'd fallen pregnant with Toby. If she picked it up, flicked through its crisp pages, the emotions she'd experienced would come flooding back.

She heard footsteps on the stairs, then a tap at the door. She sniffed, quickly composing herself as her mother entered the room.

'What's keeping you? Can't you hear that mutt barking at the back door? You better let it in and then go and see your father. Dinner won't be long.'

After she disappeared downstairs, it took all of Sandy's strength not to start crying again. How she longed for her mother to be softly spoken, not be harsh and military in her ways. She just had to get through this however difficult it was going to be, but how long could she stand it before her parents drove her completely insane, and which was the lesser of the two evils, being here or back with her husband, the man she could no longer trust?

Out of her bedroom she paused to glance through the landing window, remembering suddenly the thrill of her second date with Jasper, watching his confident swagger as he skipped up the steps with his hands in his pockets, and hurrying down to open the door, her dad bellowing for her not to let the cold in. He was good at putting on airs and graces and making it look as though he was a welcoming host.

She checked on Angela sleeping peacefully in her carrycot and then let Tibs in. After settling the dog in his basket by the back door away from her mother who was busy dishing up the dinner, she closed the kitchen door and went through to the lounge.

The room was exactly as she'd remembered. The furnishings were tired-looking and the nets, designed to stop the neighbours from being nosey, were old-fashioned and ghastly and part of that generation's style. There was one change to the room though, an extravagance her mother had railed against. Her dad had always referred to it as the idiot's lantern and yet like so many families they'd eventually given in to the modern world and purchased one. A television.

Her dad was sitting on the settee, his leg on the coffee table supported with several cushions. He was watching an old war film and turned to look at her with surprise on his face, which was shadowed with fatigue and pallid like a clay mask. She noticed his hair was greyer around the crown and he had less of it. Years of being with a difficult wife clearly taking its toll.

'Hello, love. What are you doing here?' His voice was soft, such a contrast to her mother's.

'I've come to help out.'

He shifted in his seat trying to get more comfortable and winced as if in pain. 'She shouldn't have fetched you. You've got your hands full enough as it is.' Sandy made a sharp intake of breath. He was right, but that hadn't stopped her mother insisting they needed her. 'We can manage, we always do.'

'It's okay, Dad. I can stay for a few days. Now what exactly did you do? Mum said something about you falling out of the loft.'

'Yes, old fool I am. The stepladder snapped in two. I was very lucky I didn't fall down the stairs.'

Sandy thought about how nasty that would have been, and shuddered. He could have hit his head on the wall and even tumbled to his death. 'You were lucky.'

'Could you drop into the ironmongers and buy a new pair? They will deliver. That would be very helpful.'

'Of course. I can walk up to the parade in the morning. But you won't be going into the loft anytime soon.'

'Maybe that's something you could do?'

'What did you want up there?'

'The anglepoise lamp. Your mother's been knitting a matinee jacket for the baby but the close work, especially in the evenings, is straining her eyes.'

Her mother had long enjoyed knitting, particularly for the WI, and she was in a knitting group. With her mother's presence it would be more a stitch and bitch class. Sandy wondered who had taught her to knit. It couldn't possibly have been her own mother because she had walked out. This was another question to ask––another riddle wrapped in a mystery.

IT WAS late morning the following day when Sandy settled Angela in the pram and attached Tibs's lead. What a relief it was to be out of the house and doing something useful.

At the end of the road, she stopped by the phone box, in two minds whether to call Jasper. She wasn't going to ring from her parents' house, there was no privacy there. She yanked open the heavy metal door; wedging it with her foot and keeping a tight grip on the dog's rein, she checked her purse for coins. She didn't have the right money to make the call which was just as well because she didn't know what to say to him. She'd only start moaning about her mother and then he'd tell her to leave them to it and come home. While she didn't want to be here, she didn't want to go home either. She needed time apart from her husband, to collect her thoughts and step back from the problems they were facing and work out if they were fixable.

She shoved her purse back in her bag and strolled on towards the little parade of shops. She'd let Jasper get on with his week, it was best they had a complete break from each other.

After ordering the stepladder, she browsed in the window of the knitting shop next door. On the other side of the glass, baby dolls were dressed in woollen garments. Matching sets of hats, scarfs and jackets and woollen romper suits. This was where generations of grandmas had chosen wool and patterns to knit for their grandchildren. Knots of love, slipping stitches, underestimating the amount of time it took to make something, using spare moments, round a fire or gathered as a group. With her eyes lingering on a gorgeous apricot jumper, she pondered her mother's life through her love of knitting. If only their relationship could be repaired like a dropped stitch.

On impulse she decided to buy wool and a pattern.

After making her purchase, she felt strangely lifted by the prospect of Irene's excitement--her next knitting project. Did she dare hope she could win her mother over by playing on her love of this craft?

The autumn air was welcoming, and not wanting to rush back, she deviated from the route, veering down a side alley and towards the park where she could let the dog off his lead. The bench under the tree facing the pond enticed her. Parking the pram, she sat and enjoyed watching Tibs sniff around the bushes and flowers. Soon Tibs was at the water's edge, barking at the ducks bobbing on the pond.

She glanced into the pram. There was something magical about the serenity of watching a sleeping baby, like standing on a boat after a storm and enjoying the calmness of the sea. It was perhaps the only thing more comfortable than sleep itself. Lost in thoughts of how lucky she was to have Angela, marvelling at her perfect little lashes, her button nose, and rosy cheeks, Sandy didn't immediately notice that someone was walking towards her.

'Is that you, Sandy?'

CHAPTER 10: JASPER

Nothing was going right for Jasper this morning. He'd slept through his alarm and in his rush to leave for work he flung open the wardrobe and seeing no shirts hanging on the rail, had grabbed one from the pile in the laundry basket waiting to be ironed. And now the train had been stationary for the past five minutes with no announcement. This wasn't a great start to his week, and he had a meeting with Sam, the editor, first thing to decide the next story he would be covering. It wouldn't be good to arrive late.

The train jolted and scraped and screeched back into motion. The journey was supposed to take forty-five minutes, but it rarely did. This section of the track was decrepit, beset with signalling problems and never-ending engineering works.

Jasper wished he could push the fast-forward button to the weekend and the prospect of Sandy returning, or perhaps rewind his life by a few years and handle the situation better. He hoped she would come back at the weekend, but she hadn't said, and he hadn't asked. He checked his watch, glanced out of the window. He felt tense, and loosened his tie. He was always so confident but today he felt winded. He was already half an hour late for the meeting.

There had been many moments of beating himself up since she'd gone, trying to challenge the voice inside that said, "you're a disaster" and counter it with the humbling voice of reason that acknowledged his shortcomings and begged for him to be a better husband.

The train crawled along, juddering past warehouses, bridges, past Victorian semis, and rabbit-hutch gardens facing the track. Twice a day he was offered a glimpse into the lives of those who lived there, just for a few seconds and he wondered if their lives were as complicated as his.

Joining the throng of commuters spilling out of the train at Blackfriars and towards the City; he felt as if he was floating like a ghost. Normally he appreciated the walk along Fleet Street, taking time to stop and admire the architecture. It was the architecture of Empire––dignified and elegant, symbolising prosperity and the way British industry liked to portray itself–– proud of its achievements and open for business with the world. Peterborough Court, standing halfway along the iconic street was home to *The Daily Telegraph*, a dazzling neoclassical and Art Deco temple to journalism made of fine Portland stone. And the contrast of *The Daily Express* building, number 120, with its fine glass frontage that looked like black marble and cut into curves at the corners. Built in the inter-war years it was an expression of the rise of the ocean liner. Jasper was fascinated by the history of Fleet Street, the façade of a huge world, the business of print, but today it was a blur. He didn't even wave to the newspaper hawkers standing on the street corners in their flat caps yelling the day's headlines and using familiar catchphrases to entice readers. "Extra, extra, read all about it."

He saw people walking through the City and wondered about their lives. He had a natural thirst for a story and enjoyed conversing with strangers. Yet today he stared at the faces passing him through senses that were cold. Today was going to be hard, getting back into the swing of things.

In Sam's office, Jasper plonked himself down in the chair facing his desk. Sam was standing near the window smoking his pipe. The aromatic smell wafting through the air instantly relaxed him.

'Problem with the trains?' Sam didn't seem overly bothered that he was late. He twiddled his moustache. 'You look like you need a stiff whisky, boy, a strong coffee to kick-start the day will have to do. Everything okay?'

Jasper grunted. 'I've had better weekends.'

Sam perched on his swivel chair, picked up the phone and rang his secretary. 'Two coffees please, Pauline.'

Moments later and after a few pleasantries, the coffee arrived. Jasper took a sip, the kick almost immediate as caffeine hit his bloodstream.

'What do you know about Jimmy Carter?'

Jasper hadn't expected this. He normally only covered British affairs although he had flown to New York in the early sixties to interview Dr Frances Kelsey who was responsible for stopping thalidomide from going on the market in the United States. In 1962 President Kennedy awarded her the highest honour given to an American citizen, the second woman to ever receive the award. Jasper still swelled with the pride--it had been a privilege to meet this incredible woman who'd saved countless lives through her actions. There were other reasons he'd never forget that week in New York. Sandy was there on a modelling assignment and staying at the same hotel. Through this bizarre coincidence, they'd reconnected and the rest was history.

He shrugged. 'I've read about both candidates. Why?' The presidential election was fast approaching, and the broadsheets were full of stories about Jimmy Carter and Gerald Ford. He couldn't wait for it to be over so they could focus on British affairs and all the issues that mattered to him.

'He comes from the Deep South, from Georgia. He gave up his military career to save the family peanut farm.' Sam stepped towards his desk, put his hands on the back of his leather chair and looked at Jasper. 'Imagine being in his shoes. What would you do, Jasper, to save your folk? What would any of us do? Torn between desire and duty.'

Sam's words hit Jasper like a bullet, and he froze. How could Sam know that he was in a hole, what did he know? Bile rose in his throat.

'My home is here, in Fleet Street.' Sam beat his fist against his chest. 'I love the hustle and bustle of life here. It would take a lot for me to shift focus and up sticks. I'm not a country fella as you know.' No longer smoking his pipe, he thrust his hands deep into his pockets and jangled his loose change as he gazed out of the glass to the street below. 'There's always something going on out there. Right now, I can see a row of yellow Bedfords being loaded with newspapers. And there are rolls of paper being loaded into the printing press room.' He laughed. 'They always remind me of giant loo rolls.'

Jasper smiled.

'Just about every household buys a paper and its journey into those homes starts here, with us. That flimsiest of media, here today, gone tomorrow, destined to be wrapped around a pile of greasy chips and battered cod or soaked in puppy pee.'

This was quite a speech and Jasper wondered where it was leading.

'So...' He paused. 'My question to you is, I know you've a wee baby in the house, probably giving you a few sleepless nights, but how do you fancy jetting off to the U.S. of A. and escaping all that for a few days?'

Before his problems with Sandy, Jasper wouldn't have hesitated. She accepted that he had the occasional business trip here and there. He didn't have to think about running it past her. But this time felt different. He couldn't afford to do anything that might put their relationship in further jeopardy. It was hanging by a thread as it was.

'You look hesitant, old boy.'

That was the last thing he wanted to be. His marriage might be on the rocks, but he couldn't afford to ruin his work prospects either.

'I'll go,' he said in a turnaround.

'That's my boy. You like to sniff a story out. You'll be pleased to hear your visa was applied for a few weeks ago. All you have to do is pick it up tomorrow from the consulate officer at the American Embassy.'

'Going away will work very nicely. Sandy's gone to stay with her parents. A sort of break--we're having a few problems.'

'Oh?' He looked curious.

'We'll be fine, I'm sure. She's probably just tired and rundown after the birth.'

Sam's eyes grew bright. 'Why not take her with you? Or would that be too much? No, wait, what am I thinking? She hasn't got a visa.'

Jasper couldn't think of anything worse, travelling with a baby and sadly, there was no one to mind Angela if Sandy came. What he would give to enjoy quality time in a different place, taking her out for fabulous meals and really pampering her. The timing was all wrong. No, he'd fly out, focus on getting a good story.

'Did you know, the peanut isn't really a nut?' Sam was on a roll. 'It's related to the pea. And there are over 300 uses for peanuts, including paper from their shells, shaving cream, shoe polish, axle grease and ink.'

Was he going to sit here all day hearing about peanuts?

'What would you like me to report about? Carter's background in the peanut business?'

'Yes, I'll leave that to you. Fly out to Georgia. I want pictures of his boyhood home and the peanut farm and how his experience has helped him gain the necessary skills for high office. I'm sceptical about this fella but he's riding high in the polls. Be interesting to see what you come up with. Oh and, Jasper, we also need to interview more of the thalidomide kids. It doesn't have to be the same families you covered last time. Some of them will have left school. The readers will be wondering how they're getting on, how they're making it in the big wide world. I've compiled a list of families who've agreed to be interviewed.'

'Any contacts in America, I wonder?' Jasper was keen to make readers aware of the American thalidomide tragedy because it was particularly chilling. The pharmaceutical company, Richardson-Merrell, had known little of thalidomide beyond what Grunenthal had told them. Like Distillers, they hadn't carried out any studies of their own apart from routine checks and had relied on Grunenthal's work. It repeatedly assured doctors the drug was safe, and safe for everyone including pregnant women. They went on to test the drug on rats with clear evidence it was toxic, but didn't inform the FDA of the results but instead pressed ahead with clinical trials on humans, which involved the sales and marketing team distributing 2 million tablets to doctors across America. And more shocking still, many of the doctors who dished out the tablets didn't keep records of the patients they'd given them to.

'That might be possible,' Sam said.

'Dr Kelsey is a hero over there for averting a crisis, but it's easy to forget that Richardson-Merrell had already blighted the lives of many. We just don't know how many.'

Jasper mused to himself. It might be worth revisiting thalidomide in America. The pharmaceutical companies, Richardson-Merrell and Smith, Kline & French had promoted and trialled it across the States. Richardson-Merrell made numerous applications for thalidomide's approval, but the FDA did not approve it. How many victims were there in America born because of these illegal trials? Officially, only a handful-- but this, Jasper suspected, was just the tip of the iceberg.

His interest stirred; he could feel the questions building in his head.

CHAPTER 11: SANDY

Startled on hearing her name, Sandy glanced round to see a familiar figure walking towards her.

'Blimey, I thought that was you, Sandy. Haven't seen you in years.'

Sandy stared up into his deep petrol blue eyes. The man she'd once danced with at the Cricklewood Palais all those years ago. Maybe if she hadn't met Jasper the following week, he might have asked her out. 'Eddie. Wow, fancy seeing you.'

'I see you've got a baby.' And then the question left his lips. 'Is that your first?'

Hesitating for a moment, Sandy swallowed and briefly thought about her answer. It was an awkward pause that reared up every time someone asked the question.

'Yes.' As soon as the word was out, she regretted the lie. Not wanting to acknowledge Toby's existence––she betrayed him every time—but it wasn't a story she wanted to tell. And besides, she'd been sworn to secrecy. 'What brings you here, Eddie?'

'I'm on my lunch break. I do the accounts for the ironmongers. Their office is above the shop.'

'I've just been in there to order a stepladder for Dad.'

'When it comes in, I'll bring it round for you.'

'Thanks.'

'You back seeing your folks? Bet they're overjoyed to have a grandchild.'

Sandy ignored his comment. 'Dad broke his leg falling out of the loft, so I've come back to help out.'

'Ouch. I see them pottering in the garden when I pass the house. I always say hello. Nice they remember me. Your dad speaks to me, but your mum's always frosty.'

That didn't surprise Sandy. It didn't cost much to smile, be polite and friendly.

'What are you up to these days?' Tibs wandered back and she secured his lead onto his collar. 'Are you married?'

Now it was his turn to hesitate. 'Nope. Still waiting for the right one to come along.' As she glanced at him, she thought he looked stricken. It was obvious that he'd been hurt by someone.

'There's still time. Don't give up.' She smiled.

'Any of your friends still single?' He gave her a mischievous smile.

'I don't keep in touch with anyone from round here.'

'Not even Deirdre? You girls were as thick as thieves. And what about Sylvia?'

She shrugged. 'Nope. We don't even exchange Christmas cards.' His question forced her to reflect. It was true, her childhood friends had fallen by the wayside. They'd drifted apart when she left London. She didn't feel bad about losing touch, they hadn't made the effort either.

Sandy stared at the carpet of twisted golden leaves, closing her eyes briefly against the warm October sun. The sky was ironed into an acid blue leaving a faultless page of autumn above their heads. Although she was to blame for not staying in touch with the friends who had once been important to her, she couldn't help wondering if her dragon of a mother had played her part in the demise of these friendships, or her modelling career. They were never happy about her bringing friends home.

'That's a shame. If you're around for a few days, maybe you should look them up.'

Afterwards, Sandy wandered back to her parents'. They lived on a big estate, built in the interwar years, and it was easy to get lost. The gardens were neat and presentable, and the houses, with their single gables, bay windows and occasional stained glass, were attractive and built of the toughest bricks according to her dad. She could hear him now, referring to the red bricks as tough old bones. But nothing changed in suburbia apart from the weather. Sandy found the silence debilitating, crippling. She was glad she'd moved to a village.

A sudden thought slammed into her, and she stopped abruptly.

The day she sat at the kitchen table shortly before marrying Jasper. She'd written and sent out Christmas cards to all her friends. She'd popped a change of address note into each one. Irene had seen her do this. Irene had offered to post them on the way to the shops.

But had she?

Sandy didn't trust her. Nothing would surprise her when it came to her mother. That malicious streak was dusting every part of Sandy's life. What had she done to deserve such poison? Maybe she was jumping to conclusions, but she hated being on her guard for the next assault. Her mother was cranky and unpredictable, acting out of spite at every count.

'You're late for dinner,' her mother snapped in that harsh tone of hers the minute the back door opened, and Sandy stepped into the steamy kitchen. 'I'm about to dish up.'

She wasn't late. The table wasn't laid, and several pans of vegetables were bubbling on the stove. Any excuse to have a go––it was wearing. Just for once, it would have been nice to hear some pleasantries, like thank you for ordering the stepladder.

Over dinner, Sandy chatted about her trip to the shops to avoid them lapsing into an uncomfortable silence.

'I bumped into Eddie who I used to know. He sends his regards.'

Her mother glared at her. 'That's nice.' Her words curdled with insincerity through an expression that turned Sandy cold despite the warmth of the stew in her belly. 'What did you talk about?'

'He suggested meeting up with the others to reminisce about old times.'

She watched the colour drain from her mother's face, her fork mid-air, and wondered why she was being like this. 'Did he now?'

'Would you mind looking after Angela if I go out?'

She shifted in her chair, a prim look on her face. 'I'm not sure, Sandra. I'll have to think about it.'

What was there to think about? Surely, she'd want to spend time with her granddaughter, but it didn't matter, she'd take Angela with her.

Arthur sighed. 'Give the girl a break, Irene. You used to like the lad. I remember you saying they would make a great couple.' There was a mischievous glint in his eye as he winked across the table at Irene.

Sandy glanced at her mother. Her eyes had grown brighter as if a lightbulb had pinged on, and the corner of her mouth was turned into a slight smile. There was no mistaking the devious expression on her face.

She felt an odd blip in the air, as if something had passed between the pair of them.

'Doesn't matter now, I'm married to Jasper.' A dull ache spread across her chest. On paper they were married, and they shared a house, but they were broken. That was how it felt. Had they come too far, was it too late to recover what they'd lost?

'I was reading in the paper--divorce rates have shot up in the last decade.'

Trust her dad, always quoting the news, but why say this? It felt as if he was planting a seed in her mind or maybe she was just being sensitive because it was a subject too close to home.

Irene took another mouthful of her food, then looked at him with interest. 'Divorce is a sin. I couldn't think of anything worse, the shame and neighbours pointing fingers at whoever they thought was to blame. I'd hate my dirty linen to be aired in public, or a member of my family's come to that. One scandal in your life is enough, don't you think, Sandra?' She turned her head and glanced at Sandy as if foreshadowing what was to come.

Something snapped inside her. She got up, scraped the chair back, unable to sit there any longer. Behind her mother's eyes she could see the smirking and knew she had no faith in her marriage. It saddened her to think that her mother couldn't bring herself to support her with anything she did and if she did end up divorcing Jasper--God forbid--she would either smile in glee or sneer down and tell her, "I told you so". And as for her father, she wasn't sure what he thought. He was like a closed book. He was overshadowed by Irene, henpecked, cowering in the background most of the time and sitting on the fence when important matters came along. Sandy knew who wore the trousers in that marriage. He was weak, she was overpowering.

CHAPTER 12: SANDY

Holding the baby in her arms, Sandy came down to the kitchen for breakfast. The air was filled with the aroma of toast and the kettle was whistling on the stove, a plume of steam rising to the ceiling. She lowered Angela into the carrycot.

'Morning, Mum,' she said brightly. 'Where's the dog?'

'Don't bloody morning me.' She took the kettle off the stove and didn't look at Sandy. 'I kicked him out in the garden. He jumped up at me. One of these days it's going to ladder my stockings.' Brandishing a butter knife as toast popped up, she turned to look at Sandy grumpily. 'And I came down to a puddle of pee. I don't know why you had to bring that mutt with you, it keeps getting under my feet. I wish you'd keep that dog under control.'

Her mother wasn't wearing stockings. She was still in her dressing gown. And Tibs didn't have accidents, unless of course he was so nervous around her mum that he couldn't help himself. She felt sorry for little Tibs. In hindsight it would have been better to leave him with Bill and Toby, who both loved having a dog around, unlike her mother who found things to complain about every five minutes.

The air was thick with silence as they sat at the table to eat. Even after all these years, she felt nervous in her mother's company. Butterflies danced in her stomach causing intermittent pain. She had to get out and away from this oppressive atmosphere. After a swig of tea and a mouthful of toast, Sandy got up and took her plate and cup to the sink.

'You've barely touched that toast. Honestly, Sandra, I know you and that husband of yours have money to burn. Give it here, I'll finish it,' she snapped. Sandy tilted her plate and the toast slid onto her mother's plate. At the sink she downed the rest of her tea just to keep her happy and rinsed out her cup.

'I'm just taking Tibs for a walk, I'll leave Angela in her carrycot if that's okay? I'm not sure when Eddie's dropping the stepladder off. He said it would be early. Hopefully I'll be back before he gets here.'

'Put Angela in the front room with your dad. I need to mop the floor. Why's he bringing it round? He's not an odd job boy, is he? I thought you said he works in their accounts department?'

'I don't know, Mum.' Her head felt as if it was about to explode. She couldn't wait to escape.

Irene peered at Sandy through narrowed eyes with a disdainful expression on her face, and taking Sandy's wrist, gave it another of her hard squeezes. 'You be careful what you say, I've reminded you, mind your tongue, young lady.'

Sandy shrugged her off. 'I won't be long.' She hastily opened the back door and called Tibs in before attaching his lead.

'I hope he doesn't stay long.' She glanced at the wall clock. 'I need to get ready for my WI meeting.'

Sandy was glad of the fresh air and brisk walk. Having a dog stopped the pounds from settling on the hips and she felt healthier for it. Tibs gave her the perfect excuse to get away from her mother, a chance to clear her head and reflect on her life with Jasper. Staying at her parents' was a stressful experience which was why she'd avoided coming here in all these years. She didn't feel guilty about it though. Until now they'd never suggested it—not even for Christmas or Sunday lunch. It stabbed at her heart to think how little they wanted her company. And it was only after Angela's birth that her mother had visited. Over the years, Sandy had invited them to stay, more out of politeness than anything, but they'd point blank refused to get a bus over and made a ton of excuses which was just as well because it would have been an unpleasant experience.

Sandy still hadn't heard from Jasper. It had been three days. She hoped her mother hadn't answered his call and deliberately not told her.

Enjoying the freedom, she took longer than she'd expected. Skirting the park and around the pond, taking her time to look at the ducks and the trees, she wondered how she was ever going to trust Jasper again. She didn't care about the reasons he'd kept Toby a secret, it was the fact that he had and the way he was going about trying to repair their relationship. She knew that healing didn't come quickly but his actions had severely damaged any chance of her feeling loving and affectionate––at least for the foreseeable future. With trust broken, she'd become suspicious of everything he did and that had turned her feelings sour. She glanced up at a weeping willow, admiring its long branches, like tendrils as they dipped in the pond. She knew that forgiveness would take its own sweet time to come her way. From the bottom of her heart, she really did value him and their relationship and a voice deep inside told her that the long-winding path back to gaining trust would be worthwhile. It wasn't going to be like rubbing ointment on a sore knee. It was a journey and each of them needed to plan that journey back to each other.

Back in her parents' road, she saw a van parked outside the house. As she approached, Eddie was coming up the path.

'Hi, Sandy, can't stop, just had a cuppa with your mum. Maybe I got her wrong.' He opened the gate and the dog jumped up at him. 'I've left my number on the kitchen table. Give us a buzz and we'll arrange that drink.' He gave the dog a quick pat before hurrying to the van.

'Will do, Eddie and thanks.' She stood there startled by his words as she watched him pull away from the kerb.

Her mother, friendly. *How odd.*

She looked heavenward; the corners of her mouth turned down as she pondered her mother's motives. Why invite Eddie to stay for a cup of tea when earlier on she claimed to be rushed off her feet?

Through the back door and into the kitchen, Sandy took the lead off and Tibs went to settle himself in his basket. As she took her coat off, she noticed the teapot and two cups on the table with dregs in. She took a clean cup from the cupboard and poured the remaining tea from the pot. Hopefully Angela was still asleep in the front room. She sat enjoying the peace while her mother was upstairs, probably now getting ready for her meeting.

A while later she heard steps on the stairs and braced herself.

'There you are. You were gone for ages. Stepladder arrived. You'll have to take it upstairs. I don't want it stuck down here in my way. You can store it in your room.'

Sandy sighed and looked at the stepladder. The dog, the stepladder, they had a lot in common.

'That chap, I think he's got a soft spot for you.' She smirked as she put her coat on. 'He told me he's never been married. Nice chap. I thought it very odd. He's got a good job and looks okay. Wonder why he never married. Would have thought he's a good catch. He said if you can't manage the loft, to get in touch.' She peered in the small mirror hanging from the wall and straightened her collar before applying her crimson lipstick.

'Sandy glanced at the table. 'He said he'd left his number. Where is it?'

'It's under the pot on the mantelpiece.'

Irene picked her handbag up from the counter. 'You'll have to make your dad a cup of tea and don't forget, he likes a couple of custard creams. You've made me late now.'

She dashed for the door and Sandy caught a whiff of the powdery smell of her perfume.

Sandy brewed a fresh pot of tea, and searching for his dirty mug, found it in the sink. She headed into the front room where her dad was sitting on the settee looking sorry for himself with his leg propped up on the coffee table and the *TV Times* magazine resting on his lap.

'Hi, Dad, Mum said you needed a cuppa.'

'Thanks, love.' He took the saucer and shoved one of the biscuits into his mouth. 'I've not seen her all morning, where is she?'

Sandy perched on the arm of the settee. She wouldn't have been allowed to do this if her mother were here. 'She's gone to one of her WI meetings.'

Her dad tutted and took a glug of tea. 'A gaggle of crony women.'

'What does she do at her meetings?'

'How should I know, love? It's a bunch of women who gossip about everyone and moan about everything.'

'Eddie's brought the steps round. What is it you need from the loft? I may as well go up there while the baby's still asleep.'

'The anglepoise lamp for your mother.'

'Oh yes, I remember. Got a torch?'

He turned slightly and winced. 'There's an old lamp and an extension cable on the landing. Lift the hatch and slide it to the left. Plug the lamp into the socket on the landing. The extension cable is long, so be careful. Watch what you're doing. Don't get yourself tangled up in it.'

She turned to leave the room.

'And, Sandra, only half the loft is boarded. Stay on the left side otherwise you'll come through the ceiling.'

'Whereabouts is the lamp?' She hovered at the door feeling a bit uncertain about going up there. It was more complicated than she'd thought. She didn't want to end up having an accident too. But on the other hand, she wanted to get it out of the way before her mother came home. She could just imagine Irene standing on the landing blocking her light, calling up to her, "mind the rafters, watch your step," and that would make her nervous.

'At the far end of the loft. Once you've got it, come down carefully, mind the cables and put the hatch back properly otherwise cold air will seep through and chill the whole house.'

She went into the hall and glanced up at the landing.

'And, Sandy,' he called through the closed door. 'If you feel it's unsafe, don't do it. We don't want two of us with broken legs. I can always ask a neighbour.'

She let the dog out and made sure Angela was settled before heading upstairs. She plugged the lamp in and after ten minutes figured out how to open the ladder. Bill had always done odd jobs around their house because she and Jasper were a bit clueless when it came to DIY. Holding the lamp and standing at the top of the ladder, she raised the trap up and to the left. She hadn't been expecting dust to fly out. Grains went in her eyes and mouth making her cough and blink, but she held her nerve and managed to keep her balance. It was so dark up there, but the lamp illuminated the expanse as she crawled in.

She groped around for somewhere to put the lamp. Putting it on a joist, she peered round in the gloom, her eyes adjusting to the light. The bulb was low-powered but provided just enough light to see through to the other end of the loft. One side of the loft was empty with a cold-water tank standing there like a cow's trough in a field. Old cobwebs hung from the rafters. The thought of spiders gave her the creeps. A streak of light was coming through a hole in the felt lining the roof, and bits of felt were hanging down. It was like looking at the night sky.

Boxes were piled indiscriminately, like the stock room of a shop, different shapes and sizes, no sequence, unlabelled. She wondered when the last time was that they'd had a clear-out. She thought of the day that would come when she'd have to sort this lot out for her parents. It wasn't a thought she relished.

She couldn't see the lamp straight away. She clambered along the boards feeling like a circus performer. The boards were wobbly and not screwed to the joists. She gingerly made her way past the boxes and suddenly spied the lamp lying on top of a big box at the far end. It was obvious the lamp hadn't been used for some time as it was covered in dust.

On her way back she saw an old gas mask beside a box, proof that they hadn't cleared the loft out in a very long time. It looked like a child's mask, possibly her own. Curious and excited by the find, she considered picking it up but thought better of it. She'd read somewhere that they contained traces of asbestos. The rubber straps had corroded and were flaky.

As she crawled back to the hatch, her eyes were drawn to a square scarlet red box, measuring she reckoned around a foot and a half in each direction. Being nosey, she took a closer look. Touching it, she realised it was covered in velvet material. Even in the gloom, she could see it was a special box and a glint of light reflected off a gold padlock. She wondered if it was a family heirloom or a present from her father to her mother, but why keep it up here? And what was in it? It was clearly not junk and would look lovely on her mother's dressing table.

'You alright up there, love?' Her mind snapped back to the

lamp. Her dad would worry if she took too long. She'd better get down.

'Yes, Dad, I'm fine, just on my way down now,' she called from the top of the hatch as she made her way down.

She put the lamp on the settee beside her dad and went to feed Angela who was stirring. Tibs was yapping at the back door. Poor dog, it was unfair to keep putting him outside although mostly he didn't seem to mind.

She perched on the edge of the armchair opposite her dad while she fed Angela her bottle. He stopped watching his programme and looked over at his granddaughter with love in his eyes which made Sandy's heart swell. She could see that he did care even though he hadn't shown much interest in the baby.

'Do you want to feed her, Dad?'

At the suggestion, his eyes grew wide with alarm. 'I wouldn't have a clue, love.' He shook his head, his jowls wobbling.

He needed encouragement, that was all. Standing up she went to pass Angela over. 'It's not difficult, Dad. Give it a go, I'll sit beside you.'

After a moment's hesitation, his face relaxed slightly but when he opened his arms awkwardly, he looked gauche.

Sandy didn't want to appear bossy. In a gentle voice she instructed him to hold Angela in a semi-upright position, supporting her head so that she could breathe and swallow comfortably and to lightly brush the teat against her lips. Then when she opened her mouth, Sandy beckoned him to let her draw in the teat.

The relief on his face was palpable as soon as she started to gulp. His eyes were bright as he glanced at Sandy. 'Am I doing, okay?'

'Perfect, Dad.' She rubbed his shoulder. He was wearing a bristly brown tank top, not ideal for brushing up against the baby's skin. 'I bet it's all coming back to you now. You must have fed me plenty of times when I was a baby. I can imagine Mum would have made you get up in the middle of the night.' She laughed.

'It was the middle of the war. I was usually out on fire duty.' All of a sudden, his face turned stony and even though Angela was content in his arms, he abruptly lifted her and passed her back to Sandy.

'You were doing well, Dad.' Sandy cradled Angela, who was still feeding.

'My shoulder's getting sore.'

There was something about the sudden change in demeanour that unsettled her. He made a feeble play of rubbing and wiggling his shoulder. She studied him for a moment. Something was wrong and it wasn't just a stiff shoulder.

'You're always watching programmes about the war, but you never talk about it, Dad. I'm curious to know what you both went through, how it was living through a war.'

'It's all in the past.' There was something vacant about the look in his eyes as he stared off to the wall.

Determined not to let his reticence put her off, she probed. 'Strange to think I was born in the middle of all that going on. Was I born in the Anderson shelter? Was London bombed that night? Lucky the house wasn't, otherwise you'd both have been killed and I would never have existed.' Sandy had never really thought about her own birth until now, but suddenly her head was filled with lots of questions she wanted to fire all at once.

'It was just an ordinary night. A neighbour helped deliver you.' There was something about his blunt reply that stopped her from asking further questions. She detected a reluctance to elaborate.

She remembered the gas mask and the red box. 'Talking of the war, I noticed a child's gas mask up there. Was that mine? Did I ever wear it?'

As she glanced at him, she saw what she thought was a look

of fear in his eyes, as if he were haunted by something. And then it dawned on her, the reason why he didn't want to talk about the war.

The horrors of war exist only in my imagination and on a TV screen, but Dad's generation witnessed them first-hand.

Something had happened to him during the war. In the heavy air that had settled between them she felt it and wondered what mental imagery crouched in the deep recesses of his mind.

'Maybe. I don't know what's up there. The loft's groaning with boxes and old stuff.'

She wished she could go up again, just to explore, take the odd box or two down to rummage through, but she didn't relish the prospect of going up there again, having to balance on the joists, watching out for spiders and struggling in the dim light. And where would she begin? It was an impossible task, a needle in a haystack, but the biggest obstacle of all was her parents.

Angela had finished her bottle and was asleep in Sandy's arms. 'Dad, there was also a beautiful red velvet box up there. It looks too lovely to be stuck up in a loft. What do you keep in there?'

His eyes looked brighter now that they weren't talking about the war. 'Don't ask me, love, probably where your mum keeps all her bits that she's not looked at for years. It's maybe an old jewellery box.'

'It's got a lovely gold padlock. I wonder if Mum still has the key.'

'Might be the key she keeps on one of the gold chains she wears.'

Irene had always worn several gold chains. The only time she took them off was when she had a bath. The chains were not something Sandy had taken much notice of, and she certainly hadn't seen a gold key around her neck. She was sure it was probably a locket.

'What stuff do you keep up there? The boards are groaning with boxes. Isn't it time you had a good sort out?'

'You know what it's like, stuff gets chucked up there. It's amazing the ceiling hasn't collapsed.' He gave a little chuckle.

She put Angela in her carrycot and went to check on the dog before taking a closer look at the anglepoise lamp on the table. Her mother would be back at any moment and would grumble if she saw how dirty it was. She took a cloth from under the sink and gave it a good clean. She smiled at the plug; it looked old, not like the type in her own house.

She went back into the front room. 'I've given the lamp a good clean, Dad.'

'You better put it over there on the hearth by her sewing box.'

'It's got a funny plug on it.'

'Oh bugger, yes, it's an old round pin plug. We had the house rewired a few years ago. Plug will want changing, or we might have to bin the lamp and get a new one.'

'She's back.' Sandy detected the groan in his voice when they heard the key in the door, and she had to smile. He'd be justified in calling Irene a battle-axe, but that wasn't something he was likely to say. He never complained. He put up with his lot––one of those long-suffering husbands that comedians often referred to.

Irene swept into the front room unbuttoning her coat and taking off her hat. Her eyes darted to the hearth. 'What's that doing there? You've not been up in the loft while I've been out?'

'Yes, it was a good opportunity to go up there.'

'Silly girl,' she snapped, a scornful look on her face. 'And what would have happened if you'd had an accident too?' She peered at Sandy, who morphed into her five-year-old self who was regularly scolded for minor misdemeanours. 'Who would have helped you, raised the alarm? Your father with his broken leg, the baby, or the damn dog? Honestly, Sandra, you're so impetuous, you don't use that brain of yours.'

A dull ache spread across Sandy's chest. She just wanted to rush upstairs and burst into tears. Whatever she did, she could never please her mother. She was tired, so tired of trying and failing. In that moment all she wanted was Jasper, to hold her closely and tell her that everything they'd been through was just a bad dream.

It hit her then.

He's my rock.

He supports me in everything I've ever wanted to do. He is my everlasting love.

They had a beautiful home and love had been in abundance. Their sex life had been super, in fact it had been the perfect relationship. No woman could want for more, but then the secret, it had shattered her bubble even having Angela could not hide or suppress the pain and the hurt. She felt the emotion surge in her heart and her chest. As she rushed from the room, her feet pounding up the stairs, tears started to flow like the pressure released from opening a tap. They burned her cheeks, and she could taste the salt on her lips.

Closing her bedroom door behind her, she threw herself on the bed as she had done so many times before. It felt like one of those déjà vu moments.

I can't do anything right.

When she'd calmed down, she sat up and stared at her reflection in the dressing table mirror and remembered the gold key. She was sure of it--it was hanging around her mother's neck, it had swayed when she'd shouted at full pelt.

Why hadn't she noticed it before, and how could she get hold of it and go back into the loft?

CHAPTER 13: JASPER

*A*s Jasper kicked off his shoes and loosened his tie after his long and exhausting afternoon in the American Embassy, he tried to force from his mind the image of Sandy flitting around the house and the two of them eating dinner together. It had only been a few days, but he hated coming home to an unlit house. Her desertion of him, their love sucked from the walls. The house felt cavernous and so much bigger and quieter without her, and the only noise was the ringing in his ears--the sound of silence.

He wished he could say something, do something that would make everything all right, but he felt spent, lost for words, which was why he'd made no attempt to ring her. He chastised himself for this familiar thought loop that led nowhere but craziness and frustration.

Give her time and space and maybe she'll come round.

He grabbed his suitcase from the corner of the bedroom where it had stood since his last trip and flung open the wardrobe doors. He began opening drawers and pulling shirts from hangers, but soon realised he didn't have enough clean clothes. His suit had to go to the dry cleaners and that took three days.

This is all I need.

He'd just have to pack what he could and pop into Saks on Fifth Avenue or Bloomingdales. Sandy had often told him, he was a rare species of men who loved shopping and buying clothes for himself. Over the years he'd listened to her advice, but he knew his style and cared about what he wore.

After zipping the case, he slung it to one side and with a heavy heart headed down to the kitchen to eat. Hunting through the cupboards, he felt like a scavenging racoon. Then he peered into the fridge, but all he found were three bendy carrots, a limp lettuce, and a tub of cottage cheese. The idea of whipping up a palatable meal with these scant provisions wasn't at all appealing. Feeling sorry for himself and with his stomach growling, he slammed the fridge door and then he remembered he couldn't even nip out for fish and chips because Sandy had taken the car.

The phone rang from the hallway, its trill startling him like the siren of an oncoming ambulance. His heart leapt––Sandy.

'Hiya,' he said cheerfully.

'Jasper,' came Bill's husky voice. 'I've been trying to get hold of you. We really need to go out with Toby to get this sorted.'

'What's he been like?'

'Quiet, sulky, stays in his room the whole time. Barely says two words to me, but at least he's back at school.'

'Good.'

'It's not good.' Bill sounded at the end of his tether. 'When can we meet? Something needs to change, I can't go on like this, I don't know what to do, I can't cope.'

Jeez, give me strength.

'Look, mate, I'm flying out to the States on Thursday, can't this wait till I'm back?'

'How long are you going for?'

'Not sure. Maybe three weeks.'

'Blimey, what does Sandy say about that? Bet she's not happy about you leaving her alone with the baby.'

'I don't have to worry about her for a while, she's gone to stay with her mum for a bit.'

'Thought they didn't have a great relationship.'

'They don't, but after that night you came over, things haven't been great. We needed a break--well, she needed a break.'

'I'm sorry, mate. Alcohol doesn't solve problems, but then again, neither does fruit juice.'

Jasper normally hated it when Bill came out with flippant remarks, but tonight, after the stressful day he'd had, he smiled.

'I suppose you've already eaten this evening?'

'Not yet. I was thinking of getting fish and chips. It's Toby's favourite, might cheer him up, you never know. I'm clutching at straws.'

'Tell you what, grab an extra portion for me and bring them round here.'

'Okay, great idea. In an hour?'

'I'll lay the table. See you in a bit.'

Coming off the phone, Jasper felt the tension seep from his body--this was just what the doctor ordered, company. He busied himself in the kitchen, feeling more upbeat as he gathered cutlery, ketchup, napkins. Already he was looking forward to catching up with Bill and Toby. He visualised the three of them sitting around the table like old times, taking the mickey out of each other in that light-hearted way that made them all feel at ease. They'd once joked about buying a shed and a kettle for somewhere to meet away from Sandy. The irony of it, they didn't need a shed now.

When Jasper heard the doorbell, he suddenly felt like a balloon deflating. What had he been thinking? This wasn't going to be like old times, not after everything that had happened, they couldn't go back to how they were. The evening would be fraught with unease and strained conversation. He hadn't even opened the door and he wanted the evening to be over. Toby would be moody, Bill stiff and tense, and it would be left to him to break the ice. Jasper to the rescue, that's what Bill was hoping. But after the week he'd had, he wasn't sure.

Heading into the hallway, he took a deep breath, pulled his shoulders back and glanced in the mirror above the narrow table where Sandy applied her lipstick.

They need you.

It was up to him, he had to pull them out of the hole before they descended further. Both were stubborn as mules.

As he approached the door, he reached out and grasped the cold metal handle. The hinges squeaked as the door swung open, letting in a rush of cold air. Toby and Bill stood on the doorstep, Bill clutching cans of beer and coke and Toby the handles of the bag of fish and chips between his teeth.

'Need a hand there?' Jasper smiled and grabbed the bag from Toby. 'They smell good. Hope you got me an extra big portion, I'm starving.' He winked at Toby. 'Come in, out of the cold.'

Jasper stepped aside as Bill and Toby made their way into the kitchen, greeted by the sound of the radio blaring out. Jasper set the bag on the table and switched the radio off. Toby slumped into a chair and made no attempt to take his coat off. Bill opened a couple of beers and a coke and put the other cans in the fridge.

'If you hadn't called, I was facing the prospect of three bendy carrots and limp lettuce for my dinner.' He laughed. As he opened the bag and divided portions onto each of their plates, his mouth watered with the tantalising aroma of crispy batter and big fat greasy chips drenched in vinegar––just how he liked them.

Toby raised his eyebrows, tutted, and slid down in the chair as if trying to disappear. This silent act of disrespect was infuriating but Jasper saw it as his way of asserting his independence and pushing back the authority figures in his life, a small act of rebellion. He was determined to ignore it. He'd try to get the lad to calm down; he knew what he needed, and it wasn't rocket science. He needed reassurance, to know that they all loved and cared for him––that hadn't changed and never would.

'I'm sorry, I forgot to warm the plates.' He glanced at Toby and could see by the expression on his face that he knew they were here to have a challenging chat.

As they ate their meal, Bill grumbled about his day and Toby ate in silence. This wall of silence around the boy seemed impenetrable, the most powerful scream. It had to be broken.

'Can I have ketchup, please?' Toby asked in barely a whisper.

'Course you can,' Jasper said brightly as he turned the bottle upside down and gave it a pelt. A huge splodge splattered Toby's chips.

They all laughed, and Toby muttered that Heinz should design a better bottle. Jasper smiled. The ketchup spill was just what they needed to defuse the atmosphere.

'Why is a meal always better with ketchup, eh, lad?'

Toby shrugged.

'Are you going to sit here and grunt all evening, because I've had enough of this.' Bill glared at Toby.

'How's school, Toby?' As soon as the question was out, Jasper knew what a gaffe he'd made. All kids hated to be asked about school, but adults always made the mistake of asking.

Toby groaned and said flatly, 'It's fine.'

'Is that all you've got to say?' Toby threw Bill a withering look, clearly irritated by the grilling.

Jasper knew he had to try a different tack and push through his blunder.

He looked at Toby and in a soft voice said, 'Look, mate, we

did what we did. In hindsight I wish I could turn the clock back. As soon as I found out I should have told you.' He glanced at Bill. 'And I know your dad regrets not telling you years ago that you were adopted.'

Bill sighed and looked thoughtful as he rubbed his stubble. 'Your mum and I should have sat you down when you were young. Maybe we should have come clean with the authorities years ago.'

'Toby,' Jasper said. 'The thing you'll learn about adults is that we all fuck up. When I was young, I put my parents on a pedestal, I thought they knew the answer to everything and the meaning of the universe. But how wrong I was. Adults are just children in big clothing. We never stop learning from our mistakes, we never stop screwing up. Believe me I've made some clangers in my time and I'm sure your dad has too.'

Bill smiled and raised his eyebrows.

He noticed Toby looked more relaxed. His face was less taut. He wasn't sighing or raising his eyebrows. Somewhere in the conversation, he'd sat up and was leaning across the table. While he didn't say anything, it didn't matter, because Jasper had the sense that he was taking it in and thinking about what he was saying.

'We kept it from you for all the right reasons. We had your best interests at heart, Toby, I promise you that. If this had come out, think of all the publicity. There wouldn't have been five minutes of peace, it would have driven you insane. You forget I work in the media. Those journalists would have swooped in like locusts. They'd rake through all of our lives, uncovering what dirt they could get their hands on, anything to write a good story and sell a few bucks. It would have been horrible. And that's without even considering the law. Bill and Rona, they could have been arrested and you would have ended up in care.'

Toby made fists with his hands. The poor lad, Jasper

thought, not to be able to bang them on the table, how frustrating that must be.

Toby glared at Bill. 'I'm angry that you had loads of opportunities to tell me. You should have told me, I would have coped, I would have understood, but instead you treated me like a baby.'

He turned to Jasper, his face like thunder. 'You stopped me from getting to know my real mum. All that time I could have got to know her and now she's not interested in me, neither of you are because you've now got the replacement kid you've always dreamed of.' He gave a spectacular sigh and sank in his chair. 'You have no idea, either of you, just how fucked up I feel. Quite honestly, it would have been better if I'd died at birth. I bet that's what you're all thinking.' Toby raised his voice and sat up again, his face all flushed. 'I've got a friend at school, Sue, and she wishes she was dead because her parents don't come to visit. In fact half the kids there think their parents would prefer it if they hadn't lived. That's why they chucked them into a boarding school. We're all one big burden.'

Jasper got up and pulled his chair round to the other side of the table and sat next to Toby. He put his arm round him, pleased when the lad didn't flinch or pull away.

'Okay, you little shit,' Jasper said, trying another tack.

Toby went to pull away as if he'd been burned by a flame, but Jasper drew him back, giving him a squeeze on the right shoulder. 'Let me tell you this. We aren't like other parents, and we aren't going to compare ourselves to other parents. I don't know about that lot up at the school, but there are a lot of messed-up people in this world. We do things our way here and our way is putting you first. And I'm sorry if that caused lots of hurt. Nobody comes out of this life unscathed by something like this. As life events go, this is pretty big.' He jabbed a finger at Toby's chest. 'Our way is loving you, wanting you around. You have three parents who love you very much, three people who would do anything for you. And I'm never going to stop reminding you of that.'

Bill smiled and reached out, putting his hand on Toby's other shoulder. Jasper noticed how tired and drawn he looked. There were dark shadows under his eyes and his hair was thinning.

As the three of them sat there, not saying anything for a few moments, it felt like the calm after the storm, the moment the sailor looks out over the still lapping waters and sees land ahead.

There was so much more they needed to talk about, but was this enough for now? He wanted to ask Toby if he'd given much thought to the future, where he'd go after school. Was he still planning on taking A levels at the local college? What careers had he considered? But he didn't want to overwhelm the lad by making him feel as if he was being interrogated.

'You know we'd do anything for you? Anything to ensure you're safe, happy, and fulfilled. Helping you achieve whatever you want. And we all want to be there, celebrating your important milestones. When you graduate from university, when you get married. We'll be there to navigate you through life's challenges. In our hearts, Toby, you're irreplaceable.'

When Jasper glanced at Toby, he saw the lad struggling. It seemed it was taking every ounce of his willpower to keep his emotions under wraps. Jasper's heart went out to him. In the slump of his shoulders, the slouch of his back, and the way his chin dipped––he was broken. He needed them––Bill, Sandy, and even little Angela—now more than ever.

'I love my job, but it's unfortunate, I won't be around for a while. I'd rather be here, but I can't choose when the presidential election is. And it's a hectic time for you, kid, you'll be revising for your mocks soon.'

Bill, who'd been cradling his can of beer and looking thoughtful, hadn't said very much all evening. Jasper got the sense that he was hoping for this--for him to take the lead and do all the talking. He wasn't sure if he felt resentful or pleased to be able to steer the situation. 'I'm here for you, you only have to ask. Anything. I'll do my best.'

'Your drinking doesn't help. Ever since Mum died, it's like the bottle has become your new best friend. And now, you're drinking more than ever. It's like it's all you care about. The kitchen's a tip and you can't be bothered to clean it. I'm sick of living like that.' He turned to Jasper. 'Can I come and live here? You're my proper parents, this is where I should be.'

The words hit like a bomb.

Jasper glanced over at Bill, barely able to look him in the eye as a deep sense of awkwardness and unease gripped him. He didn't want this, for Bill to feel undermined, to come across as superior, or belittle him. What he wanted was to play an equal part in Toby's life, but not to usurp Bill.

Christ, the man's done his best. He's not perfect, no dad is.

Bill scraped his chair back, stood up and stared down at Toby with sadness in his eyes. 'You don't want me, live here then, see if I care. You know what, at times you're an ungrateful little shit.'

'I suppose I should spend the rest of my life feeling grateful that you stole me from a hospital and just put up with us living like pigs.'

'Come on, mate,' Jasper said gently, 'sit down, he doesn't mean it, he's just very confused right now.'

Bill sat down with a huff.

'I'm not confused,' Toby shrieked. 'I just want him to stop drinking and not be so messy and filthy. He doesn't understand how hard it is for me without arms, I can't live in chaos. That's part of the reason I stay up in my room. It's tidy, I know where everything is. If I go home with you, nothing will change, you'll keep drinking and expect me to live in a slum. Every time I go downstairs, the smell of alcohol lingers like a dark cloud. And you just brush it off like it doesn't matter. You're slowly killing yourself.' His face was contorted as he looked up at Bill. Jasper could see the boy loved him––after all, until he had come along, Bill was his dad.

'Toby, right now you don't have a choice. I'm going to America and Sandy's not here. For now, things have to stay this way.'

The past hour had been emotionally draining, for all of them. He'd felt positive until Toby raised the issue of Bill's drinking, but now it was the main worry. Toby was right, Bill seemed resistant to change, stubborn and pig-headed. Just one evening of drunkenness had taught Jasper a lesson, but when would Bill learn from all the drinking he did, that it wasn't worth the toll it was taking on his life and the impact it had on Toby's?

Bracing himself, Jasper knew he had to say something to Bill. It felt like his duty, he had a responsibility to Toby and couldn't just ignore how the kid felt.

'Drinking's a mug's game, Bill. A vicious cycle. People drink to alleviate their worries and then end up with more problems. It starts to take its toll on your health and those around you. I know it's an escape from the stresses of life, but listen to the kid, he's not happy and I know his happiness means more to you than anything.'

'Okay, okay, you've both made your point. Maybe I have got a problem, but I know people who drink far more than me.' He sighed, let go of his can and rubbed his forehead.

'There are professionals that can help you, Dad,' Toby said.

Jasper smiled. There was warmth in his voice for the first time that evening and it was nice to hear him refer to Bill as Dad again. After finding out the truth, Jasper noticed he'd been replacing Dad with Bill, creating distance between them.

'I'll deal with my shit, kiddo, I promise. I know I've let you down.' Bill crossed his arms and looked ashamed, but Jasper detected that Bill was saddened by the impact of his drinking. Maybe he was going to try to repair bridges with Toby.

Remembering his forthcoming trip, Jasper suddenly felt inadequate. He wouldn't be here to offer support or influence events. He slumped in his chair, feeling the stirrings of a headache. There wasn't much more he could do.

With a look of resignation, Toby got up. 'Can we go now? I've got homework to do.'

Bill, who'd been gazing out of the window, jerked his head round to face Toby. 'Yeah of course, we mustn't take up any more of Jasper's time.' Was that relief on his face, that Toby wasn't persisting with the idea of coming to live at Jasper and Sandy's?

In the hallway, Jasper had a sudden idea and without giving himself time to consider it, blurted, 'Why don't we all go away, with Sandy and Angela too? The dog can go to the kennels. A long weekend somewhere? We could do with some fun, and it might help your studies, Toby, to have a break.'

Toby's eyes lit up. Abruptly, his demeanour shifted from one of moodiness to excitement, leaving Jasper feeling hopeful. 'I've always wanted to go to Butlin's. My friends have been to the one at Bognor Regis.'

Toby headed out of the door first and behind his back, Jasper and Bill shared a quick glance, recognising the positive shift in Toby's attitude.

After he closed the door behind them, Jasper took a moment to reflect on the evening. Small steps had been taken, he'd made his feelings clear to Toby and really that was all he could do for now, but they still had a long way to go to repair and build on their relationship. He smiled to himself. Like his career and marriage, it was a work in progress.

Too tired to clear the evening's debris, he switched off the kitchen lights and made his way up the stairs, stopping midway as a thought hit him.

Sandy.

She's my bloody wife and I'm making plans without running it past her first.

There was a good chance she wouldn't want to go to Butlin's, it wasn't her cup of tea. He could just predict her making a remark along the lines that it was for common folk and not for the likes of them.

CHAPTER 14: JASPER

Jasper ascended the steps from the graffiti-adorned subway deep into the heart of Times Square, the piercing sun reflecting on the towering buildings that surrounded him like a manmade forest. He stopped on the corner of the pavement to take it all in. The eclectic sights and sounds of this bustling district, in the city that never slept.

The Big Apple.

Sam had reminded him to stay alert for pickpockets. An assortment of disenfranchised youth, hustlers, drunks, drug dealers and the homeless roamed the streets and lurked in the shadows. But having experienced the loss of his camera at the Notting Hill Carnival a few years back, he was all too aware of the potential risks that came with being among large crowds and in an area where crime rates were rampant.

As he strolled along, he glanced all around him, mesmerised by what he saw. He passed a plethora of go-go bars, sex shops and peep-show establishments––symbols of the city's decay. He passed a window with two blow-up dolls on top of each other and dressed in naughty undies. He noticed a guy in a grey raincoat about to head into an establishment offering a 25-cent peep show.

A scruffy old man with his belongings in a shopping trolley paused to look at a life-size poster of a scantily clad woman. A couple were tittering as they glanced at a display of erotic magazines. Adult films and erotic merchandise were sold on every corner and a man tried to engage him in a three-card con game.

Jasper was saddened to think that Times Square, a once flourishing place for high end entertainment, now facilitated the sex market. This was like returning to the days of the Wild West when frontier towns offered all manner of sexual services to cowboys.

As he crossed the road, he noticed a man with a missing limb slumped against a building begging for money. As he passed the man, he read the board displayed beside him. *Homeless Vietnam Vet. God bless America, please help.*

This man had put his life on the line for his country and now his country had cast him aside.

Jasper dropped a few coins into the cap beside him and as he did so, another man, crossing the road shouted at him. 'He doesn't deserve it. They're all murderers, baby killers, rapists and psychos. They carried out the orders of our sick government, spraying toxic chemicals over thousands of villages, killing and maiming innocent people––and people like you give them money. You British?'

'Yes. I'm a journalist.'

He stood in front of Jasper in full rant. 'Well get your notepad out. Men like him were told to go in and kill women, children, animals, throw bodies in wells, ruin their water supply, burn the villages. Just kill. Exterminate. Our God-damn government initiated a war of aggression. What they did, it was an international crime. They used living targets to test their inventions to use in future battles.'

'What do you think of the candidates for the forthcoming presidential election? What's Carter's approach to foreign policy?'

He turned to go, shouting over his shoulder. 'I don't bloody care. Ford or Carter, they're both warmongers, they all are. Bunch of capitalists. You can't trust any of them.'

Jasper stared after the man, unable to move for several moments as the power of his words cut through him like a knife. The country was still gripped by the horrors of Vietnam, living in the shadows of the atrocities it committed. This homeless man was probably one of hundreds living on the streets. He wondered what his story was. Probably most veterans were treated with this same scorn and indifference. The man's eyes were glazed, perhaps with drug use. Jasper wanted to hold on to his feelings of compassion––the same compassion he felt towards the thalidomide victims––but he couldn't. The thalidomiders were innocent victims of pernicious pharmaceutical companies. This man faced choices. Jasper couldn't help seeing him in a new light, a man who'd probably committed the most appalling acts.

After checking into his hotel, he went up to the bedroom and opening his suitcase took out his washbag. About to head to the bathroom for a shower, he suddenly realised he'd meant to call Sandy. But now he was abroad. She had no idea that he was in the States.

He plonked himself on the bed, feeling like a fool. Leaving it until he was here was going to be difficult and expensive. International calls were at premium rate and a lengthy process. At the thought of all that hassle and getting routed to the wrong person, never mind the poor quality of the call, his heart sank in despair. He couldn't do anything right––what was happening to him? He felt so incapable.

He was so far away from her now, in spirit and in distance. In all the years they'd been married, they'd always been in contact. The silence and distance now between them loomed large and was a reminder of the unspoken issues that had driven a wedge between them. He still held a glimmer of hope that they'd find a way back to each other.

Despite the aggravation, the call had to be made. He went down to the hotel foyer where there were several booths. The operator connected him through and after a short wait, her mother answered. Sandy was out walking the dog and so he left a message with Irene.

With his spirits plummeting, he replaced the receiver. Then in the lift, it occurred to him that she might not pass on his message. Surely, she wouldn't be that callous. But it was possible, she'd been vindictive all those years ago when she'd destroyed his letters. Even though he'd moved up to Manchester for work, he hadn't meant to lose touch. There was every chance she'd seize this opportunity to hammer the nail in the coffin and destroy their marriage once and for all.

The following morning after a good sleep, Jasper headed down to the hotel's lounge where he'd arranged a meeting with Dr Frances Kelsey. He'd interviewed her in the early sixties when she was a reviewer for the US Food and Drug Administration after she'd refused to authorise thalidomide for market because she had concerns about the lack of evidence regarding the drug's safety. As he pressed the button in the lift to take him down to the ground floor, he reflected on his first interview with her. She'd refused to bend to pressure from the drug company officials. She'd told him that Richardson-Merrell's application for approval of Kevadon was unsatisfactory and inadequate. There were no complete reports of animal studies, they were not frank with her about harmful side effects, and she was unimpressed with the argument that the fact that the drug had been available in other countries was proof of its safety. Today's interview was to find out what had happened in the ensuing years. It occurred to him that it would be interesting to find out what she thought about the presidential candidates regarding drug regulation and testing.

Kelsey had prevented what could have been an appalling American tragedy, the birth of hundreds or thousands of deformed babies. He was about to have coffee with an American heroine; she was awarded a gold medal by President Kennedy.

As the lift doors swung open at the ground floor, the scent of flowers and polished wood mingled in the air as he scanned the ornately decorated foyer. An oversized chandelier hung from the ceiling, casting warm light on the onyx floors and intricate metal stair railings. The reception desk stood at the far end of the foyer, flanked by yucca plants and plush settees. As he approached the desk, a smiling receptionist greeted him, ready to assist him.

'Morning. Which way to the coffee lounge, please?' Although he'd stayed in this hotel before, he still couldn't find his way around. The maze-like layout of the place never ceased to baffle him, with its endless corridors and tucked-away alcoves. He headed towards the coffee lounge.

He spotted her immediately, sitting by the window, perched on the edge of a velvet armchair. She'd aged, but it had been fifteen years. She was petite, had a slender frame but still looked masculine with short-cropped hair like a boy and dressed in a modest, dark suit. He'd always thought that simple suits on women reflected a no-nonsense approach to life.

Turning and smiling at him, she rose to shake his hand. He remembered her delicate features––the sharp bone structure that gave her a sense of grace and poise.

After settling in their chairs and ordering coffee and biscuits, they exchanged pleasantries and she asked about his trip to America.

'Well…' he said after a short while, 'you're something of a heroine here and across the world. You must have saved hundreds, if not thousands of lives. How does it feel to be compared to great figures like Schindler and Turing?'

She laughed. 'Hardly. I was just doing my job. I was a simple bureaucrat.'

'You're too modest, Doctor Kelsey.'

'I'm someone who believes in learning from mistakes. I regret not doing anything, not being able to stop the illegal clinical trials of Kevadon that took place throughout America.'

She leaned forwarded and with passion in her voice said, 'Can you believe it, these drug companies were submitting applications for its approval but all that time they were illegally promoting it and dishing it out to doctors and medics like sweeties, claiming it was safe? It was passed among family and friends with little awareness that this was an experimental drug.'

'Jesus.'

'Women didn't know what they were taking. The pills were unmarked, came in various colours, handed out casually by doctors in envelopes with some kind of written instruction inside.'

'Nobody knows how many thalidomide births there were in the States?'

'That's right. The official numbers could be the tip of the iceberg. The true toll will never be known. So, when you and everybody else calls me a heroine, believe me, I don't feel like one. There will be children with deformities who will never know for sure whether they are thalidomide victims. And without that recognition, how are they to claim compensation?'

'Lots of ambiguity then?'

'The clinical trials were slapdash and the paperwork almost non-existent. We launched an investigation, but it was impossible. Like hunting for a needle in a haystack. Many doctors were unreachable for weeks, others refused to talk, some denied they'd handed out the drug.'

'What a mess. So many ruined lives.'

'Possibly hundreds of victims, with no definitive proof. I've devoted my life to drug regulation, but at times it's been like beating my head against a brick wall.'

'Richardson-Merrell and the other company, Smith, Kline & French--are you saying they got away with it?'

'We referred our findings--if you can call them that, because they were grossly inadequate--to the Department of Justice for criminal prosecution. Our agency lawyers listed twenty-four counts under which Richardson-Merrell broke the law, including marketing and distributing an unapproved drug and claiming it was safe.'

Jasper leaned forward and rubbed his chin. This was getting interesting. 'And what happened?'

'They concluded that criminal prosecution was neither warranted nor desirable. Their exact words.'

'Fuck.' The swear word slipped out without him thinking. 'Please excuse my language, Doctor Kelsey. I'm so shocked. Speechless.' He shook his head.

'Herbert Miller, the Assistant Attorney General, said that as far as he knew, only one malformed baby had been born in America as a result of its mother's use of Kevadon.'

Jasper scrambled to take notes.

'Richardson-Merrell's case was that they had only handed it out to physicians of high professional standing. As if that made it alright.' Her head went back, and she laughed. 'And Smith, Kline & French handed it out in packets with a code name SK&F #52627. Patients didn't know what was in the tablets.'

'How many babies, Doctor Kelsey? How many in this country were affected?'

'We don't know exactly. By the time our investigation concluded, the official number was seventeen. But some of those mothers had obtained the drug while travelling in Europe.'

Digesting her words, Jasper was left shocked to the core as he leaned forward, gripped by the realisation that she didn't actually have a bloody clue. Thousands were affected.

The hidden victims of the scandal.

If it was obvious to him, why wasn't it obvious to her? Nobody, not even Kelsey dared to admit the truth.

Suddenly he saw her in a completely different light. She was part of a machine, and it was corporate corruption on a grand scale.

Thalidomide was never available in the United States.

Just a whopping big lie.

The words violently jolted, leaving him reeling in a pit of despair and disbelief.

All that praise she'd received for stopping the approval of thalidomide––the real truth had been covered up, a government cover-up too, swept under a carpet of lies, deception and above all, inertia.

'This is a time bomb, Frances. I don't believe for one moment we're only talking about seventeen children. And I think you know it. You're basking in the praise for what you did do, but what about what you didn't do?'

As he spoke, he couldn't help but notice a man sitting on a nearby settee with his back towards them. He'd glanced round several times, each time with a frown on his face. Jasper wondered if their interview had disturbed his peace. The man now began shuffling his newspaper, creating a soft rustling sound that resonated within the room. He didn't get a clear look at him but there was something about him that looked familiar.

'Our investigation was as thorough as it could have been.'

'Does it not bother you that thousands of children are growing up without help and support?'

A cough escaped the man and the rustling of his newspaper now felt deliberate.

'I think you're being a bit dramatic, Mr Cooper. Haven't you flown over to cover the presidential election? Reporting on the FDA investigation––you're ten years too late.'

'What about the candidates, Carter and Ford? What you think they'd have to say about the cover-up? Do the Democrats or Republicans plan to reopen the investigation?' His questions were coming at her like bullets from a gun.

'I doubt it. The investigation has long concluded on the matter.' Suddenly she rose to her feet, frowning, effectively concluding the interview. Obviously these were questions she didn't want to ask.

After she'd left Jasper sat, numb with shock, contemplating what actions he could take next. He'd speak to Sam, get his thoughts.

He glanced over at the man who'd been rustling his newspaper, but he was gone.

Jasper wondered if they were connected; was he her bodyguard? The whole scandal was cloak and dagger.

The interview was over before it had begun, so many questions he had not asked. It was as if she had become defensive, part of the system. She could have said so much more but chose not to.

The man bothered him, he never got to see his face, he was there when he said goodbye to Dr Kelsey, did not see him leave as he returned to his chair, but with so many corridors, it would not be difficult to escape unnoticed. There was just something familiar about him, even from a back view.

No time to dwell though, he had to focus on the election, get what he needed and get back home. He did not want to be away any longer than he had to.

CHAPTER 15: TOBY

It was a Saturday morning, a week or so after Jasper had gone to the States. Toby stood at his bedroom window wondering what to do with his day. After weeks of studying for his O levels, he felt as though his brain was about to combust. Countless hours poring over textbooks, scribbling notes, taking practice tests. The weekends had become tedious, the minutes ticking away, yet another two days of monotony stuck in his bedroom.

From his window, he could see over the wooded lane and out across the heathland towards the North Downs. He found himself longing for adventure, a chance to break free from the chains of schoolwork and do something fun for a change. He wondered what his mates were up to. There were always friends hanging around in the school grounds at weekends--always someone to chat and laugh with.

As much as he wanted to spend time with friends, kicking a ball across the field or just messing about doing nothing in particular--it was Jasper's company he missed.

My biological father.

The man who has been missing from my life all this time.

I've gone my whole life not knowing him, I want to spend time with him.

His mind kept turning back to the image of Jasper. Ever since they'd met for the first time back in Blackpool, there was something about the man that drew him in. An unexplained familiarity that was reassuring. He'd never felt that way about Sandy, because it was hard to visualise her as his mother. He felt no connection. She was just a very attractive woman, not mother material. But with Jasper, there was a sense of connection he'd never felt before, an innate understanding. He felt it in the silent glances, the unspoken conversations and in the comforting words he offered. Jasper understood him and anticipated his needs. He'd noticed it that night they'd gone round for fish and chips. Jasper had cut through his moodiness with his calm patience––and that way he had of defusing any situation. All Bill did these days was rile him. Sometimes he couldn't stand the sight of him. He hated feeling contempt but lately it seemed to be out of control.

He eased into his flip-flops. He'd always worn flip-flops even during the winter––his feet were used to the cold. Sometimes though he wore canvas slip-on shoes he could easily remove. His feet were his hands after all, and they had to be accessible. He glanced out of the window again; the weather was good, but he'd need a jacket. With his mouth, he grabbed his tan suede jacket from the hook on the wall, twirled and shrugged it on.

About to head downstairs, there was a tap at the door. As Bill peered round the door, Toby's heart sank.

'Off out?'

Bill was wearing his frayed plaid dressing gown open over a pair of grey joggers and a vest, his hair flopping around his face, fresh stubble on his chin.

His dad had been trying to engage him in conversation ever since the fish and chip supper at Jasper's. Toby couldn't help being grumpy and distant with his sullen expressions and downcast eyes. He was lost in his own world. His responses to Bill's questions were terse and he rarely initiated conversations, preferring to stay silent. And now, with Bill asking questions, Toby couldn't be arsed.

As Bill came into the room and glanced round, the air grew thick with a palpable sense of awkwardness and tension.

'Just going for a wander, see who's about.'

It was annoying that his dad wasn't working today. He had one in four Saturdays off a month; Toby didn't keep a track of when they were. The mere thought of him suggesting they go for a walk together filled him with dread. He knew it was mean, but Bill was the last person he wanted to spend time with.

'I thought we could spend time together, kick a ball around the common, go into town.'

'No, you're all right,' Toby said in a dull tone, his body language closed off.

Bill folded his arms and stared at him. 'You spend weeks cooped up in your room and now you'll do anything to escape the house. I don't know what's got into you.'

'I don't suppose it would have anything to do with your secrets and lies.' Toby barged past him and out onto the landing.

Bill huffed. 'Not that again. I've always tried to do my best for you, you know that. Look at the stuff in this house. It's filled with all the contraptions I've made for you over the years to make your life easier. I saved bits of wood, nails, bits of plastic, anything I could get my hands on so that I could make you gadgets. That cup holder to rinse your mouth after brushing your teeth. That rod that holds toilet paper so you can wipe your arse, those special scissors I made. I never stopped thinking about your needs.' His voice was breaking, and Toby dared not look at him. 'The sacrifices me and your mum made. You don't realise what we gave up for you. Holidays for a start. One day, when you have kids of your own, you'll realise. And

I'm trying my best to stop drinking in case you hadn't noticed. You've not made any comment.'

Toby was about to head down the stairs but stopped and turned back.

'What do you want, a bloody medal?' Toby hated to lord it over his dad, but he was being pathetic.

'I don't think you appreciate how hard it is.' His voice fell to a whisper, and it sounded as if it might crack. Toby faced his dad stonily. 'You're blaming me for all your sacrifices and making out it's my fault you had to quit drinking. You're twisting my words. I know I can't carry on like I was. Why can't I just go and live with Jasper? Or live there some of the time? I could have two bedrooms.' The thought excited him.

'That's a daft idea.'

Toby knew he was being challenging by the way Bill rubbed his forehead in despair.

'I just want to get to know them better.' But it was more than that. There was a growing desire inside him to live with them, spend time with them, a desire that had taken root in the past week and woke him restless in the night with beads of sweat on his face and neck. How could he possibly tell Bill how he really felt? That his heart ached for a sense of being a part of a family––his real family. Living here no longer felt like home. His curiosity about the way they lived was insatiable. But how was that going to be possible? Bill and Jasper were both against the idea. They didn't want their lives disrupted, neither wanted to face the truth. How could they say they wanted the best for him but not follow that through?

He tried another tack. 'If anything happens to you, I'd have to live there, so I should at least have a bedroom there, somewhere to call mine.'

'I'm not about to pop my clogs.'

'You might drink yourself into an early grave.'

'Don't you worry, I'm as strong as an ox. And what's wrong with living here, am I not good enough anymore?'

It was no longer about the state of the place, although since finding out that Bill wasn't his real dad, Toby found himself walking through the house with a heightened sense of disgust and frustration. Like everything going on in his mind, the disarray seemed to be growing, from the pile of dirty dishes in the kitchen sink to the overflowing bin in the corner. He tried to tolerate it, but sometimes it was the final straw. It was as if his dad didn't care.

'I didn't say that.' As he glanced at Bill, he felt a pang of guilt. He knew he was being hurtful when he saw the sadness in Bill's eyes. He wanted to take it all back, to make things right between them, but he also knew his heart's greatest desire. He could feel the weight of his actions hanging heavily on his shoulders, the thought of the pain he was causing left him in anguish.

He tried to muster the words to explain himself, to apologise, but his throat was dry, and he couldn't explain in a way that Bill would ever understand.

'Sometimes, lad, you can be so bloody hurtful and ungrateful. Do what you bloody like, but I doubt they will pander to you like I have.'

Toby felt an ache move across his chest and glanced away.

'Besides,' Bill carried on, 'they have a child of their own now.' With fury, he stormed off, charging down the stairs, his footfall echoing through the cottage. Toby heard a deafening bang as he slammed the front door behind him as if determined to never return.

When he was gone, there was silence.

Bill's last words cut through him like a knife.

They have a child of their own now.

Where the hell did that leave him?

I feel as unwanted as a discarded sandwich, incomplete, rejected.

CHAPTER 16: TOBY

Toby had no idea where Bill was heading. From his bedroom window he heard the truck being violently revved before it sped off along the bumpy track. As soon as it was out of sight, he decided to venture out into the school grounds to see who was about.

As he stepped outside, he could feel the coolness of the air penetrate his lungs. There was just enough chill to invigorate. The sun shone brightly through the trees casting a warm glow on everything it touched. He meandered along the stony path and through a thicket of bracken as he took in the beauty of the autumn colours. The sky was a stunning shade of blue with fluffy clouds drifting lazily across its expanse. He couldn't think of a better way to spend a day. Autumn was his favourite season.

The beauty of nature and the gentle caress of the breeze on his cheeks helped his stresses and worries dissipate. Closing his eyes and stopping to gaze up at the sun, he realised he needed more days like this--away from his books and the confines of his bedroom.

The pathway through the wood led out onto the sprawling green of the lawn at the back of the school. It was easily the size of a park. A vast sea of bracken touching the fringes of the lawn spread away and into the distance as far as the eye could see. As he walked, he came across an old fountain with corroded stone statues covered in lichen and no longer spurting water.

Further on, he saw the old stables now converted into the Lady Hoare Experimental Workshop where some of the prosthetics and assisted living gadgets were made.

For a Saturday, it was quiet. It was too nice to be inside, which made him wonder if the students had either gone home for the weekend or were on an outing.

As he rounded the stable block he caught a glimpse of the rear wheels of a wheelchair, then two long arms.

Sue.

Alone again.

She glanced round and seeing him, smiled. 'Hiya, Toby, nice to see you, what you up to? Park your bottom and tell me the gossip.'

'I was bored of studying. Thought I'd see who was about.'

She laughed. 'I thought you never got bored of schoolwork. You're a right little swot you are. I can see you going to that university for toffs––Oxford.'

He let out a titter. 'In my dreams.'

'About as likely as me riding off into the sunset on the back of a Harley with Donny Osmond or David Cassidy?' She gave a pig-like snort.

'Probably.' He perched on the bench next to her wheelchair.

'So, what are you going to do when you've left here?' She glanced at him. 'Sorry, is that a boring question, type of thing a parent would ask?'

'Parents. God, who needs them?' He let out a sigh. 'I'm going to take A levels at college. And yes, I'd like to go to university but I don't know if anywhere will take handicapped students like us. I'll just have to apply and see what happens. Would be nice to get away from home. It gets stifling living with my old man.'

'Hey, stop your grumbling, I had this last time we met. As I said before, you don't know how lucky you are.'

'Sometimes I think life would be better without parents.'

'You don't mean that.'

'I wonder what it would be like to run away.' He turned to look at her. 'We could run away together.' From deep in his core, Toby began to laugh. Maybe it was nerves. His body convulsed and his shoulders shook as the laughter grew stronger.

'And how far d'you reckon we'd get? You with no arms and me with no legs. We'd look a right pair of Charlies.'

'Doesn't matter what we look like. You can be the arms, I'll be the legs, could work well as a team.'

'I wouldn't get very far in this wheelchair. It doesn't go over bumps and tree roots.'

'Maybe it could grow a pair of wings.' He glanced up and watched an aeroplane streak a fuzzy trail across the sky. 'Be nice to fly. You ever been abroad?'

'No, but my brother and sister get taken on nice holidays. Spain, Italy, Austria, Switzerland.'

'That's not fair.' Toby glanced at her. Last time they'd met, he'd seen her at her most vulnerable, but now, with her shoulders squared and her head held high, she looked as if she wanted to defy the world. He saw resilience, like a second skin protecting her from the blows of life.

Despite how strong she looked, he knew that deep inside, she hurt. To be excluded. He'd never experienced that kind of rejection. His parents had always included him in everything they'd done.

'All my life, I've watched them go off on their adventures, while I was left here, longing to be part of my family.'

'That's awful, I'm sorry.' It struck him then, how lucky he'd been. He'd never been abroad, but he had great memories of days on Blackpool beach with his mum and holidays to Skeggie and Clacton. The memories of those happy days spent with Rona on the beach were still vivid in his mind. As he recalled those moments, he felt a strange mix of sadness and gratitude. But Sue, poor girl. He couldn't imagine the crushing rejection she felt, still felt, to be excluded by those who were supposed to love and care--her own flesh and blood. It was despicable.

'I wish they'd understand how excluded I feel, rather than seeing me as a burden. I remember my mum telling me when I was quite small that they couldn't deal with my needs while travelling. To them, I'm a burden and always will be. Every year I ask if I can come too. I don't know why they bother telling me they're going. It would be easier if they didn't. They always tell me how great it's been and what fun they've had. I would rather not know. It always leaves me feeling unwanted. I don't need to know. My dad tried to act all cheery when he said, "every day's a holiday for you in that place".'

'Have they always been like that?'

'Pretty much, but something happened when I was about eight and since then they see me less and less.'

'Oh?' Toby was listening but still dwelling on his own sadness. He hadn't thought about his mother much lately, but now her image returned to his mind, the loss was deep. The memory of her left an ache in his heart. It wasn't just that she'd always put him first and all the happy days they'd had--it was how she'd made him feel. Her kindness, the way she made him feel special and valued. The way she helped him to be independent. Her determination to encourage him to try and never give up. She'd always been at his side, gently guiding him but never carrying him.

'One morning when I was home for the weekend, my sister Jackie pushed me into the corner shop so that we could buy sweets. She parked me inside because the aisles were too narrow for the wheelchair. Jackie disappeared down one of the aisles and the next minute the shop owner angrily grabbed my chair and started to push it out of the door and down the big step. He was so cross that I was in the way of his customers that he didn't bother to tilt the chair back. I tumbled out and hit the pavement hard. My face smashed into the rough concrete. I remember several people surrounding me, the stunned silence as everyone watched, their faces frozen in horror. I broke my nose.' She put a finger into her mouth. 'And my teeth got smashed. Had to have them all replaced. I remember the wheelchair lying on its side, the wheels still spinning slowly like some dance of death and blood spreading across the pavement in a gruesome, crimson puddle. After that, my parents just saw me as a burden. I came with trouble written across my forehead––or at least that's how it felt.'

'Didn't your mum complain to the shop owner?'

'I don't think so. I think they were embarrassed by the whole ordeal.'

'My mum would have complained. She always stood up for me. She fought the council so that I could go to the local primary school.'

She looked at him. 'Toby, I don't want to pry but you never talk about your mum. What was she like?'

It was the first time a school friend had asked after his mum, but they were all aware that she'd died. Toby found himself lost for words. His mind went blank, like a sudden whiteout that left him stranded at sea.

Tears filled his eyes. She had caught him by surprise as emotions welled inside.

While he welcomed the question, at the same time it felt intensely private and he felt exposed, as if someone had stripped away his layers on a cold winter's day.

After a moment or two, he realised she was staring at him expectantly and he felt under the spotlight. 'She was lovely, just the best.' It was all he could think to say, but in those few words he'd summed her up. When he thought of his mum, sometimes it was like trying to catch smoke with his hands; the harder he tried, the more it slipped away from him.

He looked up at the sky, now clouding over.

'How nice. My mum doesn't give a damn. I've never met her friends. She doesn't want me to meet her church lot, too embarrassed by how I look. Not unless I wear my artificial legs and I gave up on them years ago. Horrible things, so painful.'

'I'm sorry. That must be hard having a mum like that. I was lucky. My mum was the opposite. When people stared at me, she'd stare back. We were in a supermarket once and this kid came up to me and pulled my hand. I think he thought that if he pulled hard enough my arms would come out, a bit like a retractable umbrella or police baton. My mum very calmly told the kid why I had no arms.'

'How did she die?'

'Cancer.'

The solemn declaration hung in the air, leaden and heavy like a grey cloud.

'How painful, watching her fade away.'

He was surprised by her statement; she seemed mature beyond her years, and he wondered if she'd experienced loss herself.

The truth was, he hadn't watched her fade away. Bill had shielded him from the ordeal, hadn't allowed him into the hospice. Twelve hadn't felt young though and he wished he hadn't been treated like a baby.

He had no idea what cancer was like other than the fact it was a death sentence.

'It was a long time ago.'

He wondered what went through a person's mind as they lay dying. Could they think, or were they too ill to think? Instinct told him that his mother would have fought the illness to the end with strength and courage. He wished he'd been there beside her. Maybe they would have talked about all the things that really mattered rather than the chit-chat of everyday life, dull questions about school, no doubt.

He wondered how he would have used those last hours with her. He would have sat there and studied her and memorised every mile of her face, every mole, every wrinkle. It would have been impossible to cram a lifetime of moments into those final hours. To have been able to thank her for everything. For being such a wonderful mum.

And then it hit him. As clear as day.

The reason he'd been kept away.

If I'd gone to see her, she might have told me the truth.

Why hadn't it occurred to him before? There were numerous films and books depicting lead characters revealing dark secrets or making big confessions on their death bed. In *The Great Gatsby*, one of his favourite books, Jay Gatsby revealed the truth about his past to Nick Carraway before he was killed. And in *To Kill a Mockingbird*, the book he'd been studying for his English O level, Arthur "Boo" Radley revealed himself to Scout Finch and Sheriff Tate. And hadn't Queen Victoria confessed to having had an affair moments before she slipped away?

He could see a scenario with such clarity now and it haunted him. Rona's grip on reality would have been slipping away in those final days and hours, her words muddled and confused, her thoughts and speech uninhibited. Like the characters in books, maybe she'd needed to unburden herself before it was too late.

Bill stopped her from confessing.

Sue was rattling on. 'We should go for a walk round the town one Saturday, what do you think?' she asked him, but he was only half listening, his mind was elsewhere. He had to get home.

'Good idea, next week, I'm sorry, I've got to go, you've made me think of something. You better head off too, looks like it's going to rain.'

'I thought you were away with the fairies; you've not heard a word of what I've been saying.' She laughed and as he turned to her open-mouthed, he saw how royally cheesed off she looked. She must have said something important and all the time he'd been daydreaming. He had a lot of making up to do now. He liked her, didn't want to offend her, not when they were starting to become good friends. She was a chatty soul, easy company and had no problem filling silences.

'You going to be here next Saturday?' he asked.

'Probably.'

'I'll come and find you.'

She threw him a puzzled look. 'Good luck with that.'

He got up and after saying bye she called after him. 'Toby, if you can, bring some ciggies next time.'

'I'll try.'

As he walked back through the woods, it started to rain, a light drizzle that dampened the bed of golden autumn leaves. He stopped to enjoy his surroundings, the peace of the wood, the birds silent as he glanced up at the tall trees now nearly bare, tiny droplets of cold rain moistening his face. Despite the discomfort, there was something magical about being caught in the midst of drizzle in the middle of a wood. The scent of rain and the wet foliage made him feel connected to nature. How different nature was to humans, he thought. Humans only brought strife, discontent, pain and destruction, but nature conquered everything through its beauty and vastness.

Deep in thought, he continued to stare up at the tall branches, but after a few moments it made him dizzy. He glanced down and blinked, focussing now on the knotted moss-covered roots underfoot, twisted, and gnarled protruding from the ground like giant fingers trying to claw their way to the sky. As he took a step, his foot caught on a jagged root and his body lurched forward. His senses were jolted, he tried to right his balance, but it was too late, he was tumbling, losing his balance. He couldn't reach out, no arms to break his fall, and as his face smacked the wet ground, he was aware of an intense pain, sharp and stabbing. He must have twisted his ankle. He screamed out, it was a searing pain.

Shit, I can't get up.

The rain was getting heavier, splattering his eyes. He shook his head, trying to clear his vision. His face was covered in damp leaves and mud. He needed help. He shouted out. Somebody must hear him, he wasn't in the wilderness. He turned, inched his body towards a tree and leant against it. There was no way he could walk, and he wasn't sure how he was going to even get up. Not on one foot and with no arms to help. He hated this feeling, of being vulnerable.

Those bullies were right––I'm just a cripple, a flid, a spaz. Why was I even born?

I'll never lead a normal life. What's the point?

Mixed with feelings of hopelessness and failure came feelings of strength.

Most of the time I'm capable.

He prided himself on just how capable he was because he could find his way around most problems, but now he was helpless. With the pain growing intense he couldn't think of how to get himself out of this situation. What if he was stuck here all day, all night, his dad wouldn't know where he was.

CHAPTER 17: JASPER

After interviewing Dr Kelsey in New York, Jasper took a domestic flight down to Georgia, where he hired a car to embark on a journey to Plains, a quaint rural town and birthplace of Jimmy Carter.

When he'd arrived in the States, he hadn't known what his specific area of focus should be with regards to the election. He'd been instructed to explore Carter's background, find any dirt on the guy or interesting stories about his childhood. But Jasper wanted to focus more on the issues that drove the election, and in particular social issues, because that was where his interest lay.

As he drove through small rural towns, he thought about how remote and cut off it was from Washington. Anyone growing up in these parts had to be a real visionary, dream big, think big, for it took a particular mind to set the bar so high, to break free from the shackles of the family business, the family gene pool. But coming from these parts and diving in to rescue the family's peanut farm, Carter had shown to America he could roll his sleeves up and get stuck in. And after all, the next president had to come from somewhere and that could be a Texan cattle ranch, the Blue Mountains of Virginia, or the vineyards of California.

The sky was ironed into a denim blue, leaving a faultless fabric above his open top car, and the air was pleasantly warm. But despite this, there was something chilling about driving through the Deep South. The sudden realisation this was a state that used to lynch people. Despite the civil rights movement and legislation, had that reign of terror really stopped or did the evil people just cover their tracks better? What did Carter think about the racial issues facing his country, or any other social issue come to that?

With these thoughts running through his mind, he pulled over when he saw a welcoming roadside diner, its bright signage declaring it made the best peach pie in the whole county. His stomach growled. It had been a long time since he'd eaten. Cutting the engine, he stepped out onto rusty red soil. Powdery and dry, it was whipped by the slight breeze into a cloud of fine grain. It occurred to him then as he made his way over the dusty carpark to the entrance, that the racial questions facing America, as well as the legacy of Vietnam, the shadows of Kennedy and the cloud of Watergate that continued to hang over the political establishment were well-worn subjects to write about. He needed something fresh to explore--a scandal the press either chose to ignore, or not pursue.

The thalidomide scandal.
The subject closest to my heart.

The official line was that the country had escaped the devastation of the drug. The scandal had briefly flared, and the crisis had led to modern drug safety laws, but what about all the forgotten victims? Interviewing Kelsey, he learned that nobody knew how many victims there were.

That alone was shocking enough, a story in itself.

About to skip up the steps to the door, he briefly glanced round as a black Pontiac pulled alongside his Chevy. As there hadn't been many cars on the road, he recognised it from a few miles back.

Entering, he was greeted with a blast of steamy air mixed with the aroma of freshly brewed coffee and a smiling waitress who led him to a cosy booth. The walls were covered with movie posters coupled with bold, colourful signs featuring popular American brands such as Coca-Cola. A teenager was feeding coins into a heavy-duty jukebox in the corner and a moment later the voices of Elton John and Kiki Dee singing 'Don't Go Breaking My Heart' filled the restaurant. Jasper studied the menu and after deciding what he wanted, slotted it into the holder beside the condiments, his gaze now drawn to the lanky teenager as she wandered back to her table, sliding in beside an older woman. The girl was around the same age as Toby and a pang of guilt spread across his chest when he realised he'd barely thought about the lad in the last few days. She looked like Toby's friend Lucy, and he wondered if they were still in contact. It had been a difficult friendship, unrequited love and there had been times when he'd seen the pain in Toby's face. He'd loved her dearly, but the feelings were never going to be reciprocated.

After ordering sausage and chips and a coffee, Jasper watched them chatting, aware of the driver of the black Pontiac sliding in the booth behind him. There was a certain familiarity about him.

As he watched the girl flick her long blonde hair back, his heart skipped a beat. He squinted to reduce the glare––the lights were bright, maybe he was finding it difficult to focus. But when she turned her head, there was no mistaking, nothing wrong with his eyesight.

The girl had no ears.

He averted his gaze, knowing what it must be like to have strangers gawk, but anger had started to well inside him. He wondered if she was a victim of Kevadon.

Jesus, somebody should be accountable for the misery caused by those drug trials.

These families needed recognition and financial support. Americans liked to be seen to be setting an example to the rest of the world as the gold standard of democracy and free speech, and yet the story of these victims was hushed up in a cesspit of secrecy, corruption, and incompetence.

It took every ounce of control not to wander over and ask questions, but how rude that would be. It wasn't appropriate or professional, and Jasper always prided himself on his etiquette and sensitivity. But on the other hand, if he wasn't bold, if he didn't break social norms––how were stories ever to be heard?

As he watched them talk, the girl grew irate.

'Mom, stop treating me like a baby,' she shrieked.

The mother, raising her eyebrows at Jasper, shook her head in despair. Just then, the girl's elbow hit the plastic condiment bottle. The bottle's contents, a big dollop of thick red ketchup spurted from its mouth. It fell from the table, landing hard on the floor, exploding in every direction across the checkered tiles.

'Now look what you've done. It's all over me.' Flustered, the girl slid from the booth and headed for the toilets.

'Kids,' she said to Jasper with a tut. 'Have you got a difficult daughter too? I'm sure boys are easier.' There was a quiver of laughter in her voice.

This was his chance, and he was going to seize it. 'I have a handicapped son.'

'You're English.'

'Yes.'

'My daughter's handicapped. I don't know if you noticed. She was born without ears, not that that's an excuse for her kicking off. She's got a dreadful temper on her.' The woman lit a cigarette and sucked hard on the tip, exhaling her frustration, and sending thin plumes of smoke eddying into the air. He noticed she had the kind of diamond-patterned skin that came with heavy smoking. 'Maybe my smoking caused the deformity, I've always wondered. I should give up, it'll be the death of me.'

'Probably nothing to do with your smoking. I'm no doctor, but that's my hunch.'

'What wrong with your son?'

'He's fifteen and has no arms.'

'Holy shit. I thought my Clara had it bad. What caused that then?'

Jasper's food had just arrived, which was unfortunate, but determined to continue the conversation, he pushed his plate aside and took a swig of coffee.

'It was a drug called thalidomide. I'm sure you've heard of it. His mother took it for morning sickness.'

The woman looked blank, and the girl returned to the table still grumbling about her top. 'It's stained, ruined.'

Jasper wished the girl wasn't there. The woman might have been more candid without her, but he pressed on regardless. 'Did you take any sickness pills when you were pregnant?'

From behind him, he heard a man cough loudly. It was bizarre, but there was something about the cough that he recognised.

'Never heard of it.' The woman shrugged and took another drag of her cigarette. 'I've got a couple of friends that had babies with deformities. I think it's inbreeding. Both married second cousins. That's what inbreeding does, causes birth defects. You only have to look at the Amish in Pennsylvania. Many of their kids have deformities.' She gave a cackling laugh. 'Don't let your food go cold.'

He reached for cutlery and a napkin. 'Nice talking to you. You from round here?'

'Few miles up the highway. Place called Plains.'

'That's where I'm heading.'

'I thought as much. Place is teeming with journalists. I'll be glad when this election's over and we can get our lives back.'

She nudged her daughter to get up. 'Come on, let's get out of here, your dad will be home.'

After she left, Jasper picked at his meal, his eyes fixed on a tree outside, each bite bringing a new question to ponder. He couldn't believe that the woman hadn't heard of thalidomide. Absent ears were one of the birth defects. It was odd how she didn't seem interested in the cause and blamed inbreeding. Before William McBride's discovery, this was one among many explanations doctors gave for the deformities. But this was 1976, not 1960. If the woman was representative of many others who'd given birth to children with deformities, this was a nation bathing in ignorance.

As he sat there puzzling, an older man with a beard and wearing a lumberjack shirt sat on a bar stool at the counter to his left. The man turned and smiled at him.

'I couldn't help overhearing your conversation. You're a newshound, from England?'

'We have a reputation for aggressively pursuing stories, but I hope that's not me.' Jasper chuckled. 'Your own journos are probably far worse.'

'You here for the election then?'

'Yes. You live round here?'

The man took a deep breath. There was something about him that looked shifty. But if that was the case, why had he started the conversation? Jasper noticed his eyes narrow as he regarded him with what looked like suspicion, and he shoved his hands deep into his pockets as he rose from his bar stool and came over.

'Mind if I join you?' Not waiting for Jasper to answer, he slid into the booth. Jasper caught a whiff of stale cigar smoke and coffee breath. He wished the man had stayed where he was, but now, as they sat facing each other, Jasper had the feeling that he wanted to talk to him about something important.

'Be my guest.'

'I take it you've not heard of the Hope Canal Disaster?'

'No.'

'That's how that kid and the others in the community got their birth defects. Disasters like Hope Canal are happening right across this nation, and I very much doubt the likes of Jimmy Carter or Gerard Ford care much. Because at the end of day, it's about protecting big business. Big business finances their campaigns and lines their pockets. You'll know about the power of the gun lobby. The way they influence state and federal policy on guns is by chucking a shedload of money. The millions they donate to the Republicans. Same with the chemical companies.'

'And pharmaceutical companies, like Richardson-Merrell?'

'I heard you mention thalidomide. You're barking up the wrong tree. The FDA are the best in the world. While you allowed the drug over in Europe, we didn't.'

'But it was being prescribed by the back door, GPs were dishing it out like Smarties and without labelling there was nothing to tell those poor mothers what they were taking. There could be thousands of children out there affected.'

'I'd be careful if I were you. Like I say, you're barking up the wrong tree. Hope Canal was one of the most appalling environmental tragedies in our history. And worse, it's not an isolated event. It could happen again, anywhere, and those damn politicians don't care. The idea was to build a short canal between two rivers to generate power cheaply to fuel the industry and homes. In the 1920s it was turned into a municipal and industrial chemical dumpsite.'

'That was decades ago.'

He glanced round and lowered his voice. 'In the fifties, the owners covered the canal, and homes and a school were built at the site. It was a chemical time bomb. Corroding waste-disposal drums could be seen breaking up through the ground, trees and gardens were turning black, one swimming pool was a sea of chemicals. There were puddles of noxious substances and everywhere the air had a faint, choking smell. Children had burns on their faces. And then there were the miscarriages and birth defects. And high white blood cell counts were detected too. Whole thing was a nightmare. I'm not saying that girl's defects are down to Hope Canal, but there's a bigger picture than thalidomide. In fact, the likelihood of the birth defects resulting from a drug that wasn't even on the market are close to zero.'

Jasper was horrified. The blatant dismissal shocked him to the core, and the unwillingness to be open-minded. What hope for justice did the innocent victims of thalidomide have with these attitudes swilling around?

'I can see you're sceptical, Mr, sorry I didn't catch your name?'

'Cooper, call me Jasper.'

'I don't need to tell you, that any good journalist worth their salt will explore every angle and if you're really here to explore birth defects you should look into the chemical industry and also exposure to atomic radiation.'

'Radiation?'

'Yep. Radiation from nuclear tests. Radioactive pollution made its way into the environment and food supply. Millions have been exposed to tremendous amounts of radiation.'

Jasper stared at his plate for a few moments while he considered the theories this man was hitting him with. He didn't know much about the effects of exposure to atomic radiation. This was a whole new area of study and a path he didn't want to embark on. He glanced at the man. Instinct told him the man was hiding something.

'Peel the layers, find the truth,' the man said, looking at him through bright blue eyes before turning his gaze to the door and sliding out of the booth.

'What do you think of Jimmy Carter?' Jasper asked as the man stood and was about to head off.

He swept a hand through his hair. 'Ford only became president because Nixon was thrown out following Watergate. It left a big scar on the Republican Party. Whatever they do, they'll be kicked out.' He paused, shook his head. 'But this Carter fella. Outside these parts, he's unknown. And a peanut farmer, that's got to be a joke. The guy's a devoted family man, religious and hey, maybe it's time for change. They're fed up with scandals, whether it's the lies of pharmaceutical companies or the chemical industry, unanswered questions surrounding Chappaquiddick or Watergate, they want politicians they can trust. That's what this election is about.'

'I've heard that Carter steers clear of delicate issues. His campaign has been about open government, yet he's secretive and cautious.'

'Nobody really knows what his manifesto is. I'm not sure he's up to the top job.'

'Who are his supporters?'

'Right here, in the South. Anyway, I must get going, nice talking to you. And a word of advice, thalidomide, if that's the subject that interests you, go back to Europe. There are thousands of victims over there.'

Jasper turned to watch him go. The Pontiac driver was still sitting behind him and coughed in a false and irritating way. This was the second time in as many days that he felt as if his conversation was being overheard.

It was time he headed off. He'd booked a motel a short distance away. He went over to the till and the waitress handed him the bill. As he sorted the change in his hand, she asked if he had far to go. 'A motel not far from here. Called The Peach.'

'Everything in Georgia is about the peach. Grows well in our red clay. I hope you like peaches.' She gave him a broad smile.

'Did you know that fella I was talking to, by the way?'

'Everyone knows Doctor Wilson. He's retired now but was one of the finest doctors. He saved my auntie's life.'

'What sort of doctor?'

'Just a country doctor.'

Jasper headed to the door, puzzled. If he was widely known, surely the woman and her daughter knew him. Or maybe they lived in a different neighbourhood.

As he unlocked the car door, a new thought abruptly dawned on him. It was as if a lightbulb had switched on.

The man was a country doctor guilty of dishing out thalidomide.

Pregnant women in his care gave birth to babies with deformities.

Jasper got into the car and shuddered. Carefully shifting the conversation to other disasters, the man had tried to lead him down a different path. How easy it would be to get sucked into a vortex. In this land of freedom and democracy, this was a cover-up, another scandal to sit alongside Watergate and Chappaquiddick.

Starting the engine, he glanced in the mirror to see Pontiac Man pull away, also indicating to turn right. There was something that unsettled him. He entertained the possibility that he was being followed, but quickly dismissed it as a fanciful notion found only on the screen of James Bond movies.

CHAPTER 18: SANDY

It was Mafia Tuesday, Arthur's joke when he referred to Irene's weekly WI meeting. It made Sandy smile. Her dad hadn't lost his wit after all these years of being married to a difficult woman. As Sandy stood waiting for the kettle to boil, she spooned tea leaves into the pot and when the water was ready, poured it and watched the steam rise. The inviting scent wafted through the air, a smell that made her think of home and growing up in this house. This simple act of making tea for her dad had created an atmosphere of closeness and rapport with him in recent days.

She pondered the secret of her parents' long marriage. How had he survived? It wasn't easy living with her mother. Did he quietly suffer, accepting his lot, for better for worse, in sickness and in health, because it was what his generation did? Maybe love was a form of madness and marriage a series of volcanoes. Sandy had been married for long enough to know that the heady early days of romance--gazing into each other's eyes with longing and passion—couldn't and didn't last and anyone believing that was deluded, but she found it hard to imagine her parents in the early days, gooey-eyed and lovey-dovey.

As she carried the tea tray through, she realised how little she knew about how her parents had met and fallen in love. She nudged the door to the front room with her elbow. If they'd been in love, the love no longer burned brightly, its light had faded, and a hard wax had formed around it.

'Where did you and Mum meet?' Bringing a new life into the world had a profound impact on her mind and heart. She couldn't help but wonder about their story. She wondered about the love and care they must have showered on her as a baby, the sacrifices they made and the hopes and dreams they had when they met. She put the tray on the coffee table and picked up Angela. As she planted a tender kiss on her forehead, something overwhelming surged through her. The enormity of responsibility that came with bringing a child into the world. Had they felt this too? The notion that her own parents had once held her in the same tender embrace and had hoped for her growth and happiness added to a deeper meaning on her own parenting journey. The questions raced through her mind more quickly than her dad could answer. He was concentrating on pouring his tea while managing to keep his leg propped up. He sat back, teacup in one hand, Bourbon biscuit in the other and smiled at her. His crinkled eyes sparkled with a new light and his weathered skin seemed to smooth over, and in that moment, she knew her parents had been in love once upon a time, a love that had changed over the years to a quiet acceptance of each other's ways.

'We met at a tea dance.' His eyes twinkled as he remembered. 'I was shy, never said boo to a goose. I'd noticed her on the other side of the room. Thought she looked all right, in a red spotted dress and red shoes to match. She noticed me too and as bold as brass came marching over and insisted we have a dance.'

Sandy laughed.

'The shadow of war loomed large.' Abruptly he stopped talking. His eyes had been animated and sparkly, but they glazed over and took on a vacant expression. It was as if he was no longer in the room but miles away.

It was a few moments before he spoke again. 'The world was changing, our future uncertain. But we forgot our worries and went dancing and skating and we covered a fair few miles round the park putting the world to rights.' He shrugged and Sandy couldn't read his thoughts. 'Marrying your mum, it felt like the right thing to do.'

'You loved her though?'

He didn't answer, his eyes glazed over again, and his face had turned a shade of grey.

A strange sensation crawled over her, a sense that there was something he didn't want to tell her.

'Love.' The way he said it, it sounded hollow and devoid of emotion. 'She needed me. After what she'd been through.'

'Her mother walking out?'

'Yes, and I suppose I accepted how things were going to be.'

Sandy frowned, confused. What did he mean? His choice of words was strange. 'You did love Mum?'

He looked embarrassed. 'She can be a funny old stick, but I wouldn't be without her.'

'How long were you married before you had me?'

He shifted his bottom on the settee. 'You and your questions, love. About time you took the dog for a walk.'

'Sorry, Dad. Having Angela has made me curious. You and Mum never talk about the past.'

He slapped his knee. 'Focus on the present, girl. Get that dog walked, then how about you nip back up into the loft before your mum comes back. I need something else fetching down.'

Adrenaline surged through her, whipping her heart into a frenzy. She didn't relish the prospect of a brush with a spider, but this was what she'd been waiting for, a chance to climb back into the loft and bring the red box down.

'I'll do it now in case Mum comes back early. What do you need, Dad?'

'Good idea.' He threw her a conspiratorial look. 'When you were up there last, did you see a pile of old books? They're near the hatch. Your mum doesn't like me reading books on the war, but I get bored of the telly, be a nice change to read.'

'Why wouldn't she like you reading about the war?'

'I don't know, you'll have to ask her.' Her mother never ceased to amaze her with her funny ways. Surely, she would be glad that he was being entertained. Anything to make her life easier and quieter, seemed to be Irene's motto.

She went upstairs and positioned the stepladder under the hatch. As she began to climb, she felt excited by the prospect that she'd finally get to open the box. When she'd seen it up there it had felt like stumbling upon a long-forgotten heirloom, something special that might offer a glimpse into the past. What secrets might it reveal? Perhaps a piece of jewellery that had once belonged to an ancestor or a set of letters. Regardless of what was inside, it was the box itself that mattered. It was too lovely to be sitting in a dusty loft, unused and forgotten. It needed to occupy a place of pride on a shelf or mantel. When her mother saw it again, she'd be thrilled, Sandy was sure of that––and the smile she'd bring to her face.

Sandy was kneeling now in the loft. Excitement coursed through her as she reached for the pile of books and took them down before returning for the box. She couldn't see well in the gloom and wished she'd plugged the lamp in.

Spotting it, she moved items out of the way before nudging it gently towards the hatch. Taking care not to fall, she descended the ladder with the box under one arm. It smelt musty. Her mother had probably long forgotten it and would be delighted to see it again, or maybe Irene would simply scoff and tell her to sling it in the bin.

As soon as she was back on the landing, and with her dad

calling for his books, she slipped into her bedroom to find somewhere to hide the box. The next challenge would be the key on her mother's gold chain. Hopefully she'd have a bath that evening and leave her chains either on the kitchen table or in her bedroom.

After wrapping the box in a towel and hiding it under her bed before putting the ladder away, she took the books down to her dad.

'You better slip them behind here,' he said, pointing to the side of the settee with a wink. 'I'll be able to read them when she's not around.'

Sandy hovered in the doorway, unsure whether to tell him she had the box. Maybe it was best not to, she'd only stir up a hornet's nest if her mother found out. She went to get the dog's lead and assembled the base of the pram before clipping the carrycot onto it. She needed a walk, and the dog certainly did.

Out in the fresh air and striding along, she was able to think more clearly. Stopping at the bench by the pond, she checked on Angela and sat down, watching the Canada geese swim across the water with such grace then diving and returning to the surface as if looking for something in the murky waters. They reminded her of her quest to know more about her childhood. Her dad had been evasive and changed the subject when she had asked. Was his memory starting to fade? She wondered how long it would be before he had his plaster removed. Her mum wouldn't need her then and she could return to normality whatever that might now be.

Her thoughts turned to Jasper and a pang of guilt surged inside. They still hadn't spoken since she'd left and although she had tried to call him, he was never there. It hurt that he hadn't called; was she in his thoughts? She made up her mind to try again and if no joy she would ring the office. She also wondered how Toby was getting on.

Her stream of thought was interrupted by Tibs, who began

pulling on his lead and barking. A duck was waddling along the bank. Then she suddenly saw the figure of Eddie heading her way.

'Hi, Sandy, nice to see you again.' He breezed up and sat down. 'See you're enjoying the sunshine and wildlife. I'm just on my break.' Tibs was jumping up at him trying to get some attention. 'If you're free soon, why don't we meet up? Be great to have a proper chat. Soon you'll be gone again.'

Sandy frowned. She wasn't sure when that would be, but it would be nice to chat to someone her own age and have a laugh.

'That would be nice. This week?'

'Great. I'll give you a call to see when you're free, then we can decide what to do. Must go now, back to work to earn my keep. See you soon, Sandy, and take care.'

Sandy watched him disappear from view. She liked him, he made her feel at ease even after all these years.

She stood up, tightened her grip around the lead and headed back to the house. Irene was back and the radio was blaring generic pop and shouty ads.

'Wipe your feet,' she barked, glancing round from the sink. 'I've just cleaned the floor.' She was bashing away on the washing board trying to get a stain out of her blouse.

'You can peel the potatoes and veg. Make your dad a cup of tea and make yourself useful. You're not on holiday, my girl.' Sandy wondered why she was so accepting of the way her mother spoke to her.

'After dinner,' she continued, 'I'm having a long hot soak in the bath. I need it after the morning I've had. You can look after your dad so I can relax for a while.'

Sandy winced. Poor Dad, did he have to put up with this all day?

They ate dinner in near silence, which was the normal pattern, *never speak while you're eating. You will choke* and *it's the height of bad manners*. She could hear her mum's voice. Words that were stamped on her mind from an early age, just like Coleman's mustard and Bovril.

'I wish that dog wouldn't keep looking up at me while I'm eating. It should sit in its basket.'

'That's what dogs do, I'm afraid. He's waiting for you to throw him a scrap of chicken.'

'You haven't trained him properly. You encourage him to beg. I've seen better behaved dogs.' She sniffed and carried on eating, looking irritated at the presence of Tibs beside her.

Sandy washed up, fed Angela, and changed her nappy in the bathroom before letting Tibs into the garden.

'Make your dad a cup of tea,' her mum said as she trudged upstairs to the bathroom.

She mused that her dad must be a human teapot the amount he drank. It was a wonder he hadn't drowned in it. She made the tea and took it in, but her dad was snoring. She wouldn't wake him; it was the only time he seemed to be at peace.

She gently closed the door and went back into the kitchen. She could hear her mum banging around upstairs. Glancing round, she saw it. The glittering sparkle caught her eye. There on the sideboard was her mum's necklace in a heap next to her earrings.

She tiptoed over and picked it up, twirling it in her fingers. There on the end was a small brass key so small you would hardly notice it.

The key to the red box.

Her heart leapt.

She rushed up the stairs as quietly as she could, knelt by the bed and pulled out the box. The key fitted like a hand in a glove and as she turned it, there was a small click, and the catch sprang open. She longed to open the lid, but fright took hold. She pushed it back into its hiding place and sat for a few moments, her heart banging in her chest, unnerved by the emotions welling inside.

Why was she feeling like this? It was just an old box. Except that it was so much more than a box. It was the not knowing what was inside, her mind was running riot. She realised how little she knew about her mother's life. There might be something unsettling inside, something deeply personal, something she wanted to keep hidden, and she was invading her privacy. She didn't have permission to open it. But if her mother wasn't so secretive, wasn't such a difficult person, she wouldn't be curious or suspicious that she was harbouring unresolved issues and traumas.

She crept downstairs, and with trembling hands put the necklace back where she found it. In her mind she imagined the box contained family secrets and everything she needed to know to understand her mother better.

She stood at the sink and stared outside.

I'll never understand her. She's closed off, cold. I can't connect with her on a deeper level. There is no warmth or kindness and never will be.

That beautiful red box and what she might discover inside symbolised everything--especially hope and understanding.

The box was open, but she wasn't ready to look inside.

CHAPTER 19: BILL

Bill's legs ached. He hadn't walked this far in years, and it left his chest tight. He realised he wasn't as fit as he'd been a few years back. Despite his aches and pains, it was pleasant up on the heath. He followed the Hindhead Common trail, a stunning landscape of open heathland and shady woods, a glorious mosaic of purple, greens, and gold. He spotted grazing cattle and ponies and views over the distant London skyline.

There was so much to discover in Surrey and yet he rarely had the time to explore. The peaceful silence of the natural world enveloped him, allowing his thoughts to drift freely. It was a welcome contrast to the busyness of his daily routine where the incessant demands left him drained and disconnected from himself and from Toby. Hours at the school fixing problems, an endless grind, a never-ending cycle of work, bed, work, bed.

As he gazed out over the countryside, he realised how much of his life had been about survival rather than pleasure. He'd long given up the idea of chasing happiness as if it were a butterfly. Real life had delivered disappointment, responsibility, duty, and heartache. His happiest years had been with Rona particularly those early days of courting, planning their future, and a family. And then, years down the line, the realisation it was never going to be. Rona had felt the loss like a severed artery.

Then Toby came along and the light in her eyes shone bright again.

But their lives weren't the same from that day on.

Sometimes he felt like Dorothy caught in a tornado, unsure where he'd land, but he wouldn't have been without Toby. The boy had brought so much joy and tested every resource he had. If the human condition didn't involve struggle, what was life about?

He sat on a bench to rest and watched a feather fluttering in the air, light and carefree. Like happiness it couldn't stay in the air for long and soon plummeted to the dry earth. He sighed. What was there to look forward to? He couldn't ever imagine a point in the future when he'd be happy again. His life was about firefighting, battling through, paying the bills, just getting to the end of each year in one piece. He'd worked so hard to support Toby--for what?

His heart sank and his body flopped against the wooden slats. Being unappreciated left him with an ache across his chest. He couldn't do anything right. It was hopeless. These days all he saw in Toby's eyes was resentment and bitterness. Every parent made mistakes; no one was perfect. For all the criticising Toby did, Bill knew he was a good parent. He wasn't expecting gratitude, but he deserved respect. He was tired of his surly ways, the raised eyebrows, the tuts, the moods. Toby's world had been shattered, he got that, totally. His sense of self had been thrown into disarray and confusion--but sweet Jesus, the lad had to get over it. At some point he needed to accept. They couldn't go on like this.

He was running out of ideas--where did he go from here?

That evening at Jasper's, he'd pinned his hopes on repairing their relationship, but it had fractured even further.

And now, the worst possible scenario.

Toby wanted to live with Jasper and Sandy.

All he felt was complete despair.

Bloody Jasper. He has everything. Success, charm, charisma, wit, ambition, drive. I can't compete with any of that. I may as well give up.

It pained him––that look of admiration in Toby's eyes, all for Jasper. He knew that look; he'd always seen it in the lad's eyes. Toby looked up to him.

The rejection he felt was crushing, as if a vice was squeezing the blood from his heart. And then a new random thought came to him.

One day Toby might be a dad and Jasper and Sandy will be grandparents.

With his heart quietly breaking, he dipped his head and stared at the feather lying in the mud. The boy who had once adored him was slipping out of his life like sand through fingers.

He rose from the bench and glanced at the view. If only he'd told Toby when he was little that he was adopted, it might have helped. But the risk of people finding out the truth was too huge, and Rona had been terrified of the consequences. So had he.

As Bill walked back along the sandy track to the truck, he recalled the times when he'd nearly blurted it. Toby had been around eight years old, and they were looking through old photographs. The boy had asked lots of questions about the different family members in the pictures. And another time when he'd almost told him was when a neighbour had made a stupid joke about him not looking like either his mum or dad. "He's so handsome," the neighbour had said, "the postman must be his father".

All those years he'd kept their secret, to protect Rona.

Yet on her deathbed, had she considered him when she'd pleaded with him to bring Toby to the hospice to tell him the truth?

Rona lived a life of lies, wanted to die a death of truths.

Her last chance to set things straight, a peaceful death maybe–– but knowing I'd be left with the fallout.

And that was why he hadn't taken Toby to see her.

Now that the clocks had changed, dusk was descending early as Bill's truck turned into the pot-holed lane. Up ahead, the cottage was shrouded in darkness. Toby must be up in his room, Bill thought, reading under torchlight. As he pulled up, it occurred to him there might be a power cut. They'd had a couple of those over the past few weeks. He'd had to go to the school to reset the timers.

Guilt clawed at him as he opened the front door. It had been his turn to strop, the reason why he'd stayed out all day. But he'd needed that time alone to process his thoughts and step away from everything that was going on.

Warily he trudged into the kitchen, tossed his keys on the table, and kicked his boots off. Seeing the dirty dishes piled in the sink, he groaned, but rather than tackle it all he put the kettle on and sat down.

Christ, how could anyone live like such a pig? No wonder Toby has a go.

He finished his tea, and a voice inside told him to do it now not tomorrow. He started tidying up and clumsily knocked a pan off the side. *Damn*, he thought as the contents spilled to the floor. He grabbed the bin to scoop up the slimy baked beans only to find it full. He hadn't emptied it in days. And then he saw them, nestled among the debris––several cans of beer.

How he longed right then for a drink, but his conscience pricked. He'd made a pact with Jasper and Toby to stop drinking and he was determined to stick to it.

The next half hour was spent busily tidying up until not a cup or a plate was out of place. He stood back, wiped his hands on the tea towel and admired the cups standing like ducks in a row, feeling proud of himself. And not only had he cleared up, but he hadn't cracked a bottle open.

His mind turned to dinner; what to eat? He trundled up the stairs to see what Toby fancied.

'How are you, Toby, what do you want for dinner?' he asked on the landing behind the closed door.

There was no answer.

'Come on, Toby, I'm tired.' About to walk away, he felt something wasn't right. There was no sound coming from the bedroom, not even a grunt.

He opened the door and peered across to his bed. Switching on the light, he realised he wasn't there, and his backpack seemed to be missing too.

Back on the landing, he called out as he checked every room, but it was only a small cottage and didn't take long.

Deflated, he slumped onto a kitchen chair. He'd have to eat alone tonight. He hated eating alone and was glad of Toby's company even if his conversation consisted of grunts or short simple sentences like a Ladybird book. He was probably round at a friend's house and would come back shortly.

He made a cheese and tomato sandwich and piled his plate with crisps, had another cuppa and crashed out in the armchair, arms splayed, feet on the pouffe. As he was about to drop off, the phone rang startling him, and he jumped up to answer it, cursing under his breath.

'Hello, Bill, it's the school.'

'Bloody hell, now what's happened?' Unblocking a toilet was the last thing he wanted to deal with on a Saturday evening.

'It's not a maintenance issue, it's about your son, Toby. I'm Sheila, one of the nurses. We have met.'

'What's happened?'

'There's been a bit of an accident.'

Shock hit and he felt all floaty.

'Accident, what do you mean?'

'There's nothing to worry about. He fell over in the woods and has sprained his ankle and might have concussion. He banged his head on a tree. He's okay though. He's not in hospital. He's lying here in the sick bay.'

A tickle rose in the back of his throat, and he couldn't immediately answer. Within seconds it turned into an explosive coughing fit which rattled his whole body and left his chest constricted. 'I'll be up in a minute,' he managed to say through splutters.

'Sounds like you've got a nasty cough.'

'Sorry, didn't mean to cough in your ear. I'll be right there.'

When Bill arrived at the school, he went straight to the sick bay where Toby sat looking battered and bruised and feeling sorry for himself.

'Okay, kiddo,' he chirped, hoping to raise his spirits but he could see that Toby wasn't in the mood.

'Come in, Bill, and sit down. Toby's had a fall in the woods. He couldn't get up and lay there for a few hours. A dog walker found him. We tried ringing you several times but there was no answer.'

'I went for a walk. I thought he was with friends.'

'He's sprained his right foot and he's got slight concussion where he banged his head, but apart from that, he's okay.' She smiled.

Bill's cough returned. He could feel his chest tightening as his body was wracked with coughing spasms. Desperately he tried to suppress it, covering his mouth with his hand as the nurse went over to the sink in the corner of the room, poured a glass of water and handed it to him. After it had subsided, he was left panting and sweaty, his chest heaving as he struggled to catch his breath.

'Sorry about that,' he said to the nurse before turning to Toby. 'Come on, boy, let's get you home. If you will go chasing the birds, that's what happens.'

Toby got up, wincing as he put his foot on the floor.

'Just wait outside a moment, Toby, while I have a word with your dad.'

Bill watched Toby hobble out of the room and the nurse shut the door and turned to him.

'The lad's going to be okay? Have you got more worries about him you don't want him to hear?' She was alarming him.

'He'll be fine, just make sure he rests for a few days. It's you I'm worried about.' She was peering at him with her hands on her hips. 'I'm a little concerned about your cough. I know you've had it a few days because I've heard you coughing along the corridor.'

'Maybe a week, I can't seem to shift it, it's just a cough.'

'I don't like the sound of it. You need to get that checked out. Peace of mind. We can't afford for you to be going downhill now Toby's got an injury. You're going to have to run around more than usual in the next couple of weeks because he'll need to take the weight off his feet.'

'I'll give the doctor a call on Monday.'

'See that you do.'

Bossy woman. Why do women fuss so much? Rona was the same until she became the one who needed looking after.

He thanked the nurse and went to join Toby in the corridor. After finding a wheelchair he pushed him along the corridor to the exit.

Back home, Bill manoeuvred him through to the kitchen where Toby let out a gasp. 'Bloody hell, Dad, what's happened? I've not seen it this tidy since Mum died.'

'It wasn't that bad.' Bill gave him a cheeky smile. It was bad and they both knew it.

'Not that bad? You've got to be kidding me.' Toby let out a

full-bodied laugh. 'Steptoe's backyard has less crap. What happened? Did you fall over and bang your head too?

'Maybe,' Bill chuckled. 'So, tell me what happened in the wood.'

'I had things on my mind.' Toby got out of the wheelchair and hobbled to the armchair, sinking into it.

'What things? What's troubling you, son? What were you thinking about as you trundled through the woods?'

'Mum,' he muttered.

The air went still. All he heard was the rasp of the intake of his breath.

Bill glanced at him, saw his eyes were a glassy sheen. He quickly looked away, didn't want to see the anguish.

'I've been thinking about her too. Can't believe how long it's been.' One of the strange things about grief, he thought, was the way it ambushed when you least expected it. In those early days he'd felt like a sandcastle when the tide came in, but now, several years later, he wasn't going to fall apart but quietly accepted that grief had become a part of him, like waking up to a severed limb each morning. It was hard, but he'd learned to cope.

'What were you thinking about, Toby?' His question was almost a whisper.

'The last few days of her life.'

'Last few days, why?' He sat on the edge of the settee and faced Toby.

'I wasn't there. You wouldn't let me see her. I wanted to say goodbye. I wonder what she might have said to me, what advice she would have given. I never had the chance to say what I wanted to say.'

'We could visit her grave. You could talk to her.'

'It's not the same. I wanted to see her.'

'I know, son, it was a tough time. Your mum was very ill, and I wanted to save you from the pain of seeing her suffer.

Better to remember her as she was. One day you'll understand.'
Tears welled in Bill's eyes, his voice cracked, and he couldn't hold back the emotion anymore. Tears flowed down his cheeks, sadness hitting his heart like a bolt. So many things he wanted to say--all the pain and hurt unlocking like a lion unleashed. There was so much he wanted to share with Toby but couldn't.

Toby stared at him. Bill knew what he was thinking--he'd never seen his dad like this. He'd always managed to hold it together, at least in front of his son. Toby looked distraught too and, in that moment he seemed older, giving Bill a glimpse of what Toby might be like in a decade or two.

A tickle rose in his throat, and he coughed, trying not to sound breathless, but it felt as if he had a bus parked on his chest.

'That nurse was right, you should see a doctor. You've been coughing for days.'

'Women worry. You'll find that out when you're older.'

'The part that hurts the most is Mum didn't want to see me. It didn't matter what she looked like. Look at me, for God's sake. I don't need to be protected all my life. I have feelings too, I couldn't tell her I loved her. Why didn't she want to see me?'

'She did, son, she really did, but...' His voice trailed away.

He remembered her pleading, begging for him to bring Toby but it was out of desperation to tell Toby the truth, clear her conscience before she departed. Her twisted fingers had clawed at his hand and her face was as frail and white as an eggshell. How could he have subjected Toby to that? Death hovering in the room. All those years ago when he was younger, she could have sat him down on her lap and told him. But on her deathbed--it was the wrong time. He imagined Toby's endless stream of questions.

Why tell me now when you are about to leave me?

Bill rose and sat on the arm of Toby's chair. He put his hand on his shoulder and pulled him close. For once Toby didn't pull away.

'It bothers me, Dad, I feel like she never wanted to say goodbye. It leaves a big hole wondering what we might have said. One last touch, one last smile, one last hug.'

Bill was breaking up; deep inside he knew that he would have to tell Toby the reason why he'd refused to let Toby see her, but a part of him wanted to lock that secret away forever because why did he need to tell him? It would only bring more pain and a further deterioration of their relationship. How was he ever going to rebuild the trust, help him feel secure?

Before he went to open his mouth to speak, he had a sense the boy already knew the truth. Was it the anguish on his face that gave him away, a look in his eyes, or even his posture? Toby was perceptive, a sensitive lad, in some ways old beyond his years and he picked up on people's emotions. There was no deceiving him.

'There's something you're not telling me, Dad.'

Bill looked away.

'She wanted to tell me, that's why you stopped me seeing her.'

Bill stood up, sweeping his hand through his hair as he paced the room. 'I was losing the love of my life, I was broken, I barely had the strength to live from day to day. I couldn't have coped back then with all the questions you would have had, some of which I had no answer to.'

'Damn you.' Toby suddenly exploded in rage. He stood up, wincing in pain as his bad foot connected with the floor. 'How could you, Dad, how could you have deprived me of my last moments with Mum just to protect your feelings?' He pushed him away, but his leg buckled as he crashed back into the chair.

'It's always about you. How many other things haven't you told me? What other secrets have you got?' He looked at him then with pure venom. 'I wish Jasper was here now to hear what a shit you are.' He got up again and staggered towards the stairs. 'I never want to speak to you again, all you do is hurt me more than you can ever know. I'm going to my room.'

Bill stood back in shock; he knew that he should have kept quiet, but he wanted to be truthful, a clean slate, now all he'd done was add to the lad's pain. Would he ever learn?

Toby looked crestfallen. Bill watched him hobble on his good leg to the stairs. He fought the urge to help him, knowing he'd only bat him away. Toby sat on the step and got up the stairs on his bottom, wincing at every move. Bill knew it hurt like hell, but the pain would be nothing compared to the heartache he could see in his eyes. He so desperately wanted to help, to make things all right again. Anything, anything at all if the lad asked. It was agony to watch his boy, and he stepped forward to help.

'Stay away from me, you've done enough damage.'

CHAPTER 20: TOBY

The light streaming through Toby's bedroom curtains stirred him. He had no idea what time it was. How long had he slept? He remembered crawling into bed late, barely able to keep his eyes open.

Last night's conversation flooded back, and his heart quietly broke all over again. Another revelation so soon after the last; it was more than he could take, a step too far.

A sudden pang of pain shot through his ankle as he turned to face his bedside clock, his eyes wide in horror when he saw the time--midday. Then it all came back to him. Lying on the damp leaves of the wood, wanting to clutch his ankle, not being able to move, the cold seeping through him, wondering when and if someone would find him. Drifting to sleep against the rough bark of a tree, then waking, disorientated, panicked. Then a dog walker finding him. Luckily that had been before nightfall. The thought of sleeping in the wood had filled him with dread. The slightest noise--an owl hooting, or the flap of a bat or rustle of leaves would have sent shivers down his spine. It was over. He was at home in bed, warm and safe.

He shifted up the bed. His stomach was growling, he needed

to eat, but he didn't feel as if he could stand up. It felt as if he'd twisted his ankle. He remembered the nurse saying he might have torn a ligament. That sounded serious. How was he going to cope? His feet were his hands. Until his ankle healed, he would be using his mouth for tasks, and his dentist was always warning him not to because it was wearing the enamel down and he'd already chipped and cracked three of his teeth opening bottles and jars. He couldn't bear the thought of a couple of weeks lying in bed recovering and Bill waiting on him hand and foot. But thankfully that wasn't going to happen; on Monday morning his dad would be back at work.

He heard Bill stomping around downstairs and coughing incessantly. His cough was worse. Toby couldn't remember the last time he'd taken holiday leave. He needed a rest. He was always available when something needed fixing at the school. What a thankless job, Toby mused, fixing toilets that kept getting blocked, or fences that came down every time there was a storm.

There was a knock at the front door. Toby listened intently as someone entered the house. His dad was talking to a woman, and now they were at the foot of the stairs heading up. With each step, Bill gave a cough and along the landing he could hear him wheezing. Jeez, he was unhealthy. Probably the extra pounds he carried around his middle, Toby reckoned, and of course booze was loaded with sugar.

Hearing a tap at his bedroom door, he groaned. More fussing--he just wanted to be left alone. His ankle was going to get better, there was nothing anyone could do.

The nurse's smiling face appeared round the door. 'Morning, Toby, just come to check on you. And your dad.' Bill was hovering on the landing and looked almost too scared to enter the bedroom. Toby sussed the real reason she'd come. Her concern was more for Bill--that dreadful hacking cough.

'How's your foot today?' Her voice was all chirpy.

'Bit painful, I'm okay though.'

'How is it when you stand on it?'

Toby got up and stood in front of her. 'It hurts but it'll be fine.'

'Good. It might be an idea to get the doctor to check it out. And talking of doctors, I know it's Sunday, but you are going to ring the doctor tomorrow, Bill, aren't you? I think that cough is getting worse. What do you think, Toby?'

Toby couldn't look at his dad, let alone think about his needs. 'Dunno,' he muttered.

'Okay, well I'll leave you both in peace, just thought I'd call round to check.' She glanced at Bill. 'I'll see myself out, don't want you rushing downstairs. You should be in bed too taking it easy.'

'I'll be fine, don't you worry.'

'Well, I do,' she said in a soft voice. 'I know how hard you work.' She smiled up at him and as she spoke, she rested a hand on his arm.

In a flash, Toby saw it. An exchange between them, something in their eyes.

Yuk. She likes him.

Or maybe his imagination was running amok. He hadn't seen a woman pay attention to his dad, not in a long time. She was just doing her job, he reminded himself.

Over the course of the day, he avoided his dad. Right now, he didn't want to acknowledge his existence. Better to keep his mouth shut and be thought of as a grumpy teenager than to engage and find out more lies. He'd caused too much hurt; he deserved the cold shoulder. Spiteful words hurt, but silence broke the heart.

Sunday seeped into Monday, and Toby woke to Bill's violently coughing. Without giving it a moment's thought, he threw back the covers, twisted his legs out of bed and hobbled to his bedroom door. Maybe he still cared about his dad, or maybe he was finding it irritating, but he couldn't cope a moment longer listening to that annoying cough.

Bill was downstairs thumping around in his usual clumpy fashion, boiling water and making breakfast. The smell of brown toast and tangy marmalade wafted up. Delicious and irresistible, the slightly burnt aroma made him hungry. He headed downstairs.

'Morning, son, toast?' Bill waved a piece of bread at him.

'Yes please.' He moved a chair with his good foot and sat at the table.

'How's your foot today?' Bill came over with a mug of tea and put it in front of Toby.

'Not too bad. Your cough's getting worse.' It pained him to have to speak to his dad and took every ounce of effort, but he was worried.

'I've booked an appointment for nine.' Standing at the counter, he took the last of a mouthful of toast, cramming it into his mouth, the crumbs dropping onto the floor. More toast popped up and after buttering and spreading it with marmalade, he took the plate to Toby.

'Right, I best be off.' He wiped his hands on his trousers. 'I won't be long. Will you be okay?'

'Yeah,' he replied in a flat tone, and, not wanting him to think that he'd been forgiven, he didn't bother to wish him well.

He felt a wave of relief as soon as Bill stepped out of the house. Hopefully he'd be gone a while. No nagging, no awkward conversations, no expectations, just the freedom of being home alone. His bedroom was where he spent the bulk of his hours enveloped in his own world, but now he could relax and not worry about listening for his dad's footsteps on the stairs.

He gritted his teeth in frustration every time he thought about Bill. His very existence got on his nerves and the resentment bubbled away. And yet now, as he sat in the silence of the living room, he couldn't imagine life without him. As he slunk back upstairs, something disturbed him--just how sick was he?

CHAPTER 21: JASPER

Jasper's eyes snapped open in the pitch black, his groggy mind momentarily struggling to make sense of the unfamiliar surroundings. Then he remembered where he was, in a motel a few miles from Plains. Jerking himself upright, he reached for the bedside lamp but couldn't find the switch. Something had woken him. He wasn't sure if he'd heard a scratching noise or whether he'd dreamt it. A sense of unease washed over him as he stared at the door. Was someone trying to break in? He glanced at the clock by his bed; it was 3am.

The light under the canopy outside pinged on and illuminated the room. Someone's presence outside must have triggered it.

He still couldn't shake the feeling that he was being followed. He'd felt it in New York and yesterday arriving at the diner. He knew he was being ridiculous, but it was like a sixth sense had kicked in and he couldn't ignore it. He got out of bed, his bare feet padding softly on the floor, parted the curtain and peered through the glass.

A sense of foreboding crept over him. There it was, in the car park, a few metres from his window.

The black Pontiac.

Paranoia had set in during the previous evening when he'd made a note of the car number plate.

He shivered, closed the curtain, and stood back against the icy wall as he sank to the floor, cradling his knees, his heart thumping.

Am I losing sight of reality?

There was something about being in America. It felt safe but was that just an illusion? The gun was legal and so there was always the possibility of being caught in a deadly situation. Although America was like Britain in many ways, the right to bear arms created a cultural divide between the two countries. America was supposed to be a beacon of freedom and equality, yet there was a palpable tension simmering beneath the surface of everyday life––a fear that anyone at anytime and anywhere could pull out a gun. Knowing his luck, he'd be caught in the crossfire and never get to see Sandy again.

He'd been watching too many episodes of *The Streets of San Francisco*, *Hawaii Five-O* and *The Rockford Files*. Gritty action-packed scenes with car chases and shootouts which made America look crime-infested.

Just as calm washed over him, and he was about to get up and go back to bed, there was a sudden scratching noise at the door. The sound of metal scraping against metal. His heart leapt into his throat.

Shit, someone is breaking in.

He froze, his senses on high alert as his eyes darted round the room searching for a weapon. Reaching over on all fours, he yanked the lamp from its socket, snapping the cable. Clutching the lamp, he crawled to the other side of the bed and crouched out of view ready for whoever was about to gain entry.

His heart banged in his chest. The lampshade was no match

for a gun. A rising tide of fear and desperation threatened to engulf him, clawing at him like a beast in the dark.

With each passing moment the scratching grew closer. The door was about to give way. And then it did. His body tensed as a shadowy figure stepped into the room. He could see the silhouette at the bottom of the bed. The light snapped on.

As he cowered behind the bed like a frightened child, his heart was pounding so hard that it felt as though it was about to burst out of his chest. The air was thick with the sweet metallic scent of fear as he desperately tried to make himself invisible behind the thin valance covering the bed. He wished he was ten years old again and playing an innocent game of hide-and-seek.

The squeak of rubber soles on the floor; he looked up, to see a gun was pointing directly at him. The metal gleamed, the barrel steady and unwavering as it fixed on its target––him. When he saw the finger on the trigger ready to unleash a deadly shot, his vision went hazy, and he felt like passing out. His breathing was ragged and harsh in his ears as he waited for the end. His last thought was that he'd never get to reconcile with Sandy, never get the chance to say sorry.

The gun lowered. 'Get up, hands over your head, no jerky movements.'

Shaking, Jasper struggled to his feet feeling like a wobbly foal. He kept his eyes on the gun. *Slowly, slowly,* he told himself. His life was hanging by a thread.

'Sit on the bed.'

He followed the orders, heart still thumping and blood pulsing through his ears, all the time with his eyes fixed on the barrel of the gun.

His brain was briefly paralysed.

Just give him what he wants.

When Jasper found his voice, it sounded small and detached, as if it wasn't his. 'You want money?' He nodded towards his jeans on the floor. His wallet was in a pocket. 'Take it all.'

'I'm not interested in your money; I want to know why you're here?' With the gun still pointing at him, the man stepped backwards, grabbed the chair in the corner of the room, kicked it towards the bed and sat on it.

'You're the guy from New York.'

The overpowering aftershave the man was wearing wafted into his face, making him more nauseous than he already felt.

Jasper was sure it was the same man he'd seen in New York. His hair was dark and coarse, and his skin was rough. But was he the man in the diner? He wasn't sure. He was probably in his fifties. His bushy brows were furrowed, and he was scowling at Jasper. There was nothing about the man that made him look nervous, which made Jasper wonder if he'd threatened other people.

Who was he, what did he want?

'I'm from the UK.'

'I know that.' He crossed his leg over his knee and rested the gun in his lap.

Jasper felt relief of sorts wash through him. The man might be relaxing, but he wasn't out of danger.

Speak only when spoken to. Don't say anything that might wind him up.

'I'm here to cover the presidential election.' He couldn't deny the fact and if he lied, it might aggravate him.

'Really? Is that so?' His stare was icy and piercing.

'Yes, that's why I'm here,' he stuttered. 'To find out more about Jimmy Carter. It's where he grew up.' Bile was rising in his throat.

He didn't reply but continued to stare at Jasper as his bulging wet lips turned into a contemptuous sneer--a hateful, mocking expression that showed disdain and disgust.

It's a bloody election for God's sake. He wanted to scream at him. *There are hundreds of reporters out there interviewing and taking notes and knocking on doors.* Why was he being singled out?

What the hell have I done? I'm just an English reporter. I'm not even high profile.

Times like this, Jasper wished he wasn't a journalist––it was a risky profession. Reporters had been imprisoned for publishing stories critical of government in places like Saudi, but not here, not in the United States of America, the land of freedom and democracy.

Realising he was shivering and shaking, he clasped his hands to calm his nerves.

'Except that's just a smokescreen. We both know the real reason you're here.' He leaned closer. Jasper was glad the gun was still resting on his lap although that was small comfort. The man could turn at any moment. 'Digging up old dirt, picking at old wounds. People want to forget.' He spat the words and Jasper felt the spittle hit his face. 'Leave well alone.'

'You are the one in New York, when I was speaking to the veteran. You tell me about digging up old dirt. You've been following me.'

'What of it?'

'I'm nobody.'

'I'm warning you. There are people out there who will turn their gun on you if you chance your luck.'

Slowly it dawned on him.

Thalidomide.

'It's not your concern. The government will take care of the victims. Fuck off back to Britain and report about your own victims.' He grabbed the gun and for one awful moment, Jasper thought his life was about to end, but instead he sloped off towards the door and was gone.

Still on the bed, Jasper couldn't move as he tried to calm down. He was shaking so much and clutching his legs tight to his chest. He felt disorientated and vulnerable. He wouldn't be going back to sleep, not after that. The terror inside him started to abate, leaving him with a barrage of questions. Should he give up and go home? He had Sandy, Toby, and Angela to think of, they needed him, he couldn't put his life at risk for his job, it just wasn't worth it. But at the same time, he couldn't give up in the face of violent threats. The fact that he had been threatened was of massive significance, a story in itself, and only confirmed to him that underneath the surface of what had happened here in the late fifties and early sixties lay corruption, lies and a scandal of epic proportions. If he didn't dig, ask questions, and meet some of those families, he'd be letting them down, and the awful thing was that so many of them, including the woman and her daughter at the diner, didn't even know that the deformities were caused by the drug. They'd been lied to, fobbed off, cast aside.

Jasper unfurled his legs, the strength within him starting to flow once more as hot coils of anger burned in the pit of his stomach. As he was about to stretch his legs and go to the window to see if the car had gone, there was a noise outside his room. His heart leapt into his throat.

Fuck, he's back to finish me off.

The light switch was flipped, the room illuminated with brightness and the presence of a police officer at the entrance to his door.

'Sorry to disturb you, sir. I've just checked with reception, you're Mr Cooper?' The officer had a thick rolling southern drawl.

'Thank God you're here.' He started shivering again, maybe this time it was the relief, the release of all the fear and tension crippling his body.

'We had reports of a disturbance.' He turned to examine the door but without touching it. 'You've had a break-in?'

'Yes, not long ago. They were armed, didn't take anything.' He looked at the officer. He was an older guy with a pot belly and stubble, maybe at the end of his career. He reminded Jasper of a cross between Bill, and Karl Malden from *The Streets of San*

Francisco. The marks of his long career were etched all over him, from the lines that creased his weathered face––hours spent in the scorching southern sun––to the worn patch on his uniform sleeve. As he spoke with the confidence of a seasoned veteran, it was clear he'd seen many things in his career that had shaped his understanding of the world. He'd faced the dangers of his job and learned to keep his wits about him even in the most difficult of situations. He was old enough to have served during the Civil Rights era and in the years before. Jasper found himself wondering if this man had treated people of colour fairly or if his prejudices had interfered with the impartiality he was supposed to uphold as a law enforcement officer. He knew that here in the Deep South racial tensions ran deep and justice was not always administered fairly.

'Can you describe what he looked like? What did he say to you?'

Jasper gave a full description, everything he remembered including the car make, model and registration plate. The officer took a pad from his pocket and made notes before asking him to drop into the police department at midday to make a formal statement.

'Turn left out of here, we're about five miles east. Name's Randolf.'

'Thank you, Officer Randolf.'

Jasper had planned to leave as soon as the sun was up, but now he'd be hanging around in the area. He'd have a sniff around, find out about Carter.

It was already a baking hot day when he headed to his car. After last night's ordeal, he was still on high alert and wary. On impulse he fell to his knees to check underneath the car and around the mudguards for devices. He was still haunted by the memory of one of his friends dying in an explosion on Lower Donegall Street in Belfast after the Provisional IRA had detonated a car bomb a few years back. He wasn't prepared to take the risk but equally he had no idea what to check for. It might only take opening the door for a detonator to be triggered, or pressure to be applied to the accelerator or brakes.

He hesitated before starting the engine, closing his eyes tight but when all seemed to be well, he opened them and breathed a sigh of relief.

At the station, he asked to speak with Randolf and was taken into a small office where he waited for the officer to appear.

Randolf breezed into the room carrying a polystyrene cup. The aroma of cheap coffee wafted through the air as he put it on the table. Jasper noticed the pungent smell of cigarette smoke that followed him like a cloud. It was clear he was a heavy smoker, and the stench was overpowering, leaving Jasper yearning for fresh air. His uniform was untidy today, his shirt unbuttoned and creased, revealing a large patch of chest hair suggesting he'd been on duty many hours. Jasper hoped those hours had been spent on his case, finding out who his assailant was.

After completing his statement, Jasper looked up at the officer and asked, 'Have you been able to find out who the man is and why he broke in?'

'I was hoping maybe you could shine some light on that.'

The police were as bad here as they were in England, expecting the public to solve the crime so that it involved minimal work for them.

'You're confusing me now.' He folded his arms.

'You've never met the guy before?'

'Of course I haven't.' Irritation rose inside him.

'But you said you think he was following you.'

'Yes. At the diner I mentioned and possibly in New York.'

'Just explain again, why you're here?' Jesus, why did he have to repeat himself, wasn't it already clear enough?

Randolf leaned back in his chair as he chewed the end of his pen.

'I'm here to cover the presidential election--here in Georgia to look at Carter's background. If you know of anyone who might like to be interviewed, I'll be staying in The Magnolia Motel on Broad Street.'

'Place is teeming with reporters.' He tutted. 'Followed from New York you say?' He looked amused then, as if he didn't believe Jasper's fantastical notions. 'Seems a bit far-fetched. Are you a colossus of the publishing world? Should I have heard of your name?' he said, rubbing his neck.

Jasper felt suddenly small and insignificant. 'I've made a name for myself, a champion of investigative reporting.'

'On what sort of subjects?'

Jasper told him about his reporting of the thalidomide scandal and said he was interested in finding out how people felt about the crisis in the States.

Randolf's eyes narrowed as if suspicion was tucked behind them. He peered at him for a few seconds making Jasper feels increasingly uncomfortable. 'And what were you doing in the Big Apple?'

'I was meeting up with an old contact, Doctor Frances Kelsey of the FDA. She's a big heroine, stopped the drug from causing possibly thousands of deformed babies across your country.'

'Erm, I'm perfectly aware of who is she.' He rubbed his chin. 'She ain't the American idol you seem to think she is. There are two sides to every story, remember that.'

'But she saved lives.'

'There was a lot of bad feeling at the time, bad feeling that still lingers. Some folk still feel aggrieved. They lost lots of money because of her actions.'

'To many, she is a heroine.'

'Son, you may see it that way, but I've been in this job since before you were in diapers and I'm telling you, some folk wouldn't agree. Money talks here.' He gave a tap to his nose followed by a wink. 'People pinned their hopes on making a shed load of money out of that drug. Then after they faced charges and were given suspended sentences, they were ruined. How would you feel if the empire you'd built came crashing down, your home lost, everything you'd dreamed for the future lying in tatters?'

Jasper frowned; lots of thoughts were hitting him at once but mostly he thought of the poor victims and the public who'd be used as human guinea pigs, lied to, the wool pulled over their eyes. He thought about Richardson-Merrell and the way they'd made fraudulent claims to the FDA. They had known the drug was toxic and continued to press ahead with their trials.

'You're going into dangerous territory out there, stay away, is the best advice I can give or you may find yourself in a body bag.'

'I think that guy followed me from New York, he seemed to be everywhere, that's why I jotted down his number, I know I wasn't imagining it. How would he have known who I was? I'm going to be looking over my shoulder every five minutes, I just don't feel safe with him still out there.'

'Don't you worry about him. He's now on our radar, we'll have him. It's possible he tapped Doctor Kelsey's phone line, there are some who are still baying for her blood and would go to any lengths.'

A chill swept through him as he contemplated that thought.

Had he been targeted?

Randolf stood, signifying the interview was over. Jasper stood too. He would have liked answers and wasn't sure just how much time Randolf was going to put into finding his assailant when there were more important matters, like protecting Georgia's presidential candidate.

'Ah, boy, just you make sure you write the right kind of story about our Jimmy otherwise it'll be me that comes breaking your door down.' He laughed, flashing his nicotine-stained teeth before adding, 'We don't want another JFK, not before the election, not when our boy's so close to winning, I'll be relying on your words to help pave his way to the White House.'

'Another JFK? There are no reasons why someone would want to shoot Carter?'

'Mr Cooper, this is America. There are always reasons why candidates might be a target.'

'From across the pond, he's the butt of jokes, a peanut farmer on the road to Washington. Jimmy who, everybody is asking. Sounds like the daft title for a book.'

'He's a hard-working fella and a devoted family man. The Republicans have been in for the past eight years, they've caused hell, it's time for change.'

CHAPTER 22: SANDY

While her mother trotted off down to the shopping parade for cuts of meat and a bag of veg, Sandy enjoyed a lively natter with her dad in the front room while the TV droned in the background. She noticed that when Irene was out, he always kept the TV on even if he wasn't watching it. This was something her mother hated with a passion. "Only common people leave it on all day," "it's a waste of electricity," and "why do you want to sit and stare at the test card?" Maybe it was his rebellious streak, but Sandy rather liked the added noise in the room; she didn't like silence.

'Do me a favour, love.' Her dad handed his empty cup to her waiting hand. 'The lawn is covered in leaves, and it desperately needs cutting.'

She'd never mown a lawn, but she could rake leaves. 'I'm not sure, Dad, but I can have a go. Bill does our lawn, Jasper's not keen on gardening.'

'Huh. Why have a big garden if you don't like gardening?'

'It's just another chore, like hoovering and dusting, but we like sunbathing and having barbecues out there.'

He tutted and leaned forward to pick up *The Daily Mail*.

'It's not a problem. I could do with the fresh air and so could Angela.'

She took the cups back into the kitchen. After washing them up, she tied her hair into a messy bun, and slipped on a coat and an old pair of her mother's boots, before wrapping Angela up warm in her pram and bumping it over the doorstep into the back garden with Tibs at her heel.

She parked the pram on the patio and headed down to the shed at the far end of the garden. It had seen better years but the flowery curtains peeking from the small side window lent it a certain charm. As a young girl she'd imagined turning it into a Wendy house. With a creak of old hinges, the door protested as it was wrenched open, revealing the interior soaked in the musky scent of damp soil. A chaotic jumble of various garden tools and supplies littered the shelves, with spades, rakes and trowels hanging haphazardly from hooks, their metal surfaces dulled with years of use. Amidst the disarray, however, a small table occupied one side of the shed, its surface clutter-free, save for scattered seed packets, and a neat stack of pots. She spied the green lawnmower slumped in the corner like a fat toad; its blades were rusty and looked blunt. She yanked it out, brushing away its veil of cobwebs and pushing other items to one side.

She dragged it halfway across the lawn, the wheels creaking with each tug. She stared at it for a few moments, scratched her head and tried to figure out how it worked. She felt stupid and didn't want to go back into the house to ask her dad, because of the memory of her parents telling her on so many occasions when she was young that she had no common sense when it came to machines and practical things. The petrol tank, resting on the machine's front, was streaked with the traces of grease and grime. She had no idea whether she'd need to pour petrol in it, and starting it up seemed futile.

A voice from behind startled her. 'Hi, Sandy, I saw you in the garden, okay to come through?'

'Hi, Eddie, nice to see you.'

He pushed open the small gate into the garden. 'I've got the afternoon off, was just passing on my way home.'

'That's nice, well I'm about to mow the lawn for Dad, but I don't like the look of this old mower. I don't know anything about lawnmowers and it's a bit heavy to drag round the garden.'

Eddie strolled over. He dropped to his knees beside the mower and brushed off the dirt and dried grass to reveal the name and model of the machine. 'I thought as much.'

'What?'

'My grandad's got the same mower. This, my girl––it's a thing of beauty.'

'Steady on, Ed, otherwise I'll accuse you of being a geek. It's just an old mower. Oh, and by the way, I'm not your girl.' She giggled and picked up her rake.

He laughed at her. 'Now that's where you're wrong and I'll remind you that you were very nearly my girl. If you hadn't met your husband when you did, who knows.' He looked up at her with a mischievous expression on his face that danced at the corners of his lips and sparkled in his eyes.

In a flash, she remembered.

The kiss.

So long ago now. At the time it had been of little consequence, just an isolated kiss, 'something and nothing' as she'd told her friend, but now, as she studied his face, she knew it had meant something to him and to her as well. She turned her head away as she blushed at the memory.

His expression changed as he turned his attention back to the mower.

'It's a testament to the ingenuity of British manufacturers. When it's cleaned it'll shimmer like a polished gem. These were built to last, not like the ones they make today. Each component fits together like a perfectly crafted puzzle.'

'You know a lot about mowers then?'

'I certainly do. Every summer until I was about sixteen, my grandad took me to the British Lawnmower Museum at Southport.'

'Get away with you. There's no such museum.' She laughed and kicked some leaves.

'I'm not having you on. There's a museum for everything.'

'I bet there isn't a museum of lipsticks.'

'My sweet, I think you'll find there is, in Germany.'

Incredulous, she pulled a face at him. 'How would you know that?'

'I'm a fount of all sorts of useless information. Stick with me and you'll soon be a walking encyclopaedia.'

She smiled at how amusing he was. She didn't remember him being like this when they were at school. 'How do we get it working? It looks as dead as a doornail.'

'Never give up on an old piece of equipment.' He glanced up at her, a cheeky expression on his face. She looked away blushing; was there a double meaning tucked behind the comment? 'It just needs a drop of oil and some petrol to get it going. I'll nip home, change into the right togs, and bring some oil and petrol back with me and my tools in case there's a loose cable. I won't be long.' He turned to go.

'But it's your afternoon off, you've got better things to do than help me.'

He made a clucking sound as he glanced back smiling. It was a warm smile that made him look handsome, the same smile that had briefly charmed her all those years back.

'You don't change, Sandy. You've always been Miss Independent. Remember the time I offered to fix the puncture on your bike tyre? Sooner I go, sooner I'll be back.'

She laughed as she remembered her flat tyre while out one day not far from home. It had been easier to push it home and get her dad to fix it than put Ed to the trouble.

She picked up the rake and began to gather a pile of leaves, all the time thinking about how refreshingly different he was to Jasper. There was something comforting about him, homely, grounded, qualities she found reassuring.

And there it was--the quality of greatest importance to her. Trust.

Ed is the type of man I can trust.

He was dependable, and there was something about him that set him apart from her career-driven husband and the people Jasper worked with. She smiled to think of Ed and his grandad journeying by train each year to Southport to look at lawnmowers. How quaint, how earthy he was. He seemed content to enjoy life's simple pleasures, disinterested in climbing the corporate ladder, opting for a local job rather than joining the throng of commuters on the station platform. To some he may have seemed aimless, a drifter and that might have been the case with Sandy years ago, but now she admired all these qualities. As she raked the leaves into disorderly piles, she wondered what it might have been like if she'd married Ed. He would have challenged her values, made her see what was important and it wouldn't have been keeping up with the Joneses. He wouldn't be away on business all the time, working long hours, bashing away at his typewriter at weekends, taking calls late into the evening. She cringed, thinking about her enjoyment of showing off their big detached house with its gravel drive and long back garden.

Her eyes fixed on the lawn as she reflected on her adult life--the pursuit of beauty and wealth, prestige, and recognition--it had left her with nothing but a hollow shell of a life. Jasper's drive to be successful, to leave his mark, was it really the be-all and end-all? The conversations he had at parties, telling people where he'd be in five years' time. Climbing the career ladder, what was it all about? It just meant time away from family, the people that mattered, only to realise the view from the top wasn't all it was dressed up to be. She doubted very much if Ed was wrapped up in these misguided priorities. He was a simple guy, uncomplicated, just nice.

She'd always admired Jasper's work ethic, but would he lie on his deathbed and wish he'd spent more time at his desk?

Or would he regret destroying his family?

The thought shook her, and she threw the rake aside, her heart banging in her chest.

Was that what they were––over? She peered down at Angela sleeping so peacefully, unaware of the strife between her parents, the situation she'd been born into. She was just a tiny baby, if they split now, she'd never know her parents together. Her childhood would be marred, shunted between two houses. She couldn't do that, she'd caused Toby enough pain, she couldn't do it to Angela too. But Jasper hadn't rung, not even once. He didn't care, he wasn't thinking about them.

Damn him.

Hot tears of anger welled, and she picked Angela up, burying her face in the sweet scent of the baby's warm pink blanket.

The sadness of her thoughts was broken by the reappearance of Ed wearing a pair of shorts, his arms loaded up with cans and his tool kit. 'I'm back.'

'Aren't your legs cold?' He reminded her of Toby who wore flip-flops all year round so that he had easy access to his feet for everyday tasks.

'I don't get cold, I love being in the fresh air, makes me grateful to be alive.' He was leaning down pouring oil into the mower.

She pretended to shiver. 'I like to be wrapped up. I'm more of an indoors person.'

'Is your husband an outdoor type?' he asked as he topped up the tank with petrol.

'Jasper.' She laughed. 'God no. He's always busy at his typewriter.'

Ed looked at her in a strange way and she wondered if he sensed they had marriage problems.

'What's he like? You don't talk about him.'

She realised she didn't want to answer because right then all her thoughts were negative.

'He's different, different to you.'

'Is that good or bad?' He held the mower's handles, about to start it up. 'Better clean the spark plug first before we give it a try, a clean plug makes all the difference. Bit like your mum saying make sure you clean behind your ears, lad.'

'You're both different, like choosing a toffee or a Brazil nut in a box of Quality Street.' She put Angela back in the pram.

'And did you choose him over me?' What an assumption, Ed was barely in her life back then.

'Ed, you and I, we never courted.'

'I was just teasing you. I wish I'd asked you to step out with me, but I was shy.'

'You weren't that shy. I remember that kiss.' She looked at him and giggled.

'The kiss. Oh crikey, now you make me feel awkward. I know. I remember it as if it were yesterday.'

Changing the subject before they dwelled any more on the kiss, she said, 'I might do some weeding now.' She glanced round at the beds and scratched her head. 'How do you tell the difference between a flower and a weed?'

'Sandy, you mean to say you never watched *Bill and Ben the Flowerpot Men?*'

They both laughed. 'I preferred *The Magic Roundabout.*' She did an impression of Zebedee and jumped in the air. 'Boing.'

'I always wondered about you, Sandy, now I realise, you were high on something.'

When they'd finished laughing, she watched him start the mower. It sputtered and coughed to life, belching smoke into the damp air. Its blades groaned as they began to spin. Ed gripped the handles tightly as he guided it over the soggy lawn. With each line, the mower spat out a cloud of clippings and a rich, heady scent that filled her nostrils. She realised then, as she watched, how deeply satisfying it was to be doing something together. It had been so long since she'd done anything with Jasper. She watched Ed turn and head towards the fence. Jasper was always so busy working and in the last few years he had spent most of his free time with Toby and Bill. She realised then how lonely she'd been.

After Ed had finished the lawn and put the mower back in the shed, they stood back and admired the garden.

'My grandad loved a nice lawn. He'd go round clipping the edges with a pair of scissors. You busy tomorrow evening for that catch up? We can grab a drink at the Fox and Hounds and maybe a bite to eat.'

She felt instantly brighter at the suggestion. An evening out was just what she needed to take her mind off things. 'You know what, yes, that would be nice.'

'Super. I'll leave you to it and come round at seven tomorrow and we can walk up there together.'

'I'll look forward to it and thank you, Ed, for everything.'

Having enjoyed the afternoon, Sandy found herself looking forward to the following evening. Pushing the pram back into the kitchen and removing the grass from the wheels before her mother could complain, she remembered the last time that Jasper had taken her out for supper. Hard to believe, it was over a year ago. It hadn't bothered her before, but now the disappointment slammed into her and only added to the emotional disconnection she felt. A feeling that he no longer valued their time together, that their relationship had become nothing more than a routine, with each day following the same pattern as the one before. It stabbed at her as she headed for the kettle.

What did she most long for? To connect with her husband or

to rediscover her past? She took a tea bag from the caddy, popped it into a cup and remembered the red box.

It's upstairs waiting to be opened.

She thought about going to open it, but her mind was drawn back to Eddie all those years ago. Why did they never get together or go out on a proper date? She liked him and hoped he would ask, but he never had. She chuckled at the innocence of youth and how everything seemed so awkward back then.

CHAPTER 23: SANDY

It was early the following morning after Angela's feed when Sandy slid the box out from under the bed. It had been preying on her mind all night and she was dreading this moment, but she wanted to get it over with, her mind needed settling. She peeped round her bedroom door to check all was quiet. Her parents weren't yet up. Tibs was quiet too. She'd already let him out for his early wee.

Back in bed, she pulled the box towards her and in the dimly lit room she used her finger to trace the contours of the broderie anglaise trim around the edges. She wondered if the box was her grandmother's rather than her mother's--the grandma she'd never met, whose name she'd unwittingly given to Angela. She wondered what Grandma Angela was like, what sort of mother abandoned their child? It seemed inconceivable to walk out on a small child, leaving her grandfather to raise her. A thought fluttered through her head. It would be like handing Angela over to Jasper and going off with Eddie. She shuddered.

She couldn't imagine putting her own life before her child's. It was unthinkable, hideous, monstrous. Yet that was exactly what she had done with Toby, unknowingly of course, but the thought was planted now, a seed in her mind, and she shuddered. The act of a selfish, irresponsible, and cowardly woman. Yet Sandy was filled with curiosity. She wanted to see a picture of the woman. Would her eyes be cold and icy? Would she see her lack of emotion in her face?

As emotionless and cold as Irene?

Maybe there would be a photo in the box, but she wasn't sure how she'd feel when she saw it and she braced herself for a rush of pity, disgust and outrage.

Her fingers brushed against the soft velvet. It was such an ornate box, it had to contain special keepsakes. She was excited, drawn to it as if it contained a missing link to her past. Would it provide answers and was she ready to face them? Her stomach churned; all this time she had waited, wanting to know, and just as she was about to find out, she was scared. There had always been an underlying grief of sorts inside her. But nobody had died. It felt like a dark cloud, that was the only way she could describe it. Maybe it stemmed from the cold way her mother treated her. She knew she'd never change and over the years she'd learned to live with that cloud and accommodate it like an unwelcome visitor. God knows, she'd wasted many years hoping her mother would change. It was time to focus on her own life. She was good enough. She needed to care less about what her mother thought and accept the way she was.

The excitement welling inside her dissipated as the dark cloud returned––the fear that the box would contain something painful and traumatic.

I must open it. I will open it.

She took a deep breath and slowly lifted the lid, as the musky smell hit her. The box was full and the first thing she took out was an envelope which looked as if it had been carefully opened with a paperknife. She knew it must be old because it had turned a brownish yellow. It was addressed to Irene. The writing, in black ink, was elegant and sophisticated. She carefully took out the letter and unfolded it to find a photo inside of a couple standing in a garden holding a baby and smiling. She turned it over but there were no names written on the back. Could this be her grandparents holding her mother? She stared at the photo, absorbing every detail. This was the first picture she'd ever seen of her grandparents, and nostalgia washed over her. And then she realised her own stupidity as it dawned on her it was the wrong era to be her grandparents. Because of the clothing and the fact that it was black and white rather than sepia-toned, it had to have been taken in the late thirties or forties. She had no idea who they were, she didn't recognise them, although there was a vague familiarity in their faces. She frowned; maybe they were relatives.

Turning her attention to the letter, she smoothed the pages and began to read.

Dear Irene,

It was a pleasure to have tea with you the other day and as promised I enclose the photograph. I hope it won't make you feel too sad. At least you now have a picture.

Little Sandra is really blossoming into a beautiful girl, she's just like her mother. Such a happy child and so well behaved, she's a credit to you and Arthur. You should both be very proud. She's thriving and healthy. She's a very lucky child to have you both.

I went to visit Wilfred again. He doesn't know who I am, and I know you think it's pointless visiting him, but I'm sure he gets some comfort from my visits.

All my love,

Ivy

SANDY PUT the letter back into the box and sat back against the pillow as she thought about the difficulties of bringing a child into the world during the war years. She'd never really thought about this before. Although she was a war baby, born in 1942, her childhood had been about growing up in a world that wanted to forget the horrors of the past and look to a brighter future. How hard it must have been for parents. Simply staying alive during a war was a challenge, but being pregnant and staying healthy as your baby grew inside you, the worry about adequate medical care and giving birth in wartime, it must have been horrendous. So many thoughts hit her at once. She could have been born in an Anderson shelter. The challenges of planning a family when all around London was being bombed, suddenly became apparent to her.

She peered again into the box and pulled out an old teddy bear. Stored away in the attic, it smelt musty. At one time it must have held a special place in a child's heart, her mother's, she imagined. It had had bright white fur but now it was the colour of yellowed antique lace, its stuffing was hard, and its button eyes were scratched and dulled. She put the teddy gently to one side.

An old letter and a bear, what a disappointment.

About to close the lid, she decided to delve further. Something was drawing her in, she needed to know the secrets of this box. As she rummaged through the box finding a tarnished comb, a damaged baby's rattle and a silver necklace, she came across a cutting from a newspaper. Her excitement peaked; this could be the window into her mother's history she'd yearned to discover.

There was no date and no indication of the name of the newspaper, but the headline read:

Fly-Bomb Baby

An infant was found alive in the rubble after a flying bomb incident on Friday morning. The child, believed to be around two years old, was handed out of the window of a wrecked house by a rescue worker to the waiting arms of a neighbour. It is believed the child's mother was killed in the blast. Her father is alive but suffered serious injuries and was transferred to hospital.

As she slid the box into its hiding place under the bed, she could hear the clinking of dishes and the gentle whistling of the kettle. It was Mafia Tuesday and Irene would be getting ready to go out––a perfect opportunity for her to talk to her dad alone. As she dressed, she wondered why they'd kept an article with no reference, no detail, no note on it as a reference to the past. What was so special about this Doodlebug? Tons hit London and thousands were killed and injured. Yes, it was sad, but what did it mean, who was it, who was the baby, what was the family's name, the street name? No nothing. What was the significance of the article? She felt a sense of unease but didn't know why. How was she going to ask them without telling them she'd sneaked the box from the attic? Her mum would go mad.

CHAPTER 24: SANDY

For as long as Sandy could remember, she'd struggled to connect with her mother. She was closer to her dad, felt more bonded to him. He was easier to talk to even if he was a man of few words and a bit of a dreamer. There were times when his distant demeanour intimidated her, but she'd long thought the aloofness was his way of coping with Irene, and imagined he might have been a very different person if he hadn't met her.

After Irene left for the WI, Sandy joined her dad in the front room, plunging onto the settee beside him. His leg was getting better, and he could hobble around the house without being in pain. He was engrossed in the paper.

As she glanced over to see what he was reading about, she pondered over how to broach the topic of the newspaper article. It was so hard to even talk about the trivialities of her day with her mum, let alone discuss the deeper questions that troubled her. Her hostility was wearing, disconcerting and left her confidence in tatters, but she stood a chance with her dad. While his comments could be bland and noncommittal, at least he listened and didn't judge.

'What are you reading about, Dad? News is full of the American elections.'

'Not something you'd be interested in, love.'

'Go on, try me.'

'Something good had to come out of the war. Do you realise the rockets that Germany developed in the war, the V1 and V2, became the basis of the space programme? I can't believe how far some of this stuff has come.'

Here was her chance. 'Weren't they given a funny name, flying bombs, or Doodlebugs?'

'Yes, they were bombs with wings and they sounded like a motorbike. It was a strange tearing, raspy sound, then the frightening silence.'

'I remember people talking about them. Did you ever see one?'

'Yes, love, I did, but it was a long time ago, best left in the past.'

'You must have known of people killed by them. Any houses round here destroyed?'

'As I said, love, best left in the past. Shouldn't you be out walking the dog? You better get a move on, it's due to rain soon.'

This habit of his, of abruptly changing the course of the conversation, irritated her. She could never work out whether it was avoidance of a difficult subject that made him like that, or whether he preferred to be left alone in his own company with his thoughts and his newspaper. How she craved to know more about the flying bomb article, but he clearly wasn't up for talking. She felt a stab of frustration and disappointment as he picked up his paper and resumed reading. Maybe it was just not the right time to discuss it. But when would it be the right time?

She left the house and went for a walk like he suggested and focussed her mind on the evening ahead with Eddie. They'd agreed for him to call round at seven and they'd walk together down to the pub. He had suggested a meal but that sounded too formal and too much like a proper date. Two old friends meeting for drinks was more relaxing.

As she strode along pushing the pram and with Tibs trotting along beside her, she pondered what to wear. Although it wasn't a date, she couldn't help feeling both excited and nervous about the evening ahead and wanted to look her best. It would be the same if she was meeting a female friend though––she cared about how she looked and wanted to make an impression. She had barely gone out in the evening since Angela was born, this was a rare treat, and she was surprised that her mother had agreed to look after the baby.

Hours later, Sandy stood in front of the wardrobe rifling through the small number of clothes hanging on the railing, wishing she'd brought more with her. Jeans felt too scruffy and casual and a dress too formal. Finally, she settled on a floaty cheesecloth blouse and a pair of red bell-bottoms. She stood back and admired her reflection in the mirror, hoping the outfit would strike the right balance. Slipping on her shoes and checking her hair one last time, she felt her nerves rise. She wondered what they would talk about and if they would still have some of the rapport they had shared in the past. The afternoon in the garden had been fun, but they'd been busy then, and sitting in front of him at a table would be an entirely different experience. There was only so much she could say about Angela without boring him silly and she didn't feel comfortable talking about her life with Jasper.

Grabbing her bag and heading downstairs, she pushed aside her doubts, there was no need to be nervous. But as the doorbell rang through the house and she saw Eddie's shape behind the glass, a new thought slammed into her.

Jasper.

Suddenly, it didn't feel right, she was being disloyal. But what did it matter, he hadn't bothered to ring, and was guilty of his own betrayals.

She opened the door. 'Hi, Eddie, wait there a minute, I just need to speak to Mum about Angela's feeds.'

Eddie had a beautiful bunch of flowers for her which only added to the sense she was betraying Jasper. Taking the flowers, she thanked him and went back into the kitchen where her mum was already feeding Angela. 'I'm off out now, I won't be late.'

Irene regarded her through hawk-like eyes and gave her a critical once-over. Sandy saw a glint in her eyes. 'I see you've made quite an effort––you trying to impress someone?'

Heat rose to her cheeks, and she crossed her arms defensively. 'I wanted to make an effort, I haven't been out in ages, and look, Eddie's bought me some lovely flowers. Can you put these in a vase for me?'

She returned to Eddie, and they headed up the path.

'Rather than go to the pub, I wondered if you'd like to go ten-pin bowling instead? I've driven over.' Sandy looked up to see a sparklingly clean blue Hillman Imp. He unlocked the door and then went round to the passenger side and opened the door for her. 'I've not been bowling for ages, and it was always such fun, what do you think?'

'Sounds like a great idea, I need something to take my mind off things, will be just good to get out of the house. How has your day been?'

Eddie started the engine and glanced in the mirror before pulling away from the kerb. 'You know me, the normal errands that one does, always trying to do good. Mum and Dad are always the first to volunteer me when something needs doing. I don't mind, it gives me something to do. Hate sitting down and watching telly and all that, so glad to help if I can.'

'Yes, Dad said you were the go-to chap when something needs fixing.' Sandy chuckled. 'You could have made a fortune by now if you had charged everyone.'

They drove for about thirty minutes listening and singing to the music on the 8-track stereo, Sandy lost in her thoughts and Eddie singing out at full pelt. She smiled to herself. She felt carefree, all the daily tasks of looking after a baby melted away. She knew that her responsibilities would be waiting for her when she returned, but for now she was enjoying feeling young again, being in the moment--it was fun, and he was fun. She'd never seen him so relaxed and confident. He had a good singing voice, and it was as if he was singing to her.

They parked the car and walked towards the entrance. As they turned the corner, they saw the long queues. 'Don't worry, love, we won't be joining the queue. I've booked a slot for 8pm for a couple of games. We didn't want to drive all this way and miss out.'

The last time they'd been bowling was when they were teenagers and she remembered breaking a nail.

It was as if Eddie could read her mind. 'I hope your nails are not so long and precious these days.' They both roared with laughter as the memories flooded back.

'Your nails were so long back then, I thought the police were going to arrest you for an offensive weapon.'

'How the hell did you remember me breaking a nail? It was years ago. And no, long nails are not a great idea when you've got a small baby.'

'Not unless you want to poke the little mite in the eyes. How could I forget, Sandy? You were a little drama queen when it came to your nails.' He smiled at her and winked.

'I never forget, I have a memory like an elephant. My dad always said if you need someone to remember something, tell Eddie, he never forgets a thing.'

They entered the alley and changed their shoes, grabbed a coke from the café area and trotted down to the lane where others were just finishing off. She felt relaxed, but the thoughts of the day kept crowding in.

'You seem lost in thought, Sandy.' Her attention was pulled back. 'Do you want to go first or second?'

'It doesn't matter. I'm not that good.'

'Don't know about that.' He sprang back with a grin. 'The last time you beat the pants off me. It's my turn to get some pride back.'

The first game went by in a flash and Eddie won.

'Hey, what happened to the girl with the golden balls?' he quipped. 'I didn't expect you to let me win.'

She laughed. 'I'm out of practice, the next one is my game, and I can feel it in my coke.'

In the next round she scored two consecutive strikes, winning the game. 'That's better,' she whooped, 'I enjoyed that.'

Afterwards, they returned to the car and drove back. 'Thanks, Eddie, I've had a great evening, I'm glad you suggested ten-pin bowling. I haven't had so much fun in God knows how long.' She laughed, not wanting to make it sound as if her life was dreary.

'I guess your life is so different now, Sandy,' he prompted as he turned onto the main road. 'The local girl made good. I often wondered how you would get on in the modelling world. You always had that drive and ambition, far more than I did. I've only been as far as Calais, a few day trips on the ferry, I didn't move away, I bet you've travelled the world with your modelling. Have you enjoyed your life?'

'You make it sound as if we're old codgers. We've many more years left in us yet. What about you, Ed, do you mind, still living at home with your parents? Do you get lonely?'

'Sometimes, but mostly I'm too busy. Only wimps get lonely.'

The car pulled up outside the house and he cut the engine. Sandy was quiet for a time, mulling things over as she glanced up at the house. 'It's been an interesting time coming back here. I've enjoyed seeing you again very much, but there are sad memories here too. It's like being in a time warp, Mum and Dad are the same as ever, it's as if nothing has changed in twenty-five-odd years.'

He turned the light on so that she could look for her bits. 'You seem to have something on your mind tonight, is everything okay?'

'Yes of course. Just a lot to think about. Things never turn out as you plan them to, do they?'

'I guess not.' He was frowning at her; she could tell that he wanted to know what was on her mind. 'But then after twenty-five years, I would think things have moved on. You can always tell me, Sandy, the one thing I would never do is betray a confidence, so if you want to talk about it. You know the saying, a problem shared is a problem halved.'

Sandy went quiet for a moment. 'Eddie, there is something, I've been helping Dad with a few bits in the loft. I came across an old cutting from a newspaper back in the war.' She told him about the article and finished by saying, 'It's really strange, and why would they have kept it locked in a box for so many years?'

'I guess that it's a keepsake to remind them, after all it is not every day that a baby is rescued from a bomb blast. It may well remind them of how lucky they were.'

'Do you know about this, Eddie?'

Sandy's brain was dancing; what did he mean, lucky? What did that have to do with her parents?

'It was strange. There was no detail.'

Ed had a grave look on his face that was disturbing her. 'I'm afraid the only people who can answer that are Irene and Arthur, why don't you ask them? I'm sure they will tell you after all these years, Sandy.' Eddie had been relaxed all evening, but now he was fidgeting with his hands and looked uncomfortable. It was as if there was something he was holding back, something he was hesitant to share with her, and couldn't wait to get away.

'It's just odd. I'm intrigued to find out more.'

'If you find out more, I'd love to know, I'm as intrigued as you are. Sorry to be a pain, Sandy, but I have to be up early tomorrow for work, I'd better say goodnight. If you find out more, let me know, you know where I am, and I am always here for you.'

She got out of the car in a daze, and he walked her to the front door, turned quickly and was gone. Alone with her thoughts she entered the house, which was shrouded in darkness, everyone in bed. She checked on Angela who was sleeping peacefully in her cot, and headed for the bathroom before undressing for bed.

So many questions, but they would have to wait till tomorrow. Yes, Irene and Arthur would know, but how was she to tell them that she had seen the cutting? Her stomach cramped; her mum might go mad if she knew that she had opened the box and been snooping in her private possessions.

That was for tomorrow. Right now, she needed sleep even though her mind was buzzing.

CHAPTER 25: JASPER

Jasper finished his coffee and looked at his watch; it was now around eight in the evening UK time, the perfect time to give Sandy a call. Angela would be fed and bathed by now and Sandy would be just finishing watching *Coronation Street*. A pang of sadness washed over him. Babies changed––every day he was missing out on significant moments.

Sandy had been on his mind all night and most of the morning and he was finding it hard to focus. They had not spoken in days. They'd always been so close and normally spoke every day when he was away. Not this time. Things were different. He found that hard, but understood she needed time apart.

As he sat staring into his empty coffee cup, he thought about their relationship and wondered if they could ever go back to the way they were. Would she be able to trust him again or would they never recover from this? He understood the hurt he'd caused and that she'd reach out when she was ready, when she'd healed. It was all he thought about in the small hours.

A lump rose in his throat as he realised how much he missed her presence, especially now, after the attack, it put everything into perspective. It was hard to believe what had happened to him, a close brush with death, but God had been looking after him and it wasn't his time yet.

What an idiot he had been, the more he thought about it, the more he kicked himself; *why could I have not waited just a little longer, what is wrong with me?*

She hurt and I just got pissed and waded in, most unlike me, but hey, cannot change that now.

I just need her and want her so much, need to tell her I am sorry and that I will do anything to get her to forgive me and love me again.

He wanted to know how she was. Had she cooled down, was she missing him? He so wanted to speak with her, but now she had no way of contacting him, so the ball was in his court. Why had he left it so long since the last call? Work could wait, he needed to speak with her, his love, his life partner, his world.

He went to find a phone in the diner and keyed in the number, pushed a few quarters into the slot and waited for the tone to purr. He hoped that she would answer, not that dragon of a mother. His gut twisted as he waited in anticipation.

When he heard the click, his heart leapt.

'Yes, who is it, what do you want?'

His heart sank when he heard the voice of the dragon. 'Hi, Irene, it's Jasper, how are you?' he muttered, feeling totally deflated.

'Oh, it's you, what do you want? I'm busy looking after your daughter, so hurry up.'

'Why, where's Sandy?'

'Not here.' His stomach collapsed, as if he'd just eaten a dodgy burger. 'She's out with her friend Eddie, won't be back till late. Bloody pain, Angela's playing up tonight, as if I don't have enough things to do without looking after your daughter too while she is out swanning around. You should be here. She's your responsibility not mine.'

'Who the hell is Eddie?'

Jasper tried to stay calm, but he had a flash of anger.

'He was around before you came on the scene. She's seen a lot of him since she's been back. You should have looked after her better, been more of a man.'

Jasper stuttered, 'Never heard of him, she's never mentioned him, when will she be back?'

'God only knows, I am not her keeper, I will leave a message that you called, where can she get you?'

'I'm in the States moving around, so not sure when I will be able to call again, when is the best time to catch her?'

'Your guess is as good as mine, she is always flitting here and there, I will give her your message. Got to go now, I'm busy. Maybe you should have put her before your job, always knew you were no bloody good. Goodnight.'

Irene hung up.

Bloody hell, what's going on?

Sandy couldn't have moved on already and as for Irene, she never missed an opportunity to stir––all those wooden spoons she must have in her kitchen. She'd never taken to him, thought he was too much of a gigolo. What was wrong with the woman, could she not see love when it stared her in the face?

Panic set in.

I've got to get back, need to see her, tell her how I feel, beg for forgiveness.

Bloody Eddie, what did he know about Sandy? She was his and he would do anything to show her that. He felt crushed, on the other side of the Atlantic, and his mother-in-law was playing silly buggers with his life and his wife. He had to get back before it was too late.

He replaced the receiver feeling helpless. All those miles between them and Irene making things difficult. He headed to the loos. After using the toilet, he leaned over the basin and splashed water on his face. Looking up, he stared beyond his reflection in the mirror straight into the eyes of a man leaning against the tiled wall behind me. He was wearing different clothes, but in an instant, he recognised him.

Pontiac Man.

He froze.

Fearing for his life all over again, the cold glint in his eyes and the hard look stamped on the man's face left Jasper in no doubt that he meant business. He spun round to face him.

With a forceful push, the man slammed him against the cold, hard surface of the basin. The sudden impact sent a shockwave of pain coursing through his body causing him to gasp. He braced himself for what was to come. The man stepped closer, his breath hot and foul against Jasper's face and he spoke in a low and menacing growl.

'I told you not to mess with me.'

His mind went blank in terror. Clenching his fists behind his back, he was desperate to recover his strength. He could turn this around, he knew he could, he had the guts to pull it off. But at what cost and without putting himself in danger? It was all about building trust, even with the enemy. There were always two sides to a story, he had a story too. He was angry enough–– it had to be a powerful one.

'Look, mate, I don't know what your problem is, you obviously know who I am otherwise you wouldn't be here. I'm just doing a job. I don't deserve to have my brains blown out. I've got a wife and kid back home depending on me.'

The man lunged towards him, grabbing him by the collar. Another physical confrontation—this was the last thing he needed. Mentioning his family was supposed to invite sympathy, not trigger anger.

Jasper could feel sweat dripping down his back and wanted to grab some hand towels to wipe himself. 'Christ, what a life you must have, do you always go around threatening people?'

The man let go of his collar, stepped away and stared at Jasper. Sweat was beading on his forehead. 'I had a wife and kid too, a long time ago. They were my world. People like you, you come along and remind me of everything I've lost. You journalists, you're the scum of the earth.'

'I listen to everyone's story; you've obviously got one that needs telling.'

'I want that woman to step down. Then we can all forget and move on. Little Miss Hero, basking in her glory. How much d'you pay her for the interview?'

'Nothing.'

'Jesus wept, she had her moment of fame. Now she's spending the rest of her life revelling in her success. It's just one long round of interviews for her. Smug bitch. The people I worked with, they called her a hair-splitter, a stupid bloody bureaucrat. It's not the fact that she was an obstructionist, it's the lasting impact she's had. They painted us as ruthless, heartless bastards, a bunch of evil men. And that's stuck. Some employees were able to move on, get different jobs or ride it out.'

Jasper listened intently, not wanting to interrupt while he was in full flow.

'Most people who work in the pharmaceutical industry are principled men and women. They're committed to public welfare more than people in politics. Just look at Nixon. We believed the company propaganda, we were just doing our jobs, collecting our wages, supporting our families. She and her cronies, they make us out to be crooks, every one of us. Don't think for one minute we ain't suffered too.'

Jasper glanced at the door. It was only a matter of time before someone walked in and then the conversation would end. 'Can I buy you a coffee? Be easier to talk in a booth, somewhere at the back of the diner where we're not overheard.'

The man slumped against the wall, hunched over, resting his back against the cold tiles. His face was contorted with despair, as if his world had collapsed and left him nothing to hold on to, the weight of the past having taken its toll. He grunted and glanced up.

'If you want to talk, I'll listen,' Jasper coaxed. 'But point a gun at me again, we both lose. Violence is for cowards.'

'I doubt you'd want to listen. Go and find a few deformed children. I'm the bad guy. Public don't want to read about me.' His tone was sarcastic.

'Try me.'

'Listen, pal, what's your name, what shall I call you or do I call you Pontiac Man? You can remain anonymous if you want.'

'Mike.'

'Mike, well let's start again. Pleased to meet you, Mike.' Jasper extended a hand. 'And you obviously know who I am. And that I want justice. Let's talk man to man, then I can understand what challenges you face.' Mike's handshake was limp but at least he was responding.

Out in the restaurant, they found a quiet spot at the back and slid into the booth. It was empty apart from a couple of truckers scoffing burgers and chips.

After ordering coffee, Jasper asked, 'Did you work for Richardson-Merrell?'

'Yep. I was a quality control manager, my job was to make sure the drugs weren't adulterated. I monitored compliance against the requirements of the approved procedures. Not as if I was a director, I was just a manager, a cog in a system. And can I remind you, there were only seventeen recorded cases of children with thalidomide damage and nine suspected. Most cases originated from mothers who'd got the drug abroad.'

It wasn't the time to question the figures; he didn't want to rile him or stop his flow by dropping the truth into the conversation––that thousands of pills were dished out by physicians across America and there were probably hundreds of victims.

'Did you enjoy the work?'

Mike eyed him suspiciously. 'By the end, it was just a job.' He glanced out of the window. 'I suppose I did, until the shit hit the fan.'

He paused. 'Kevadon.' He stared out of the window and looked a million miles away, then he swivelled round and faced Jasper. 'I'm a trouble-shooter, I learn fast, people respected me, I knew everyone, the scientists, the pen-pushers, it was rewarding leading a team. My work had an impact and best of all, my salary was rising. I even had shares in Merrell.'

Jasper was making notes. When Mike stopped talking, he put his pen down and stared at the man who could have ended his life. He looked so broken.

'If only they hadn't encouraged us to take the tablets home and give them to people we knew. It was a big responsibility. We weren't doctors, we were just employees. I suppose it was all part of their great experiment and they were expecting Kelsey to wave it through. After all, it was widely used in Europe, it was just a matter of time before she gave it the seal of approval.'

Mike looked down at his hands. 'Every one of us who handed it out to our friends and our families, we were rogues. Thalidomide, it was a wrecking ball in the embryo.'

Jasper lowered his voice and asked the question bound to open wounds––but a must. 'Did you know of any families with deformed babies?'

His eyes filled with sadness. 'Yep, school pal of mine. But we had a big falling out.'

He dropped his gaze and fell silent.

'I was godfather to his eldest. That was when he lived a normal life––before he went off the rails. But then he and the missus moved up to the woods and everything started to turn bad.' He glanced down at his lap before continuing. 'They lived in a trailer deep in the forest, well hidden from the eyes of the law.' He glanced up, a grey tinge in his cheeks. 'The whole area was a tip, full of trash and the way he was living, it was awful for the kids. He wanted me to come and work for him, but I refused. I think he thought it was easier to have me on his side, than turn on him and turn him in.'

Jasper frowned but didn't speak.

'He was running a pot camp. He had some pretty dangerous men working for him. The family's water well got affected by pesticide contamination of groundwater. Their young son died of poisoned water. It was a terrible tragedy, but another secret I was expected to keep to myself. Then when his missus got pregnant, she started chucking up and I was very worried. I thought, she'll lose the baby too. We didn't know if it was the pesticide making her ill or morning sickness. That's when I gave her a few tablets. I just wanted to help.'

'Thalidomide?'

'Yeah. I wanted to do something, and I could, I worked in pharmaceuticals, and thalidomide was being hailed as a wonder drug, a cure-all.' He shrugged and leaned back against the vinyl seat.

'I'm sorry.' Jasper tried to imagine the parents' horror and Mike's remorse.

Mike fell silent and stared at the table as if it held all the secrets to the universe. 'The baby, a girl, she had no arms and bowel atresia.'

Jasper frowned.

'The bowel has no opening,' Mike clarified.

Jasper kept his composure even though shock was seeping through him. He decided not to pry about the deformities. The weight of Mike's guilt had to be huge, he didn't want to add to it. 'You still in touch with the family?'

'I don't want to talk anymore. It's too painful.'

Jasper looked at him, seeing for the first time the depths of his sadness. His eyes were glazed over, misty with the weight of his sorrows, then he downed his coffee and slid across the seat. About to get up, he stopped, put his hand on Jasper's arm and said, 'You need to get hold of the local newspaper, the library will have it on microfiche. *The Tribune.* October 19th 1965. Then you'll understand and you'll be able to put two and two together.'

'Thank you for sharing all that with me. I know it's not easy, but your voice--the voices of the employees, they need to be heard too.'

'Maybe, I can see you're a good man and I'm sorry I threatened you the other night, but I'm scared, scared for my life. Once you read the article, you'll understand.'

CHAPTER 26: SANDY

When sunlight streamed through a gap in the curtains, Sandy hauled herself out of bed and glanced into Angela's cot. The baby lay there, so still that she had to assure herself that the little angel was still breathing. Fear crept up her chest as she wondered whether her precious child had slipped away to the other side in the silent embrace of the night. But when she brushed her finger across her warm cheek, she let out a sigh of relief. The baby stirred but didn't wake.

Was it normal, Sandy wondered, to feel panicked, were all mums like this or just the ones like her who'd been through a traumatic experience the first time around? This was yet another question that burned inside. The motherhood journey was challenging, but what made it even more daunting was the fear of not being good enough. How she longed to be able to turn to her own mother for guidance and reassurance. She wanted to know if her own babyhood was anything like Angela's and if she was doing all the right things.

Sometimes she felt like a ship lost at sea, so alone, no anchor to hold her steady, as if she were the only woman in the entire world to give birth. Her mother was supposed to offer pearls of wisdom laced with humour to soothe her doubts and build her confidence, but every word that came from her mouth was negative. She could guarantee strings of put-downs as long as a gold chain, and constant jibes and criticisms, but never happy words. Just to be able to hear a few stories of how she'd coped, or hadn't coped, would be wonderful. It was only in those stories that she would find meaning to parenthood that would make her feel alive. It was as if a crucial part of her life was missing. There was a loose connection, as if an electric cable had been severed. An overwhelming sense of emptiness consumed her, there was a void, a gap that needed to be filled. The absence of any stories about her own childhood left her feeling as if a part of her had never taken root in the world and left her feeling isolated and detached from her whole, as though a puzzle piece was missing and made her feel incomplete.

Damn you, Mum, why can't you be loving, why can't you be supportive, why can't you be like every other mum?

As she dressed, she remembered Ed's words. She'd had an unsettled night tossing and turning--he seemed to know something but was reluctant to share it with her. It was his shifty body language, the way he'd been cagey, telling her to speak to her parents.

When she heard her mum clattering around in the kitchen, a sense of unease travelled through her.

She shouldn't have taken the box, Irene would go loopy and accuse her of theft. No misdemeanour in this household was ever forgiven and everything was blown out of proportion with a drama to follow. Nervousness swirled like a storm as she descended the stairs playing out countless scenarios in her mind, wondering how her questions would be received. It was like being a child again and horrible to be so unsure of herself.

Trembling hands and a churning stomach were signs of the

turmoil brewing inside her. Yet she knew the only way to move forward was to ask about the newspaper clipping even if it meant admitting to snooping in the loft.

At the bottom of the stairs, an idea came to her. There could be another way. What if she popped into the local police station or library? It was a long time ago, but maybe there were records. Of course, the best source of information would be the police. But as quickly as the idea came to her, it slammed shut. She couldn't just breeze in and ask about something that had happened years ago, they'd think her batty. Besides, she had no details. No road name, no date, no nothing. Her enthusiasm evaporated when she realised how many bomb blasts there had been––literally thousands. Many people had been displaced including children. She began to think that digging around in the past was a fruitless exercise, best forgotten.

Irene was busy cleaning the worktop when Sandy entered the kitchen. That was her. She'd still be cleaning up while life was falling apart around her.

'Morning, Mum.' She tried to sound bright.

Irene glanced round with disdain on her face as if Sandy was a piece of dirt. Without bothering to ask how her evening had been, she was her usual blunt, cold self.

'He phoned last night, that husband of yours.'

Sandy's heart soared but her joy was rapidly replaced with panic when she predicted the conversation they'd had. She would have been sharp with Jasper and tried to put him off ringing again.

'Did he leave a message? What did he say?'

'He said to tell you he'd called.' She wrung a cloth out in the sink, as if it was Jasper's neck she was squeezing.

'Was that all? How is he?'

'He's in America.'

'America, what the hell is he doing there?'

She mopped the draining board, not bothering to turn round. 'I haven't the foggiest, Sandra. It was a bad line, the baby was crying, how should I know?'

'When did he say he'd call back?' Her heart was screaming, desperate to know something but as usual she was faced with an obstinate roadblock. She could tell by the vigorous way Irene was cleaning that she was enjoying Sandy's pain. 'Did you write his number down?'

'I didn't have a pen to hand.'

How convenient.

'I'm not your secretary,' she said primly. 'Strange that you didn't know he was going to America. What sort of husband keeps their wife in the dark like that and goes gallivanting off round the world? Your father would never have done that. He always supported me.'

'Mum, it was 1942 when I was born. Most men didn't have a bloody choice. They were off fighting a war.'

'Not your father.' She was impossible––had an answer for everything.

'I haven't a clue, Mum, you never talk about the past, it's as if it never happened.'

'The past is a place to learn from, not live in. That's what my dad used to say.'

Irene abruptly turned and picked up a broom standing by the back door. As she flicked the floor, Sandy knew she'd hit a sour note.

She grabbed the broom from her, compelling them to face one another. 'You're like a slippery fish, Mum, slipping and sliding from the past.'

She put her hands on her hips and scowled. 'I don't have any happy memories.'

'But what about bringing me up?' Motherhood had to be a turning point in her life, the ultimate joy and fulfilment. Hadn't she cherished every moment and savoured every milestone?

Although it was not always easy, with countless sleepless nights, never-ending nappies and endless worries for the safety of her child, Sandy wouldn't have exchanged Angela for anything. She felt blessed.

As Sandy looked into her eyes, it was as if a knife had pierced her chest. Not a twinkle of joy or any positive emotion radiated from those cold, dull bullets.

Regret. That's what she saw.

Her heart quietly broke.

All those years of feeling unloved and unwanted were now confirmed. A burden, an inconvenience, that's what she'd been.

Why?

She thought she probably sounded slightly unhinged as she rattled off a string of questions. 'I'd love to know what it was like for you. Does Angela look like me? Did I have colic too, what did you do to calm me, how did you feed me, did I sleep well, what were my first words? I want to see some photos.'

Irene stared at her, her face turning to thunder. She grabbed the broom and resumed sweeping the floor.

'Why are you so bloody horrible? Just because your own childhood was bad.'

She huffed and carried on sweeping.

'Fine, be like that. I'll ask Dad instead. At least he talks to me. I'm fed up with you pushing me away.'

Irene stopped sweeping. 'You do that. Call him in for breakfast while you're at it and put some toast on. And mind you don't burn it. Nobody likes burnt toast.'

Sandy popped bread into the toaster and called Arthur in. He hobbled through. His leg was getting better, and he could walk with a stick. He pulled out a chair with one hand and propped his stick against the table.

They slathered their toast with butter and Arthur opened a jar of homemade marmalade while Irene poured the tea.

'Nice evening, love?' Arthur took a bite of his toast, crumbs settling in his moustache.

Before she could reply, Irene scowled. 'Course she did, she had a night off from the baby bawling and she has a new admirer. You should know by now that Sandra likes attention.'

Prickles rose across her back. These barbed comments seemed designed to stoke a fight.

Sandy realised then, their relationship had been a slow and insidious drift of hurtful words and small betrayals. She was at breaking point and as she glanced across the table, she saw her mother in all her ugly glory. What the hell, why was she so scared to admit to prying in the loft? Being interested in her family's past; it was hardly a crime.

'I was talking to Ed about something I found in the loft.'

'What were you doing up there? I thought I told you not to go in the loft.' She slammed her cup down, spilling tea on the plastic table covering.

'The past interests me,' Sandy defended. 'I want to see photos of our family.'

Irene stared at her through daggered eyes. 'You had no right. You always were an insolent child and you're no better as an adult.'

Arthur didn't look as if he was about to come to Sandy's rescue, which didn't surprise her. He'd always been the cowering husband.

Taking the newspaper clipping from her pocket, she dived straight in. 'Ed seems to know about this. The story of a baby, found in the wreckage of a bomb blast during the war. Who was the baby?'

Her dad stared into his tea and her mother scraped her chair back and prepared to get up.

'You had no right to go up into the loft,' she screeched.

Arthur glanced up. 'Don't have a go, Irene, this is her home.'

'She moved out years ago.'

Arthur sat up and faced her. 'You drove her away.'

'She had a baby out of wedlock. What did you expect me to do, give my blessing?'

'Whatever happened to forgiveness, Irene?' He looked weary, as if a thick fog had settled around him. Years of being with a difficult woman had taken its toll.

Irene's lips curled into a vicious snarl and her eyes glinted with a fiery intensity. 'You must have known she was up in the loft. You haven't left the house in weeks.'

Whether she'd been in the loft or not, it was irrelevant. "The baby, Ed said to ask you.' Her chest felt tight, and she paused, as if tasting the words before uttering them because they seemed so bizarre, so out of place. 'Was it me?'

Irene stared unseeing into the middle distance.

A blanket of silence descended.

'You going to tell her?' Irene's tone was sharp and biting.

The air was tense, like static electricity, and she could feel anger radiating off her mother in waves. And then the air stilled, nobody spoke, and all Sandy could hear was a strange whooshing noise through her ears.

A sense of foreboding crept over her.

My God, they're not my real parents.

It was as if she were outside her body hovering above the table, watching the scene unfold like in a movie. She tried to speak but was finding it hard to swallow, and all that came out was a little gasping sound.

The truth, that was all she craved. 'Nothing's going to shock me. All my life you've pushed me away and avoided difficult conversations.' She glared at Irene, seeing her in a new light and for who she truly was--odious.

She was aware of Arthur sitting beside her, his shoulders slumped; he was gripping the sides of the table with both his hands as if it were a life raft, his knuckles turning white. He looked up into Sandy's eyes. 'Your parents were killed after a bomb hit their house. I was on fire duty that night and I found you.' He stood up, his gait heavy as he stepped to the window, his back to them.

'Are you going to tell her who her real parents were?' Irene shouted.

Arthur stared out of the window in silence. Sandy rose to her feet and put a hand on his shoulder. 'Dad?'

'If you're going to tell the story, tell it all.' Irene jabbed her finger in the air. Her mother sounded like a witch.

As he turned and looked at Sandy, she saw deceit and regret in his wet eyes. 'Your parents were your mother's sister Gwen, and her husband Jeff. I'm sorry, love, we should have told you years ago.' His voice was weak, like a battery losing charge.

'Jeff?' Irene chortled. 'She looks nothing like Jeff.'

Sandy's mind froze and the room blurred. Suddenly everything that had ever happened to her and in this house made perfect sense. Lightheaded, she reached for a chair and collapsed into it just as her mother rose.

'Right, I've got things to do, are you going to see to the baby, she's crying up there.' She glared at Sandy.

Her eyes darted between both. 'Dad, what's Mum saying?'

'Angela's crying.' He stared out of the window and looked a million miles away.

She touched his arm. 'I know that.'

Irene stood at the door. 'I'll see to the baby, take your cups into the front room, you need to talk.'

Sandy felt as if she was falling down a deep, dark well, and as the floorboards creaked above them with her mother's heavy step, all she could do was gape in complete disbelief as she struggled to process the news. And now she was being asked to sit down with her father.

Why?

For the first she felt that she did not want to know. Where was Jasper when she needed him? An inner drive pushed her on;

who was she? Suddenly Toby sprang to mind, she was reliving his nightmare too.

She fell into an armchair and looked at her dad. He could not look her in the eye but gazed out of the window as if wanting to be anywhere but here.

'Dad,' she mumbled, 'what the hell is going on? Tell me, I need to know, no more lies, please, I cannot take any more lies.'

CHAPTER 27: TOBY

Bill had only gone for a regular check-up at the doctors. He had a cough––that was all, and yet he'd been gone for four hours. As the minutes dragged by, Toby couldn't help but wonder what was taking so long. At first, he'd enjoyed having the cottage to himself, being free to do as he pleased, but now he was checking the lane every few minutes from his bedroom window. All was quiet outside and there was no sign of the truck trundling down the pot-holed lane.

He slumped onto his bed, one eye on the lane, his mind foggy as worst-case scenarios flashing before his eyes.

If something happens to him, it's my fault.
My limitations, I'm nothing more than a burden.
He's tried his best, would give me the world if he could.

Toby returned to his desk and tried to continue reading his book, but he couldn't focus for the worries kicking round his head.

He nipped downstairs to make a mug of tea, a simple exercise for most people, but not so easy for Toby. Bill had always bought household items that made Toby's life easier, and the kitchen worktops were at a lower level so that he could easily reach up to the sink to turn the tap on with his foot. There was a stool beside the sink, and he sat down, lifted his leg up and turned the tap lever with two toes. He then reached towards the kettle and clutched it to his chest to fill it with water before grabbing a mug from the cupboard--again using his feet.

He popped a straw into his mug, and sipping his tea glanced round the kitchen wondering what to eat. The specially designed can opener with long handles that Bill had made for him years ago caught his eye. He was suddenly overcome with emotion, remembering the hours he'd spent designing and making it. Sketches spread across the dining room table and welding the metal in the school workshop. It was more sophisticated than any in the shops, but it worked. For all his flaws, Bill had a kind heart, and a practical mind. He was clever and yet Toby took him for granted.

A strange feeling overtook him; it was fluttery, so foreign he didn't recognise the emotion right away.

I don't appreciate him; all I do is moan and complain.

He felt wracked with guilt and tears blinded his eyes.

In that moment as he continued to stare at it, the can opener took on a character of its own and represented everything that was good about his dad. He almost wanted to pick it up and hug it.

His thoughts were broken when he heard the crunch of tyres on gravel, footsteps, and a rap at the door. His heart surged.

He lifted his leg and turned the doorknob with his foot, pulling the door inwards. The sight of the school nurse standing on the doorstep sent a jolt of surprise coursing through him. She was wearing her full uniform and looked very smart.

'Toby, are you okay?' She smiled.

'Yeah, why? Dad's not back yet though. He only went to see the doctor.'

'Can I come in?'

He stepped aside to let her in with an ominous dread radiating across his chest.

She pulled out a chair and sat down.

'The doctor sent your dad up to the hospital for an X-ray.'

Confusion and a cold eddy of fear rose inside him. 'Is his cough really bad then?'

'I'm afraid he's got pneumonia and they need to keep him in for a week or so.'

'Isn't that something only old people get?'

'You can get it at any age, Toby. It's a common illness, but it can't be taken lightly. It can be very dangerous and needs to be treated immediately.'

A fist of panic squeezed his insides. 'Is he going to die?'

A sickly kindness spread across her face like sunshine. He wasn't a baby, he wanted to hear it straight or not at all.

'Your dad's a strong man and he's young.'

'He's not that young.'

She smiled. 'Compared to some, he is. He's not old and frail, that's for sure. He needs to rest, he's probably been overdoing it, working too hard.'

And why did he work so hard? To support me––ungrateful shit that I am.

When she wagged a finger at him, it was as if she'd read his mind. 'You're not to blame yourself, Toby, these things happen.'

'I said some mean things to him.'

'We all say things we don't mean, pet, I'm sure he still loves you.'

Toby looked away. 'I hope so.'

'Don't look so downcast. He's going to be as right as rain in no time, but we need to think about who's going to look after you while he's away.'

'I don't need looking after.' He straightened up to his full height with a sense of determination to prove to her that he was more than capable.

'Lovey, I know you're more than capable, but we all just want you to be safe. Your dad's suggested your friends Jasper and Sandy, but they're both away. We're going to try and get hold of Sandy. I understand she's staying at her parents' house.'

'Because her dad's ill. Can't I stay at the school?'

'I'm afraid not, but I'm going to come back later to make your dinner.'

'Thank you.'

'And do you need help getting washed this evening?'

'I can manage, I've had sixteen years of practice. People serve less time for murder.'

She tutted and shook her head before smiling. 'I can see you're a stubborn mule, like most of the kids over at the school.'

The thalidomiders, Toby included, had always been fiercely independent and if someone said they couldn't do something, they set out to prove them wrong.

After she'd left Toby collapsed onto the settee, his body sinking into the soft cushions as he stared ahead at the TV, too wracked with worry and fear to think about switching it on.

Losing his mum to cancer all those years ago had left a deep emotional scar. She was his anchor, his comfort, his fire. The thought of dealing with another loss, it was inconceivable, too painful to bear. In those early days after she'd died, his grief had felt like waves crashing over him, so strong they almost swept him away. But he'd found a way to ride those waves––not like a skilled surfer on the crest, but more like a small canoe paddling like fury across choppy waters. And now, in the silence of the cottage all those feelings of loss and fear crowded in once more, enveloping him like a shroud and tightening their grip across his heart.

The prospect of losing Bill as well––it was too much to bear, cut free, wandering the earth alone. He leaned forward and let out a cry. Facing the future without either parent, he couldn't do it, he hadn't the strength.

Except that he wasn't alone. He had family.
Jasper and Sandy and his sister, Angela.
His flesh and blood.

All those daydreams he'd indulged in, curious as to what it would be like to live with his birth family. And now, it could become a reality, but all he felt was hollow inside. This wasn't how it was supposed to be, Jasper and Sandy picking up the pieces because his dad had died.

An old saying suddenly came to him.
Be careful what you wish for, it might come true.

Yes he was angry with him, yes he was a slob, but he was his slob and he did not want to lose him.

He tried to flip the script on his fear and stay positive, just like his mum used to tell him. Instead, he focused on the days ahead. He wasn't sure how he felt about Sandy looking after him. It would be so awkward, so weird. He'd never spent much time with her alone and it made him feel nervous and uneasy. He couldn't get it out of his head that she'd rejected him, he was the unwanted baby and that coloured everything. If she'd rejected him then, as a cute baby, why would she want him now? To have a spotty obnoxious teenager foisted on her was hardly appealing. He couldn't see her rushing to return, but hopefully that wasn't going to happen. Maybe the nurse could pop in from time to time; he'd cope.

The afternoon passed quickly, and darkness fell. A rap at the door and then a key being turned in the lock startled Toby. His dad must have given the nurse his key. He stood up and waited.

'I'm back,' she called. Her voice ringing out like a spoon against glass made him think how relaxed and friendly she was, and reminded him of his mum. Perhaps it was her warmth and kind demeanour, but whatever it was, it made him feel at ease, like he had known her for years. She breezed through into the kitchen area as if it was her own cottage and set down a steaming casserole dish on the counter, as the aroma of herbs and lamb wafted through the air. As he caught a whiff, his mouth watered; he'd not smelt something so enticing in a long time. Steam rose as she lifted the lid. She grabbed a ladle from the hook on the wall and dished it onto waiting plates.

'How do they know Dad's got pneumonia?' Toby asked between mouthfuls, savouring every morsel. It was so good, and aside from the delicious taste of the meat, what made it extra special was the fact that she'd gone to so much effort.

'They saw a shadow on his lungs when they did the X-ray.'

'What are they going to do to make him better? He will get better, won't he?' He tried to steady his voice but he was struggling.

She put her knife and fork down, and still chewing her food, reached across the table and took his hand. 'Oh, lovey, I know it's hard, but please try not to worry, he's in the best place. He'll be getting plenty of rest and they'll put a drip up so that they can give him antibiotics straight into his vein. They work much better than taking tablets at home.'

It felt like history repeating itself. 'Dad said that about Mum, that she was in the right place, but she still died.' He dropped his gaze and let his body slump.

'That must have been very hard for you, Toby. I lost my own mum at a young age, I do know what you're going through.'

'Did they let you see her?'

'I was only little, I don't remember much.'

He gazed off to the window. 'They didn't let me see, Mum. Dad made excuses, Grandma made excuses, I just wanted to see her, I didn't care how sick she looked. So if you or Sandy are going to stop me seeing Dad, I'm going to go anyway. I'll walk to the hospital if I have to.'

She jabbed her fork in the air. 'You, young man, need to get it out of your head that he's dying because he's not.'

'You don't know that. You're a nurse, not a doctor.'

'True, but I have a good feeling, I think he'll pull through.' She winked.

Toby didn't agree. Bill's days were numbered, he was sure of it. The drinking didn't help, and his slobby ways and big belly. All the indicators were there, like warning lights on the Starship USS Enterprise: the lines etched deep on his face, the grey tinge to his skin that morning, the rattly cough--everything, ominous.

An abrupt flare of anger coursed through him.

Dad, you should have looked after yourself, for me, for yourself.

A dull ache spread across his chest. He was helpless, powerless, just a teenager. The truth was, the loss of his wife had taken a heavy toll on Bill, and despite efforts to pull himself together, they always seemed to fail. Over time he'd neglected his health and succumbed to his self-destructive tendencies. He'd long stopped caring about what he ate and how much he exercised. Toby didn't want to have to explain all this to the nurse, she wasn't family.

'That's what Dad used to say about Mum, that she'd pull through. He was lying, trying to protect me. I don't need protecting. I just need...' The words trailed off. He didn't know what he needed. And as for the truth, it was too scary to face, he wasn't ready.

'You were a lot younger then, Toby, it must have been hard for your dad. He was probably barely coping himself. It's difficult telling your child the person they love most in the world is dying. And how to explain death? None of us knows what happens after we die. It's sugar-coated with angels and a man with a white beard sitting on a cloud and all that nonsense.'

In that moment, he felt like laughing--the absurdity of it all, the avoidance, but better to see the humorous side of death than to think of his mum eaten by worms and rotting to a skeleton under the ground.

Again she reached out to him and he gratefully clutched her

hand as if it were a safety rope dangling from the edge of a cliff. The warmth of human touch, it felt good, healing, like a balm.

After she'd taken her hand away, he felt cold and alone, the distance between them widening. New thoughts circled like crows and he found himself wondering just how much Bill really cared about him. It had always been clear, Rona was number one. She'd stolen his heart and in death hadn't relinquished it. Even though she'd been gone for years, he couldn't compete with a love so deeply entrenched in his dad's body and soul. As a baby, Toby had been foisted on him, he'd only taken him on because it was what Rona wanted.

He wasn't a replacement for her. Bill would literally have given his life for his wife. And that was why he'd allowed his body to go to rack and ruin, he was willing his own death so that he could be reunited with her. Toby was convinced of that, but this nurse wouldn't understand any of that. She didn't know the family.

His thoughts were broken by the loud rap at the door and the chair opposite him being scraped back. They looked at each other; she was as surprised as he was by the sudden interruption. They weren't expecting anyone.

The nurse frowned as she rose from her chair and he stared after her as she headed for the door, the anticipation mounting inside him. Maybe it was Bill, discharged already, false alarm. Reaching the door, she hesitated, glanced back at him and shrugged before turning the handle.

'No idea who this is, but it won't be Sandy. I spoke to her this afternoon, she's coming in a couple of days, so until then I'll help out.'

CHAPTER 28: SANDY

Sandy towered over her dad unable to process what she'd just heard in the kitchen. She felt as if she'd been hit by a ton of bricks. Was her thinking correct or completely confused? Her dad had slept with her mother's sister. It couldn't be true, it was so far-fetched as to be completely ridiculous. He just wouldn't do something like that. He was a good man, kind and loyal. He'd put up with so much over the years; she knew Irene was an impossible woman to live with, yet he'd stuck at it. To betray her mum in the most despicable of circumstances, it just beggared belief.

Her mind was screaming––was this true? Her mother was good at twisting the facts, she was cruel and found any way she could to plunge the knife. But would she really stoop this low and make up something so fantastical? A crushing feeling like a hot iron felt as if it would suffocate her with each passing moment. And then she felt as if she was drowning, unable to catch her breath as she stood in the lounge beside the settee looking down at him and wondering what on earth to say.

He looked shifty. His face was flushed, and he was avoiding

eye contact, staring through vacant eyes at the headlines of yesterday's newspaper.

'Dad, who are my parents?' Her tone was sharp.

Beads of sweat were gathering on his forehead. He shook his paper and continued to avoid eye contact.

'Damn you and your newspapers and TV. Will you look at me, Dad?' She was trembling. She'd never spoken to him so harshly before and it didn't feel right. Her tone was alien to her, as if the words were coming from someone else.

She snatched the newspaper with force, knocking his empty cup over in the process, the dregs of tea pooling on the table. She hurled the paper across the room, its sheets fluttering to the carpet. The headlines were resting beside a framed picture of the pair of them. She rushed over, grabbed the picture, and thrust it in his face.

'Look at this.' She jabbed her finger at the faces beaming out. She was about four and sitting on her dad's lap.

'No wonder Mum isn't in this picture. Or any other picture in the house. It's always the two of us.' She was shrieking. 'I always assumed Mum hated having her picture taken.'

He cowered from her and continued to look shifty and uncomfortable as if he wanted to disappear into a puff of thin air. A bead of sweat travelled down his face.

Between her rants, she could hear her mum upstairs, pounding the floorboards, soothing Angela with a song, and suddenly her heart went out to her. She'd sacrificed her life for her, she'd been the dutiful wife, kept quiet all these years, carried the secret like a millstone around the neck, keeping up appearances because it was what she did. She'd endured the pain but, in the process targeted Sandy, punished her for the wrongdoing of her husband. She was the scapegoat. And worse—she'd never loved her. The thought slammed into her like a bus, as clear as day. Every time her mother looked at her, she was a painful reminder.

'I'm sorry, love.'

'That's all you ever say, sorry, love. They're wooden words with no meaning. I want to know all the details, however sordid, I want to understand, but God knows I don't think it's possible to understand.'

'It was the middle of the war.'

'And that's your excuse.' Her words came out as a screech. 'How many times have I heard people blame the war? How could you do that to Mum?'

'It was just the once.'

'You're admitting to it?' She was incredulous. 'That's what they all say. You're a slug. God, if Jasper ever did that to me, he'd be out, no two ways about it, but not only did you sleep with another woman, once, twice, fifty times, it doesn't matter, you still ratted on her, and you did it with her sister and you knocked her up. Jesus Christ, it's disgusting.' She was shaking so much she couldn't control herself and as she shouted, spittle hit the picture. 'I've never felt so sick in all my life.' She struggled to control the shaking and felt her body temperature drop as if she'd stepped into a fridge.

'It's not certain, love, we don't know for sure.' Other than looking sheepish, there was no emotion in his words. Sandy hated that. Where was the remorse? Where was the recognition that he'd wronged his wife and her for keeping quiet all these years?

'Liar, we do know.' She hadn't noticed Irene in the doorway holding Angela. 'Gwen and Jeff were trying for years. He was firing blanks.' Sandy stared at her mother, shocked by her choice of words, it was so unlike her to be so coarse. 'You look like each other, it's plain to see.'

'It was just the once, but you've never let me forget it.'

'How can I when I had no choice in bringing up your daughter?'

'Sandra, love,' her dad said, the tone of his voice soft and placatory. 'When Jeff was called away to war, she was so distraught and Irene showed no sympathy, told her to get on with things, but I was a shoulder to cry on. But one night that went too far. It didn't mean anything. It wasn't an affair. It happened in the moment. I regret what I did, but I don't regret you, I love you, and when your mum here calms down, she'll tell you she loves you too, because I know she does.'

Irene stayed silent and as Sandy glanced at her, hoping for words of love, all she saw was a hardening of her face, the lines around her mouth deepening like ripples on sand. There was no love, not even the merest trace.

Sandy felt hollowed out inside but in the briefest of moments as she glimpsed up at her mother again, she saw her eyes mist over as if tears were threatening, before she quickly turned and walked into the kitchen clutching Angela tightly to her chest.

The shrill sound of the phone ringing in the hallway shattered the silence. Irene darted to pick it up, as if she welcomed the interruption.

'Could you nip down to the shops, love, and pick a paper up?'

Trying to be quiet while her mum spoke on the phone, she hissed at her dad. 'Is that all you're bothered about, your bloody paper?' She felt like ramming the paper down his throat.

What was wrong with her parents? This stifling, starchy atmosphere, it was Victorian. Every difficulty, every disagreement or challenge glossed over or left unspoken. Underneath the inner turmoil of this house, it was suffocating. They were the façade of a couple struggling to maintain the face of perfection even as they crumbled within their own walls.

Sandy realised then; it was time to go. She'd done the Mary Poppins routine, the wind was on the change. It was time to face the music at home and await Jasper's return. She had to put a sense of perspective on the situation and the fact was, her marriage was far more important than her parents' marriage, and the longer she stayed away, she'd never repair it. There now became urgency to return home. She couldn't be around her parents a moment longer.

There was hunger in her heart to get back to the people who loved her, who appreciated and cared for her. She couldn't believe how desperate she now was. Two shocks in a short space of time, she couldn't be here.

'Sandra,' Irene called. 'It's for you.'

Her heart soared.

Jasper, at last.

She'd tell him she was heading home. God, she'd missed him; for all his failings, he'd never cheat on her, deep down she knew he loved her too much and wouldn't want to risk it. Marriage was hard, but she'd face the challenges.

She went to pick up the receiver. 'Sandy, it's Nurse Sheila from the school.'

'Hello.' Sandy's heart plummeted and her voice sounded flat. She'd so hoped it was Jasper.

'Bill the caretaker's been admitted to hospital.'

She took a sharp intake of breath. Her first thought––Toby.

'He's got pneumonia.'

'That's awful, poor chap.'

'You and Jasper are down as the next of kin.'

'That's right.'

'Toby.'

'You don't even have to ask, of course I'll come straight back, he'll need me.'

'Thank you so much, Sandy. He's a determined lad, thinks he can manage and I'm sure he can with some things.'

'How long do they think he'll be in for?'

'We're not sure yet, could be a couple of weeks.'

Thinking on the hoof, she came to a decision. 'It's probably best I go to him and stay at the cottage, with Angela, he's familiar with his own environment, our house isn't geared up for his needs, I think they have lots of gadgets there.'

'That's great, that's a weight off my mind. I've been so worried. He's a smashing lad, but he does need an adult there. I'd feel awful if anything happened to him. How soon can you come? There's no rush, I can help for a couple of days.'

'I'll aim for the day after tomorrow or earlier if I can. I've a few things to sort out first.'

She put the phone down.

What the hell have I agreed to?

He's my son, but I barely know him.

'What's happening?' Irene asked when she'd come off the phone.

Her dad hobbled through to the kitchen, grabbing his jacket from the hook, and looking sorry for himself.

'Toby needs me.'

Irene glared at her, throwing a warning look to stay schtum. She had no intention of doing that, not after everything that had happened.

'It's time Dad knew about Toby.'

He wheeled round facing them both. 'Toby, who's that?'

'Your grandson.'

Irene's cheeks flared. Sandy knew she was upsetting her mother, but she didn't care. The truth was a long time coming.

Something awakened inside her––a deeper understanding of herself and her values, and they certainly didn't align with those of her parents. For too long she'd put up with her mother's cruel ways, and now, finally standing up for herself was empowering. Toby's existence was real, he was her flesh and blood and she was fed up with the pretence.

'What are you talking about?'

Irene stared at the ground, her fisted hands rigid by her sides.

'The baby I had sixteen years ago, he's alive.'

'He died. He was deformed.'

She watched as he reeled in shock, his face a mix of disbelief and amazement; this moment would stay with him forever.

'Mum, I think you can explain to Dad, you've kept it a secret ever since you found out; one way and another, you two have got a lot of talking to do, so I'm going to leave you both and be on my way. It's time I went. I've been here too long.'

She knew then the reason why Irene didn't want Arthur to know. It was revenge, retribution, her way of getting back at him but looking at her now, the triumph wasn't bringing her much joy. To deny the existence of a grandchild though, it was despicable. He had a right to know.

'I have a grandson?' He still looked shocked. 'I thought he'd died, that's what the doctor told us.'

'He's a great boy, Dad, you'd be proud of him.'

Irene scoffed and Sandy could tell she was irritated. His grandson––nothing to do with her.

She'd leave them to it, being around them was toxic and pointless. They weren't about to open photo albums and fill her in on who her family were. Now was not the right time while feelings were running high. In any case, she still couldn't get her head around the whole thing. She just wanted to be alone, to cry, to scream, to process.

'I'm going to gather my bits and head off. Dad's much better now, you don't need me, it's best I leave you to talk.'

She piled up the car, going in and out of the house several times, and finally tucked the blankets around Angela and slid her carrycot along the back seat.

There were so many unanswered questions, but that was for another time. She was exhausted and just wanted the comfort of her own bed and surroundings.

Neither of them came out to the pavement to wave her off like normal parents. It was small things like that, that made her despise them. She turned the key in the ignition and felt so let down, by both her mum and dad. As she indicated and checked her mirrors, she glanced up at the house where she'd spent her formative years through to early adulthood. Sadness seemed to wrap itself around the bricks like a glove, and it was as if it was watching her depart with a dismissive air. It conveyed the same detachment as those who dwelled within. There was a deadness within those walls that had turned sour. She wouldn't be coming back, not soon, maybe never.

As the house faded from view, she turned her mind to Toby. Looking after him, how the hell was she going to cope and, in that poky, dirty cottage of theirs? She didn't do dirt or grime or mess. In fact, the cottage was the last place she wanted to be, she just wanted to go home.

It was annoying that there was no one else to look after Toby. She hadn't minded being on Bill's medical records as next-of-kin but hadn't expected to ever be called. Surely Bill had family?

Her heart lurched.

What am I thinking? I'm his mum.
But he's not a small child anymore and I don't feel like his mum.
What will he say when I arrive on his doorstep?
What will I say?

CHAPTER 29: JASPER

Jasper drove the short journey over to Georgia Southwestern College in Americus to look at old copies of newspapers on the microfiche reader at the campus library. Parking the car, he got out and looked over at the immaculate emerald lawns that adorned the front of an imposing building. The sky was a deep shade of azure and although it was early it was already pleasantly warm. He took a few moments to enjoy his surroundings, wandering the impeccably maintained pathways through the garden, enjoying its explosion of colour and neatly tended beds, pausing to take in the intoxicating scent of violas, pansies and snapdragons that wafted through the air. The splendour of it all inspired ideas for his own garden, but back home the gardening season was long over. He knew that when he returned, he'd be faced with a carpet of damp, mushy autumn leaves to rake.

He thought then of home and wondered when Sandy would return and how it would be between them. Would they be like strangers after this fortnight apart? The thought made his stomach sink and a heavy weight spread across his chest. He looked at the flowers for inspiration, soaking up their cheeriness. He hoped with all his heart their relationship would grow stronger because of this time apart, be renewed and they'd appreciate each other more. He was so far away, and communication was virtually impossible. He desperately wanted her to have missed him as much as he'd missed her, but there was no guarantee. She was strong-willed, stubborn, and that independent streak of hers, it was frustrating as hell.

He perched on a bench and admired the impressive college building taking in every detail. He'd read that the original building had been burned in a fire, the cause never determined.

As he thought about how impressive the entrance was with its imposing portico of four white columns, a girl flew out through the large double doors. She tore down the steps and across the lawn in his direction, her head bowed and looking agitated. As she got closer, a flicker of recognition sparked inside him.

The girl from the diner.

He could see how upset she was, thundering over the lawn as if she couldn't wait to get as far away from the building as she could. Reaching the adjacent bench, she dropped her satchel with a thud on the wooden slats. He glanced over as she plunged her bottom down and covered her hands with her face as if tears were imminent.

Through wet eyes, she glanced up at him. 'You're that English reporter my mom was talking to in the diner.' She sniffed and clutched her leather satchel to her chest as if for comfort.

'Has someone upset you?'

She looked away, embarrassed.

'Sorry, none of my business.'

'I've just been for an interview here. I want to study psychology and sociology. They turned me down. Said I needed higher grades, but I'm not a complete idiot, I know why they really turned me down.' She sniffed and stared angrily at the college building. 'It's what I've had my whole life, nothing surprises me, I'm used to disappointment. Why am I telling you all this?'

'I'm a good listener, it's what I do for a job, and I have a kid at home, your sort of age who's handicapped, so I know some of the challenges.'

She didn't immediately answer, maybe collecting her thoughts.

'The principal and this woman interviewed me. They sent me into another room while they decided. None of my friends had this hassle. Their offers were waved through with slightly worse grades. When they called me back in, they said about my grades and then started talking about my personal safety. Their duty of care, something about protecting vulnerable students, that I might be the object of curiosity and get attacked because I look different, and they didn't feel they'd be able to protect me.' She scoffed and looked defiant.

'And how do you feel about that?'

'Annoyed as hell. And they asked about my ears. What's that got to do with my academic ability?'

'Could you appeal?'

She uncrossed her legs. 'I'd get nowhere.' She gave a sarcastic laugh. 'I'm going to face this everywhere I apply for, and jobs too just because people don't like the way I look.'

Jasper stared at a bed of yellow roses, his mind briefly wandering to Toby. He was going to face these same difficulties. He was waiting to hear whether he'd been offered a place at the local college to study Politics and English A levels. Had they taken it for granted that he'd secure a place, and what would happen if he didn't?

'Will your parents do anything? Will they fight it?'

'Doubt it, they're just as bad, always wanting to protect me from ridicule. And another thing, they started going on about minorities, how they've had attacks on blacks since they started coming to the college ten years ago. Like they couldn't be bothered to cater for another outsider. The students they prefer are perfect white blondes, like my friends.'

Jasper leaned forward and rubbed his head. 'Is there anyone you can speak to?' He wanted to help, to at least point her in the direction of help. 'Do you know of other handicapped students?'

'I'm the only one who looks like me, with no ears. My mum used to say, it's just the way God made you, kiddo, you gotta accept God's plan for you.'

Jasper didn't reply, he was angry at all the excuses. There was every chance the kid's mother had taken thalidomide along with hundreds, even thousands of mothers across the States and yet it was being hushed up or dismissed under the mantra, "Kelsey stopped a disaster".

The official line was that thalidomide had not hit America. They wanted to portray to the world they'd handled the scandal, they had a grip of the situation and succeeded where the rest of the world had failed. Kelsey had become an idol. Underneath though, the situation stank. Jasper was so looking forward to returning to the UK so that he could write up his thoughts and publish his story. As for Jimmy Carter and the election--maybe he had enough to write a short piece, keep Sam happy.

The more he thought about it, no wonder Mike hated Dr Kelsey. All that praise that had been lavished on her. She hadn't stopped the drug trials, she wasn't dealing with any of it: the innocent children born with deformities, the doctors and pharmaceutical workers like Mike, who'd dished it out like sweeties and were now suffering from the trauma of knowing what they'd done unwittingly.

He rose from the bench with an aching heart. How he wished he could do something to help. And then he realised he was helping, in the only way he knew how. He'd be writing about the people he'd met and their situations and hopefully that would make a difference. Knowledge was a powerful weapon; to remain ignorant of the truth was dangerous, better to know the worst than to wander freely believing the official narrative while ignoring the rot. All he could do was chisel away.

He looked down at her. 'Hold fast to your dreams, kiddo, if dreams die, what's left?' Then he turned and headed across the lawn, through the grand entrance to seek directions to the library.

In the gloom of the library, he sat hunched over the microfiche reader squinting at the small print. It didn't take him long to locate the article, *The Tribune*, October 19th, 1965.

The headline read:

Horrific house fire claims lives of mother and two children. Possible arson. Motives under investigation.

The sub-headlines read:

'A devastating house fire broke out late last night resulting in the tragic loss of a mother and her two children. The authorities are trying to locate the whereabouts of the children's father. An investigation is underway, there's speculation this is arson and the motives for this unimaginable act of violence are unclear.'

Jasper read on:

'The blaze erupted within the quiet neighbourhood of Plains, Georgia. Firefighters responded swiftly to the alarming scene, their efforts hampered by the ferocity of the inferno. Despite their valiant attempts, the flames proved too relentless and ultimately claiming the lives of the innocent victims.'

He continued to scan. The article was long and ended with:

'The authorities are urging everybody with any information to come forward, no matter how insignificant it may seem.'

He scrolled on, searching for further references to the fire, his eyes strained. And then a headline caught his eye.

'Father arrested for the death of his wife and two children.'

He stared at the screen, barely able to read on.

Shit, poor sod, he lost his family, served time for something he didn't do.

Jasper felt sick to the core, his heart racing as the words blurred before him. How many horrific stories like this were out there? The countless tales of horror interwoven with the tragic repercussions of thalidomide, wreaking havoc on countless lives, the physical and emotional toll endured by everybody involved, repercussions that would last a lifetime. The aftermath of the medical catastrophe extending beyond the individuals directly involved. A shadow had been cast--people like Mike and his family were unwittingly caught in the treacherous web of the drug's legacy. This appalling and tragic story served yet again as a harsh reminder of the immense suffering and devastation inflicted on so many innocent lives.

As he stared at the screen, the words continuing to blur, mirroring the haze in his mind, his eyes filling with salty tears as a wave of intense emotion surged through his entire being. He found himself immobilised, unable to move as the sheer power of his feelings overwhelmed him.

As the storm of emotions subsided and he regained control of his body, a profound sense of catharsis and release washed over him. In that transformative instant he realised the power he had. Without people like him, investigative journalists, some of the most significant stories to impact the world would never see the light of day. Suddenly he felt tremendously humbled. And for all the flack that journalists got, people were surely grateful for waking up to the realities of the world.

With a positive spirit but still reeling in shock, he rose from the chair knowing that he needed now to find Mike to hear the rest of his tragic story.

Mike had given him his number, and from the nearest phone box Jasper made the call and they arranged to meet in the diner. Jasper arrived early, and chose a booth at the back where they wouldn't be overheard. He was waiting, cradling a mug of coffee when Mike slid into the seat opposite him.

Jasper didn't smile, it didn't feel appropriate. He let out a big sigh and nudged his arm with his knuckles. 'Mate, I'm sorry, truly I'm very sorry.'

'You're a reporter, you have to let the world know, the official line, that thalidomide didn't affect America, it's a pack of lies. I lost my family; it doesn't get much worse.'

The weight of his words settled into the air and both dropped their gaze, falling silent for a few moments.

When their eyes connected, Jasper saw the same haunted look he'd seen before. Bleak despair and loss had taken root inside him. This man needed justice.

He took a sip of coffee and waved at the waitress to bring Mike one.

'You served time?'

'No, there wasn't enough evidence to convict me. I had a solid alibi.'

'Your mate in the woods, he was responsible?'

'I couldn't prove it, but yeah, course he was. He disappeared. They lived in a trailer, they could go where they liked. They lived off-grid.'

'How did your mate put two and two together that their baby's deformities were caused by the tablets you gave her?'

He stared at Jasper. He saw the harsh raw truth behind those eyes. 'I told them. It was the most honest thing I've done in my entire life. When it hit the deadlines, the truth about thalidomide, I was beside myself with guilt. The kid was three, they were facing a challenging future. They wouldn't have made the connection, the pills weren't labelled, as far as they were concerned, I was a professional working for a reputable drug company. I told them it was safer than Alka-Seltzer and at the time that's what I believed. And besides, they didn't read the papers or watch the news, they didn't know what was going on.

But I'd kept up with developments, I read medical journals. I was in the know.'

The waitress brought two coffees and Mike took a gulp as if it was strong whisky rather than plain old coffee.

'I offered them money to make it right, but how much could ever make it right? No amount.'

Jasper frowned and offered a sympathetic half smile.

'This country is in denial. That's what you've got to get across. Thalidomide did not hit America. Kelsey stopped it. Yes, it did hit America. No, Kelsey did not stop it. We are still suffering.' His words were forceful and Jasper felt spittle on his cheek. 'We were discouraged from finding the truth. Families were in denial or feeling shame, parents were duped, gaslighted by obstetricians and professionals trying to cover their tracks. Our news media were aggressively pushing forward the narrative that we had been spared this tragedy. But two and a half million tablets were distributed. Jesus, I handed out a fair few myself. What a fool I was to believe, but hindsight is a great thing.' He looked down at the table, his shoulders were slumped.

'The distribution ahead of FDA approval was not a story the media chose to report.'

'Why? I don't understand.'

'My theory is, the public were desperate to hear a success story. We had civil unrest going on, cities were burning, Luther King was shot, we were fighting a thankless and costly war in Vietnam, we had the Cuban Missile Crisis, JFK was assassinated. The public wanted to hear Kelsey's story and that's precisely where the story stopped. It was easier to pretend the whole bloody thing never happened.'

'Strange, the story wasn't deemed important.'

'You'd be frightened by the impact of that drug. There are bound to be a hell of a lot more like me but sadly we're not going to hear their story unless they go public. They're isolated, how can they contact each other, find out about each other, they are out there.'

'It's a minefield, especially in a country so large.'

They swigged the last of their coffee.

'Jasper, the only thing I will ask of you is that you never give up asking questions and investigating. One day the truth will come out and the country will know the full story.'

They shook hands. 'Keep in touch,' Jasper said.

'Never give up the fight for justice in your own country.'

After they'd said their goodbyes, Jasper headed for the nearest payphone to call Sandy to tell her he was on his way home.

He pumped some coins into the slot and after what felt like an age, heard Irene's voice at the other end.

'Irene, it's Jasper again.'

'You've just missed her.' Her manner wasn't blunt.

'She's not gone out again?'

'She's gone home.'

'Good, because I'm on my way back too.'

'Jasper, before you go, there's something I need to say.' Her voice was different, it was much softer than normal. There wasn't the usual starchy tone. He wondered what had happened. 'I'm so sorry for all the pain I've caused.'

And then his coins ran out before he could reply.

CHAPTER 30: SANDY

Sandy stepped over the threshold into a chilly house, the familiar scent of home and the damp odour of emptiness enveloping her. She'd only been away for a few weeks, but it seemed like forever and suddenly she felt daunted by the prospect of being here alone and with all the memories of the events leading up to their parting.

On impulse she decided to go straight to Bill's. She penned Jasper a note and left it on the hall table. She dashed upstairs, collected clean sheets from the airing cupboard and clothes from drawers, dumping the dirty laundry in the basket on her way back downstairs.

Back in the car, as she turned the ignition, a wave of anxiety clenched inside her chest.

What the hell am I letting myself in for?

She inched down the drive, panic taking hold as doubts hit all at once. She was his mother, yet she hadn't a clue. For sixteen years she hadn't been involved in his life, what if she was useless? She had no idea how she'd cope or how he would take to her. She wanted so much to make a good impression and didn't want to come across as naive and stupid. What was she going to find when she arrived?

I'm the adult, he is the teenager, but it doesn't feel like it.

Adding to the weight of her doubts and insecurities were the questions she had. Just how sick was Bill? How long was he going to be in hospital? Two days, two weeks? And what about when he came home, would she need to help him convalesce too? She still had no idea when Jasper would be returning. When he did, he'd find her still away.

Nerves danced across her stomach as she drove down the road and indicated to turn left. The whole experience of living at Bill's was going to be strange. She'd spent several weeks at her parents trying to fill the void that was her childhood, all those missing puzzle pieces, all those unanswered questions, but that was nothing compared to this void. It was much greater. She had some recollections about her own childhood, but she knew nothing of how Toby had grown up and the challenges he'd faced. For all those questions she'd asked her parents, to her shame she'd asked Toby virtually nothing about his childhood. The realisation appalled her. Time to make amends, but how?

The car bumped over the rutted lane towards the cottage. As she slowed, her gaze fixated on the cottage ahead. The lights were on downstairs, and she wondered if he'd be alone or if the nurse would still be there. She hoped the latter, it would be easier to break the ice. A surge of adrenaline coursed through her body, her heart racing frantically in her chest as her uncertainty threatened to overwhelm her.

How to talk to him, connect with him, her own flesh and blood? She had no idea. He was her son and yet his essence remained shrouded in unfamiliarity, a stranger she longed to unravel. She was so anxious of making the slightest mistake and ruining everything. Their bond was as fragile as a spider's web. She had to tread carefully.

To be relaxed, natural, her normal cheerful self--that's all she wanted, but nerves would take over and prevent that happening. She was bound to come across as wooden or crass, stumble over her words, struggle with conversation. It was going to be strained and painful. In that moment, she hated herself for the internal battle inside her. All she wanted was just to be natural, confident, her normal cheerful self, but she was fighting so many insecurities.

She got out of the car and lifted Angela from her carrycot. She wrapped the sleeping baby in a blanket and headed up the path. She gently rapped her knuckles against the door, her heartbeat echoing in her ears as she anxiously waited for it to open.

Greeted by the nurse, her face full of surprise, she could see Toby sitting at the table. It looked and smelled as if they'd been eating.

Hell, what does he eat, what will I cook?

'Sandy,' she beamed. 'We weren't expecting you so soon.'

'I should have rung first.' Panic gripped, her first mistake, *what an idiot*, she thought. He needed time to mentally prepare himself for this strange situation of his real mother coming to stay.

As she stepped into the house and passed Angela to the nurse while she took her coat off, suddenly she was on her guard, careful about what she said. The nurse didn't know that she was Toby's mother.

'How are you, Toby?'

She smiled at him and then turned to the nurse who was cooing at Angela, now awake. 'Can you fill me in, what's the situation with Bill?'

'He could be in for a couple of weeks, depends how he responds to the treatment. It's going to be a challenge, he's not going to be straight back to work, he'll need help when he comes out.'

'I'll do what I can, but I'm not a nurse, I've no skills and I've got Angela to look after.' Already she was making a complete idiot of herself, coming across as uncaring and putting her own concerns first. This wasn't going well.

'Don't worry, there are certain things you'll know how to do.' She winked at Sandy. Whatever did that mean?

How am I going to cope? I need Jasper. Where the bloody hell is he?

Toby piped up. 'I'm not completely useless. I can help too, you know. I wish you'd both stop fussing.'

After the nurse had left, turning to Toby, she said, 'Where am I going to sleep? I have some bedding in the car and Angela's carrycot. Better get the bits in from the car. Then perhaps you can tell me what you've been up to.'

She went to the car with Angela and carried her back in the carrycot. As she glanced round, looking for somewhere to put the cot, she thought how lovely and cosy it was to have everything in one room: lounge, kitchen, and dining room. It was a bit poky though and needed sorting out, but with a woman's touch it could be a lovely cottage. She put the carrycot on the floor beside Toby who was sitting on the settee.

As she headed to the door to collect more things from the car, she glanced back to see Toby kneeling beside Angela. 'Hey, little sis, aren't you cute.'

Sandy's heart jolted and she stopped in her tracks and smiled at him.

Suddenly he looked sad. 'I wish I could stroke her, but without arms I don't know how. You might not like it if I touch her face with my toe.'

How desperately sad, how will he ever have a physical relationship?

She could see the longing in his eyes to caress her delicate, soft skin.

The desire to stroke a baby was the most natural and joyful

thing in the world, but to stroke with your toes rather than your fingers was not the norm.

She recoiled. An instinctual resistance surged inside, but a moment later she chastised herself. Why should he be excluded because his ways were unconventional? And then she found herself wondering, how was he ever going to be physical with another human? Poor kid, what a life, there were so many challenges ahead.

'Can I hold her, do you think?' She saw such yearning in his eyes and wanted to find a way.

'What about if you sit right back on the settee and I lay her on your lap?'

Toby sat further back on the settee and Sandy gently put her on his lap while she went back to the car, returning moments later, her arms full. Angela was sleeping peacefully in Toby's lap.

Sandy's eyes swept round the room as she wondered what to do first.

'I'll clear up.' It was easier to be busy even though she knew she should sit down and chat to Toby. She hoped her nervousness did not show.

'I'll help, or I could just hold the baby.'

'Let's put her back in the carrycot for now, you can hold her again later.' Sandy took Angela and put her back in the cot.

'I'll get the Hoover.'

'Really?' She stared at him, incredulous.

'I can do things around the house, you know. I might be a teenager but I'm not completely useless.'

She felt herself blush with embarrassment; he'd seen her surprise.

She put the tea towel down and watched him push the Hoover out of the cupboard with his foot. 'I've missed sixteen years of your life, bear with me, I know so little about you, but I want to know so much.'

He shrugged and put the plug into the socket so deftly with

one foot. 'I don't know much about your life either, Mum.' He put emphasis on the word, mum. 'Mum, it doesn't feel right, should I just call you Sandy?'

'Of course.'

'You've just been helping your mum look after your dad. My grandparents.' The way he said grandparents, the word was like food he was tasting for the first time. He savoured the words.

Oh my God, of course they were. 'Yes, yes they are.'

'What are they like? Can I meet them?'

She thought she wasn't ready to talk about what she'd discovered, but in that moment, she knew it was the one thing they had in common. They'd both been let down by those closest to them, their lives had been a lie. She was still grappling with the news; he'd had several months to come to terms with it. She wondered how he'd coped, the emotions he'd gone through. That was a future discussion.

'Why don't we tidy first, then we can chat. Oh, Toby, there's so much I have to learn about you, I want to know everything about your past.'

She gazed in amazement with tears in her eyes as he depressed the lever of the Hoover and pushed it across the carpet with his chin, gently guiding it into corners like an expert. He was incredible, a real credit to Bill and Rona. They must have taught him so much. She felt inadequate then. How had they known what to do, where to start? She would have done everything for him because it would have been easier to take control than watch him struggle and feel frustrated for him. They had the right approach.

'I'm impressed, Toby.'

'Us lads can vacuum, better than you girls can.'

'Is that the case?' She put her hands on her hips. 'In that case I'll have to get you to do my house.'

'Only if you pay me,' he shouted about the din of the Hoover. 'And I don't come cheap.'

He stopped the Hoover and they both let out a laugh. It was a pressure release moment.

'What can I do?' she asked, glancing round.

'Make me a cup of tea, this housework is hard, no wonder Dad never did much.' He puffed. 'You can change Dad's sheets, if you're staying, that's where you'll have to sleep, but good luck to you, there is a government health warning on his door, so don't say you haven't been warned.'

She headed upstairs.

What have I let myself in for?

She pushed open the door. He hadn't been joking about the warning label. She smiled to herself. It couldn't be that bad, surely. A grimy smell hit and she clamped her hand over her nose. She weaved through the mess on the carpet and threw open the windows, pushing back the grubby curtains that had come off their hooks in places. She turned to survey the room. A bare lightbulb hung from the ceiling and there were no feminine touches, and mess on every surface.

Oh, Bill, how could you live like this, doesn't my son deserve better of you?

She tidied the room to make enough space for Angela's carrycot, then whipped the bedding off. The cream pillowcases had black grease marks and the sheets were grubby and looked as if they hadn't been washed in weeks, if not months. *What a state to get into*, she thought, no wonder he was ill. He definitely needed a woman to look after him.

Do I really need to stay here, can't I just drive over here?

She didn't know how capable Toby was, she had to make sure, but she'd just seen him Hoover, so wasn't that evidence enough?

She'd stay just for tonight and then see in the morning.

Before she went back downstairs, she gave the room a few sprays of her perfume, grabbed the dirty sheets and on her way along the landing stopped to glance into Toby's room. She gasped. It was the bigger room and immaculate.

Downstairs, Toby was putting the Hoover away and asked, 'Manage to find some space, it's pretty small, isn't it? Lucky I've got the bigger room.'

'How did you wangle that?' She picked up the tea towel and started drying dishes.

'My needs are greater.' He pulled a face and flapped his hands. 'Pouf, those sheets are rank. Sandy, you don't snore, do you? Dad's like an elephant.'

'I haven't a clue, I'm asleep.'

As they chatted more there was a relaxed atmosphere between them, allaying her initial fears and making her realise how daft she'd been.

'You don't have to stay if you don't want to,' he said. 'I'm sure you'd prefer your own room at home.'

'It's the least I can do, Toby, it's a bit grim here alone, down this dark lane. If nothing else, I'll keep you company for a couple of days.'

He went over to gaze at Angela who'd now woken and was red-faced. He sniffed. 'Pongy, I think she's just pooed herself,' He laughed. 'Would you like me to change her nappy?'

'You're more than welcome to that, young man.' She smiled.

'I'd have no idea where to begin. How did you learn?'

'The nurses at the hospital showed me but I also went to ante-natal classes.'

He looked amazed. 'I always thought it was mother's instinct to know what to do.'

She smiled. 'No, Toby, not at all.' She chuckled. 'There are even classes on how to breastfeed.'

He blushed and quickly looked away.

She made two mugs of coffee and brought them over to the settee. Tibs had made himself at home and was curled up in Bill's tatty armchair.

'How is your dad? Is his leg better?' Toby asked.

'He's much better, still hobbling though.'

'Bit like me then, I twisted my foot in the woods but it's better now.'

'That sounds painful.'

'Bet it was nice spending time with your mum, I miss mine.' He looked away.

His words jolted her, made her realise there was another mum, Rona. Rona reminded her of Rebecca in Daphne du Maurier's book. She felt the weight of Rona's allure. Like Rebecca, she'd always be this enigmatic figure whose memory lurked in every crevice, a mystery, an intrigue.

'It must be hard for you, Toby, but sometimes life can have strange twists as you well know. Life isn't always as it seems.'

He frowned. 'That's an odd thing to say.'

She hesitated, uncertain whether to go on. This was a conversation she needed to have with Jasper first.

She cradled her mug. 'I found out things about my childhood that have been kept secret from me.'

'Can't be as bad as mine,' he quipped.

Is he capable of taking on my concerns, should I share this with Jasper first?

She took a deep breath, deciding yes, she'd tell her son. 'Like you, Toby, I was adopted. I've only just found out.'

He turned to look at her, his face a picture of horror. 'You're kidding me. How could they not have told you in all this time, why did they suddenly tell you? Oh my God, that's two things we have in common.'

'I found a box in the attic, I wanted to know more about the past.'

'What did Jasper say?'

'He doesn't know. You're the first person I've told. I've only just found out he's in America.'

'I've not heard from him either.'

For the rest of the evening, they exchanged small talk until Sandy finally said, 'Right, I'm going to hit the sack.' She took the cot upstairs and then put Tibs on a lead to take him out for a quick pee.

The next morning, Sandy came downstairs to find Tibs fast asleep in Bill's armchair. Not having a clue what Toby ate for breakfast, she opened cupboard doors for cereal and bowls and was just laying the table when he came down yawning, his hair ruffled and still in his pyjamas.

'You look like you've been dragged through a bush. Would you like me to brush your hair? You've got school soon.'

She had assumed he couldn't brush it himself, but when his eyes lit up and he threw her a look, she knew she'd be in for a surprise. He picked a brush up from the coffee table with his toes and leant down to style it. Her heart swelled with admiration.

'I don't have school today. It's a revision day.'

His words took Sandy aback. She hadn't been able to sleep. Bill's bed still smelt, and the mattress was too hard, so she'd spent the night tossing and turning and planning how she was going to set about making small improvements to the cottage to make it more welcoming. She wouldn't be able to do that now. She wanted it to be a surprise for Toby. But she would cook a few meals to freeze.

'How did you find exams when you were at school?' he asked between mouthfuls of cornflakes.

She was feeding Angela her bottle and looked up at him. 'I didn't sit many exams, I wasn't interested in school, I just wanted to be a model.'

He looked shifty and went bright red. 'Why would you want to be a model and take your clothes off?'

'Not a stripper, silly. Toby, you've been reading too many dirty magazines.'

'What do you expect when my dad leaves them lying around.' He spluttered out his cornflakes.

'Yeah, I had to shove them under the bed.' She tutted.

She winded Angela and after putting her back in the cot went over to the washing machine. 'There's some washing to do, I don't suppose you know which programme to use?'

'Chuck it all in and I'll show you.'

'Blimey,' she said, glancing round at him. 'I can't even get Jasper near a Hoover let alone a washing machine.'

Over the course of the day a remarkable ease and sense of familiarity enveloped them. Their conversations flowed effortlessly, tinged with humour, and Sandy was able to help Toby with some of his exam revision. It was as if, in these moments, time faded away. She could feel the warmth of a connection developing between them and it transcended their relatively brief time together. She was glad she'd made the decision to stay. Bill was in hospital, and she'd never have wished illness on him, but it had given her this precious and much needed time with her son. It was a long time coming. As they finally closed Toby's books before teatime, she sat back with a feeling of satisfaction.

She longed to know more to better understand him, his quirks, what made him tick. There was so much she needed to catch up on, but there was no rush, everything in its own time; for now she felt close to him and she was at the beginning of a journey of discovery.

CHAPTER 31: JASPER

Jasper arrived home, a feeling of emptiness engulfing him as he stepped through the door. He dumped his suitcase in the hallway and tossed the cellophane-wrapped bouquet of flowers and duty-free gifts on the kitchen counter. There was an eerie silence, as if the presence of Sandy had vanished without a trace. The absence of any signs or clues only deepened his bewilderment. There was no sign of the bed having been slept in and no food in the fridge. His heart sank and anxiety gripped. She wasn't back, but where was she?

He smelt like an old goat so dashed off to the shower, stripped and enjoyed the warm water needling his skin. Afterwards, he threw on some fresh clothes and unzipped his case. About to feed the laundry basket with all his dirty washing, he found it full to the brim with Sandy and Angela's clothes. She was back, but where had she got to?

He padded down the stairs, poured himself a Scotch and flopped onto the settee. After a short doze, he checked the time, then rang Irene.

'She'll be over at Bill's,' Irene said.

He called a taxi to head over to Bill's. As the taxi turned into the lane, he saw Sandy's car parked in front of the cottage. His heart jolted. He was about to see his wife again. But then dread clenched his stomach and by the time the taxi came to a halt, it was all knotted up.

What if she doesn't want to see me, what if she pushes me away?
Whatever will be, will be, at least Toby will be glad to see me.

He paid the taxi driver, got out and headed up the path, his heart banging in his chest as he knocked on the door. When she opened it, their eyes locked and in that moment, time seemed to still as the weight of the mistakes and hurt and unresolved emotions that had torn them apart disappeared and they closed the distance between them, their bodies melting into each other. The world around them faded into insignificance--Tibs was jumping up, Angela was crying, the bouquet of flowers crashed to the floor. As he looked into her eyes, the windows to her soul, the warmth of her skin, the smell of her scent, the tears on her face held more power and intensity than any words. The damp autumn air became filled with love and joy. She buried her face in his chest, and he felt the relief wash over her while he held her tight. Aware of Toby in the background, he fought to control his emotions, didn't want to break down in front of the lad.

When they finally pulled apart, their faces wet with tears, he said, 'God, woman, you silly sausage, I've missed you so much.'

Their reunion was quickly shattered by a cough in the background. 'Hello, Jasper, how was America?' Toby looked on in utter confusion and wonder, embarrassed but with nowhere to escape. 'This is all a bit soppy.'

Tibs was nipping at his trousers, barking excitedly and the baby was still crying. They all laughed.

'Come 'ere, son,' Jasper said, and Toby strolled over, an awkward look on his face. Jasper threw his arm around him and gave him a slap on the back. 'Missed you, boy, and I've got a few pressies for you too, back home in my case.'

There was so much to talk about, but now was not the right time. For now, Sandy and Toby were his concern, and getting Bill back on his feet.

'How's Bill?' Jasper asked.

'He's in hospital. Can we go and see him tomorrow? I never got to see my mum; I want to see him.'

'Christ, Toby, your dad's not dying.'

'Yeah, that's what Dad said last time, and I never got to say goodbye to Mum.'

'We'll all go in the morning,' Sandy said.

THE END
Book 5 pre-order now! 'Fear to Fearless'
My Book

THANK you for reading *Every Daughter's Fear*. If you enjoyed the story, I would really appreciate a short review on Amazon.

To find out about Joanna Warrington's other books, please visit her Amazon page at:

https://www.amazon.co.uk/Joanna-Warrington/e/B00RH4XP16

EVERY DAUGHTER'S Fear is book 4 in a series entitled *Every Parent's Fear* which was inspired by the thalidomide crisis of the 1960s. Please follow this link to buy the other books in the series: My Book

OTHER BOOKS BY JOANNA WARRINGTON

SLIPPERS ON A FIRST DATE

Donna's love life is a mess. Years of online dating has left her self-esteem in tatters. Now 56, she can boast a list of failed relationships longer than a grocery bill.

When her spiteful daughter Olivia makes a scathing remark about her mother's love life, Donna sets out on one last quest to find Mr Right. Is it too late to find lasting love, or will she just repeat the same mistakes?

It's 2020 and England is in lockdown, presenting a whole range of new challenges for daters.

Donna's forays into the world of dating lead her on a series of calamitous adventures involving an unwanted gift, faking her identity, and getting arrested. And finally, her job as a nurse is on the line. When things go horribly wrong, Olivia decides to take matters into her own hands.

The love that Donna has always searched for isn't the type of love she needs. Her journey reveals a few home truths, and ultimately she discovers that real lasting love has been staring her right in the face all along.

Inspired by true dating experiences and world events

Book Link: *https://amzn.to/3PoofEG*

Don't Blame Me

When tragedy struck twenty-five years ago, Dee's world fell apart. With painful reminders all around her she flew to Australia to start a new life. Now, with her dad dying, she's needed back in England. But these are unprecedented times. It's the spring of 2020 and as Dee returns to the beautiful medieval house in rural Kent where she grew up among apple orchards and hop fields, England goes into lockdown, trapping her in the village. The person she least wanted to see has also returned, forcing her to confront the painful past and resolve matters between them. Weaving between past and present, this emotional and absorbing family saga is about hope, resilience, and the healing power of forgiveness.

Book Link: https://amzn.to/3aaeJ72

Holiday

Determined to change her sad trajectory, Lyn books a surprise road trip for herself and her three children through the American Southwest and Yellowstone. Before they even get on the plane, the trip hits a major snag. An uninvited guest joins them at the airport, turning their dream trip into a nightmare.

Amid the mountain vistas, secrets will be revealed and a hurtful betrayal confronted.

This book is more than an amusing family saga. It will also appeal to those interested in American scenery, history and culture. This is part of a loosely related family drama collection. Book 2 is *A Time to Reflect*

Book Link: https://amzn.to/3p1mtfV

Time to Reflect

When an aunt and her niece take an epic road trip through Massachusetts, their relationship is changed forever.

It's a trip with an eclectic mix of history, culture and scenery. Seafood shacks. Postcard-perfect lighthouses. Weather-boarded buildings. Stacks of pancakes dripping in syrup. Quaint boutiques. A living history museum showing how America's early settlers lived. Walks along the cobblestone streets of Boston, America's oldest city––the city of revolution. Everything is going well, until a shocking family secret is revealed. In a dramatic turn of events, Ellie's father joins them and is forced to explain why he has been such an inadequate parent.

An entertaining but heartfelt journey through Massachusetts from Cape Cod to Plymouth, Salem, Marblehead, Boston and Rhode Island.

Book Link: https://amzn.to/3uyhtUe

The Catholic Woman's Dying Wish

A dying wish. A shocking secret. A dark, destructive, and abusive relationship.

Forget hearts and flowers and happy-ever-afters in this quirky unconventional love story! Readers say: "A little bit Ben Elton" "a monstrous car crash of a saga."

Middle-aged Darius can't seem to hold on to the good relationships in his life. Now, he discovers a devastating truth about his family that blows away his future and forces him to revisit his painful past.

Distracting himself from family problems he goes online and meets Faye, a single mum. Faye and her children are about to find out the horrors and demons lurking behind the man Faye thinks she loves.

Book Link: https://bit.ly/3PGjXwk

Every Family Has One

Imagine the trauma of being raped at age fourteen by the trusted parish priest in a strong 1970s Catholic community. Then imagine the shame when you can't even tell the truth to those you love, and they banish you to Ireland to have your baby in secret.

How will poor Kathleen ever recover from her ordeal?

This is a dramatic and heartbreaking story about the joys and tests of motherhood and the power of love, friendship and family ties spanning several decades.

Book Link: https://bit.ly/3PGjXwk

Printed in Great Britain
by Amazon